EXPOSURE

Also by Louis Greenberg and available from Titan Books

Green Valley

EXPOSURE

LOUIS GREENBERG

TITAN BOOKS

Exposure
Print edition ISBN: 9781789090291
E-book edition ISBN: 9781789090307

Published by Titan Books
A division of Titan Publishing Group Ltd
144 Southwark Street, London SE1 0UP
www.titanbooks.com

First edition: November 2021
10 9 8 7 6 5 4 3 2 1

A CIP catalogue record for this title is available from
the British Library.

Printed and bound by CPI Group (UK) Ltd, Croydon CR0 4YY.

1 The falling man appeared out of nowhere, in the middle of the air, right before Petra's eyes.

Not for long, because then he was at her feet, crumpled on hands and knees. Time slowed, stilled. It was like a dream. She knew she should move – either leap back from this large shape that was about to send her sprawling to the cold, damp pavement; or, a moment later, when she realised it was a human man, and that he had finished hurtling, that she should reach down and help him up. But the instant stayed frozen for an uncounted time, lost to the world, as if her life was telling her to take note of this moment.

A loose black knitted beanie, the back of a honey-yellow jacket with a sheepskin lining at the neckline, dusty jeans and black work boots. A pair of old men had stopped across the road and were looking at them, and she imagined the scene through their eyes – a man supplicating, a woman staring down at him like some sort of pharaoh queen. On Brook Street at lunchtime on a cold, clear Tuesday in February.

'Sorry. Are you okay?' It was him talking, him apologising, when it should be her.

The man pushed himself up on his hands and knees, and finally Petra forced herself to move.

'Jeez, are *you* alright? I'm just standing here like a...' She squatted down and tentatively went for his waist to try and help him up, but her tote bag slipped from her shoulder and she didn't know if she should touch him without his permission. A hesitance she'd picked up in England.

He had soft eyes in a gentle face, the skin of his forehead slightly care-weathered, Petra fancied; a trim beard with a bit of salt in it. He could be anything between thirty and late forties.

Petra forced herself to snap out of her stare again – this wasn't the way she normally behaved, but there was something about this man that spoke of deep things, like home, familiarity, and love, and acceptance. In his eyes, she felt she didn't have to choose a pose. If he could just keep looking at her like that, with those kind and open eyes, then she'd know that she belonged. She spent a lot of time later trying to understand this sense. Some people might call it love at first sight.

By this time, he had stood up and was gingerly swivelling his neck, crackling his spine back into place. On his right knee his jeans were ripped, but she didn't know whether they had been before the fall. Because that's what it had been, she now realised, piecing together the evidence of the fully extended metal ladder propped against the wall beside them, leading up to an open sash window on the first floor. A large canvas sack, heavy with something angular, was swinging by one handle from the top of the ladder.

'What happened? What were you doing?'

'Stupid,' he said, brushing himself off. 'I thought it would be easier to lower the stuff out the window than go all the way round the stairs. I was leaning too far out the window and I was distracted. I thought I saw someone… The rope slipped and I couldn't let go and…'

He stopped talking as he turned his attention to Petra. He scanned her down, then up again, frowning. 'Do I know you from somewhere?'

'I don't think so,' she said. 'I would have…' She tried to stuff the words back in her mouth but failed. '…remembered.' She was blushing, she was sure. It felt hot in her clothes. She lowered her eyes and saw blood drooling from the muddy graze at his knee. 'Oh, God – you're bleeding. You'd better sort that out.'

He followed her gaze and waved it off. 'Ah, it's nothing. I'll wash it off inside.'

'Can I help you?'

'Uh, I'll be alright.' He smiled. 'Thanks.' He bent and picked up her bag and offered it to her.

'Okay. If you're sure.'

He nodded and disappeared through the house's red front door.

Petra stood watching the closed red door for a minute, as if it was going to do something remarkable. It was an English door, like you see on TV – a heavy, panelled and bevelled townhouse door – but it was freshly lacquered in good-luck red. At first glance the knocker set in its middle was like the others on this gentrified terrace of Victorian solid-brick abodes, but Petra noticed that it wasn't a stylised lion or bull holding the iron ring in its mouth, but a mean-looking goat-horned imp – Pan, maybe. It looked at her, grinning, and she looked back until a man hurried past along the pavement towards town and Petra started to move off, not wanting to look like she was loitering.

For a moment she'd forgotten where she was going. Oh, right – to the MyHealth to check in on her mother. But now, jolted off her path, the idea of a surprise visit to her mother before a scheduled routine day procedure seemed odd and invasive – much the same as a surprise drop-in to her changing room or gynae appointment.

Just after Petra had finished university here, her father had died, and they'd agreed that Helena should come to England to be closer to her only child 'in case anything happened'. Rod, her father, had been an Englishman – a Staffordshire mining engineer deployed to the Witwatersrand goldfields in the seventies – and they had all the requisite documents. At first Petra worried about the effect Helena's arrival would have on her social life, but she needn't have. Helena had always been able to look after herself, and made friends easily. Helena didn't seem to need Petra's looking-after – in fact, she didn't need much of anything from her.

There were only twenty-five minutes left of her lunch break. Suki wouldn't care if she was late back, of course, but Petra would. Keeping her dignity and sticking to her contracted hours in that mercy job was akin to a depressive getting dressed every morning – proving she still had some purpose in the grander scheme of things. The problem was, reality often didn't match her expectations. She was self-aware enough to know she tended to drift through everyday life with her mind in a soft fantasy of what things should be: work, love, duty, fairness, belonging. Her fancy was far more compelling than mundane reality – she liked to hope, she liked to feel worthwhile, she liked to feel needed; she liked to wait for inspiration, which didn't hit her all that often.

This tendency to impracticality, she knew, didn't make her a prime candidate for a *career* in anything. Bless Suki – she'd saved Petra from post-arts-degree destitution, and Petra wasn't going to abuse her kindness.

Twenty-five minutes, now twenty-four, may not be enough to visit her mother, but it was enough to do something impetuous. She spun on her heel and strode back to Brook Street. At the red door, she tried to lift the knocker, but it was welded down, ornamental. An electronic keypad on the left side of the frame spoke subtly of the modern world. Before thinking too much, Petra pressed the buzzer button at the bottom and heard it sound loudly in the hall. A few heavy clatters and a volley of hammering answered her. No footsteps.

Come to think of it, the falling man hadn't keyed in as far as she could remember. On the replay, he had swept inside, away from her, without a pause. She pushed at the door – and it swung open.

The hallway was longer than she'd imagined from the outside; it was more of corridor, the only light spilling from a bright doorway down the end, illuminating the dusty bootprints on the sealed-wood floor. Picture frames leaning against the skirting and a paint-flecked dropcloth draped over the open door of a closet, which had disgorged an assortment of weathered cardboard boxes brimming with files and papers and knots of what looked like electrical flex. The banging, then a heavy grate of shifting furniture, was coming from upstairs, accompanied by a loud, echoing phrase and a brief, barked laugh of men at work. Petra glanced behind her at the door, which had swung shut behind her. Maybe this wasn't a good idea. But her feet carried her onward, inward. She'd go as far as the lit room at the end of the corridor, and if she hadn't found the stairs or any hint of the falling man, she'd turn back.

As she advanced, the creak of the floorboards mercifully swallowed up by the heavy noises from upstairs, Petra noticed that the frames leant against the skirting held album covers and photographs of musicians. 'Two-Tone Zone', a Madness-like group of zoot-suited jazzmen posing against a chequerboard backdrop; 'The Sign of Six', a collection of Rastas seated around an oil-drum fire under a graffitied urban bridge; some more modern-looking pop stars, with full-on glamour shots; and a long-haired, be-jeaned rock-folk guy she half recognised. Finally, a couple of framed golden records shyly facing the wall.

A recording studio, lined up here alongside the tidy homes? It shouldn't surprise her, a lot of creative stuff happened in Leamington – games companies mostly, but also design and art and advertising and future tech, even some artists and novelists lurking. The hard part was knowing where to look. Since she'd come to England, she'd enjoyed imagining all the endeavour behind the narrow housefronts, all the private lives and public functions that happened behind those doors and those slender, serried windows. There was teeming variation behind those doors, and it was rare to get a look inside: a dentist's appointment, that time she went with Helena to the solicitor's office to witness her will, and the visits to those friends who'd invited her over. A small plaque, perhaps, a discreet name tag, would indicate a multi-million-pound enterprise rather than the brash steel, Perspex and neon signstacks you'd get in Joburg office parks. So, yeah, why not a recording studio too?

Petra had just squatted down to read the label on one of the gold records – The Specials – but she didn't have time to take in anything else before the air reverberated like the building was imploding and a man careered around a corner she hadn't even known was there.

'Watch out, love!' he called to her, and then was basically through the front door bearing the armload of planks or shelves with which he'd been hurtling down the stairs as if they were propelling him.

Her surprised exclamation died unheard and the air swirled by the plank-carrier settled. The banging and dragging upstairs had stopped and Petra could hear a lower conversation somewhere ahead of her, on this floor, and maybe one of the speakers was the falling man. She'd let him finish his conversation then say what she'd come back to say – before she lost her nerve. She hoped the conversation wouldn't last too long.

She headed towards the bright room, thinking that was where the voices might be coming from, but when she got to the room, it was empty. The glow was coming from a blend of arc light filtered with cloud-grey cloth reflector hoods, as if this was a photographic studio, and the dull daylight coming in through vast bay windows looking out over a surprisingly large and open garden. The corridor jinked ninety degrees to the right here and the conversation was coming from the next room over, audible now.

'You'll have to get this stuff out, too. By tomorrow, yeah?'

'Tomorrow?' That was the falling man's voice.

'That should be enough time, shouldn't it? You can just unscrew it and cart it out.'

'Wait. Listen. I thought you'd agreed with Gloria that we'd have till the end of the month. We need to find a buyer. We can't just rip out the whole console and… I've got nowhere to keep it.'

'Why don't you just flog it online?'

'It's an Audient Eighty Twenty-Four… you can't just *flog* it. It's high-end kit. Nobody will just…' The falling man paused, breathing in, clearly gathering himself to speak calmly. 'It needs to find the right buyer.'

Petra was inching along the corridor as they spoke, trying to get a view through the door without being seen. She peered through the hinge-slit to see a short guy in a pinstriped suit and emerald-green braces showing her falling man his phone.

'Here's one on eBay for five hundred quid.'

The falling man took another deep breath and forced his voice to stay level as he looked at the man's phone. 'That's one single preamp module, man. It's a tiny part of the setup. The whole console goes for tens of thousands.'

'Whatever. It needs to be gone. Tomorrow.' The guy in the suit shrugged and Petra, sensing the conversation was over, scurried back into the light room next door as he answered a silent call.

'I've got to ask Gloria what she wants to do with it,' the falling guy said. 'I'm clearing this place for her, not for you,' he added, less confidently, to his back.

But the suited man was already talking on the phone, making it halfway along the corridor before stopping, as if he'd found himself a private-enough bubble. 'Yeah, I hope so,' he said, deliberately loud. 'The boy's dragging his feet and making excuses, but we'll get it sorted.' He listened for a moment. 'Yeah... yeah.' He laughed. 'Yeah, you're right. In a few a days this place will have a lot less soul... and all the better for it.' Swallowing his chuckle in response to something said on the phone, he started off towards the front door again.

'Don't worry. Ned will sort out the electrical compliance.' Pause. 'Yes. These old buildings are always a little dodgy but there's no reason to trouble the authorities. We'll make sure it's safe without their involvement.'

The last thing Petra heard of the conversation was, 'It's a great location, Curtis. It's a great choice.' He banged the door shut behind him.

Petra knew she should just go. She'd got in the middle of something she shouldn't be involved in, and she didn't want the guy to know she'd overheard what that arsehole had said. She thought she heard him moving something in the room next door, so she'd just hurry back down the corridor and leave. The moment had passed – or been punctured – anyhow.

She took a breath and stepped out of her hiding place behind the door – and straight into the falling man.

He frowned for a moment, and then smiled, and his expression – of happiness-to-see-her, of welcome, of hospitality – made her buzz inside, made her organs literally resonate with him.

'Oh, hi... I...' She pointed lamely down the corridor, as if that would explain her decision outside on the pavement to ditch her mom and come in here and offer this man her phone number.

He looked at her, but didn't help her fill in any words.

She straightened up, put her shoulders back, cocked her hip, would have flicked her hair back if she'd had the arm room: he was standing quite close, neither of them had really moved apart since they'd almost run into each other. 'I didn't want to leave without, you know, swapping numbers.'

'Why?'

'For observation purposes, you know. You were injured and I'd fail in my duty of care if I left you without following up.'

'You have a duty of care?'

She looked into his eyes, he looked back. It was still there, that gut-pull. She hadn't imagined it.

He thought for a moment, studying her face. He took his phone out of his pocket. 'I guess it wouldn't hurt,' he said. 'Duty of care and all.'

She handed him her phone, an act of trust that struck her as unspeakably intimate the few times she had done it. He typed his name and number and handed it back, the plastic slab completing the circuit between them. Falling Guy would be known as Vincent Rice from now on. She texted him back. *<Petra. Care and observation.>* By the time she thought that sounded a bit cringey and stalkerish, it was too late, but the corner of his mouth twitched.

'Okay,' she said. 'Duty done. I'll call you about our follow-up appointment.'

'Yeah, there might be, you know, after-effects.' He walked her to the door.

'Who was that idiot on the phone?' she said as she opened the door. Leaving things unsaid was not a good way to start a friendship.

'Oh. Just an idiot.'

'I heard what he said. I'm sure you did, too.'

He shrugged, unwilling to be drawn out.

'People shouldn't be allowed to act like that.'

'Of course not, but they do.'

'What's happening here?' Petra asked. 'What are you doing?'

'Dismantling the studio, clearing everything out. My grandfather died last year and those guys just bought the place. I'm clearing his things for my nan, then helping them subdivide.'

'Sorry. That must be hard.'

'Yeah. But I'd rather be involved. If Picton and Worthing had their way, they'd throw my granddad's whole life's work in the tip.'

2   When Petra got back to the shop, there were a couple of browsers – one a woman with a restless child of about five or six, who Petra immediately red-flagged. A student-looking guy was waiting at the vacant counter. Suki was probably doing something in the back, and Petra felt unnecessarily guilty about having taken a lunch break.

'Sorry to keep you. Can I help?'

'No worries. I haven't been waiting long.'

Petra sold the guy a pack of Sammi Superstars baseball cards from Korea, scanning the CCTV screens for Suki as the debit card machine connected. There was an old couple upstairs flicking through the racks of prints, but no Suki yet to appear on the cycle.

Needful Things. When Suki had named the shop, Petra thought it was named after the Stephen King book about a shop where each item has its true spiritual home. But when she asked, Suki said she'd never heard of *Needful Things*. Her business plan was to stock the store with 'things that speak to me' and wait for the style-starved customers to flock in and buy everything. But Petra couldn't help thinking, not so deep down, that most of the crap they sold was absolutely needless. There was so much *stuff* per person in England, you couldn't even give decent clothes or books or furniture away. Most of it ended up in the charity shops that lined the high streets, a fraction being rehomed. Nobody *needed* more pointless bric-a-brac in their lives, especially here – not one more designer plastic kids'-movie doll for grown-ups, not one more wine-glass charm, not one more fake neon diner sign, not one more gilded 'Love' mantel sculpture.

The shoppers seemed to agree. The business had languished in the red ever since opening. Sales income barely covered a quarter of the rental, never mind Petra's decent salary or the other overheads. But Suki was a Barlow – the Barlow black sheep no less, as she told it, refusing to go into the family 'law-slash-finance-slash-fostering-massive-state-corruption-in-third-world-countries' business. It was irksome for the family that she'd refused to come back home to Hampshire-slash-Kensington from Leamington after studying sociology-psychology-anthropology at Warwick University, of all places. At least she could have taken philosophy, politics and economics, the arts stream for the moneyed student with ambitions. Nonetheless, Needless Things, as Petra heretically thought of it, kept her occupied, and for that reason the relatively tiny write-off was worthwhile to her family.

The restless boy was beginning to act up now, his whining and flopping becoming more intense as his mother continued to ignore him, and from the way he was swinging on her sleeve it was clear to Petra that he was going to knock something over – her bet was on the glass-fronted display cabinet of US Congress Funko figures. As it happened, it was the dump bin of *Hot Tattooed Dudes Taking Their Shirts Off* colouring books – Suki had ordered fifty copies, no return, and even she had given up the hobby after three and a half pages.

'Charlie!' the mother scolded, dragging the kid out into the cold afternoon without an apology or a glance at Petra. It could have been worse. It might have been the Funkos, and although the cabinet was fitted with safety glass, it could have caused an injury. Or it could have been milkshake, or vomit, or piss, all of which she'd cleaned up in the five years they'd been open. She couldn't blame the kids for getting bored, and she couldn't blame the parents for wanting a moment's peace to browse in the shop. It was a blameless situation.

As she gathered up the books, the old couple came downstairs, the man apologetically putting a pack of Cartier-Bresson notecards on the counter as if they ought to buy something after browsing. Petra rang up the sale, made change for the ten-pound note, and the couple left. The shop descended into the stillness of vacancy.

The air circulated differently when there were no customers. Two-thirty now, and the sun had sunk behind the buildings on this side of Regent Street. Without the reflected light from the buildings over the road, it was suddenly dusky inside. Petra resisted turning on the lights. She watched the people passing by the shop window, and for a brief, magical moment she felt transported to fifties Paris, the monochrome silhouettes and shadows composing themselves into stark phrases like those on the old man's cards.

But the shop was not entirely vacant – from somewhere in the back offices, Petra could hear the low murmur of Suki talking on the phone, the jagged rhythm of half a conversation. More to indicate that she was back from lunch, rather than from thirst, she went through to the kitchen to boil the kettle, and picked up a mug, intending to stand in the office doorway and mime an offer of tea-drinking.

Suki was sitting at her cluttered desk with her chair turned to face the window, the phone pointed at her mouth, not pressed against her ear, as if she didn't want the other party's voice in her head. That and her tone, which had become extremely high-bred and formal, meant that it was a family call – most likely Ben, the youngest of her three brothers and the one they delegated to translate the Barlows' home truths into a language Suki might abide.

When Suki sensed Petra in the doorway, she wrapped up the call. 'Yah, fine. We'll talk later.' The irony never escaped Petra: people like the Barlows said 'yah', while she'd soon learned to change the South African 'ja' to 'yeah' to blend in just a little more. Suki swung around in her chair, setting a pill bottle on the desk in front of her.

'The meds again?' Petra asked.

'Yup.'

'Couldn't they just get the prescription filled and deliver the meds to you without you asking every time?'

'You'd think so. It's in their power. But they enjoy my mortification, my debasement.' Suki spoke these words in a deliberately hammy way, and smiled, flicking the pill bottle to the side of the desk.

'How's it feeling today, Sook?'

'Much better. Getting there. I was this close to not calling Ben. Sticking to over-the-counter, but I think I'll need the special medicaments for another month.' She winced as she turned in her chair.

Three months ago – blame her new metal-flanged biker boots – Suki had slipped down the stairs in the shop and popped a disc and nicked a vertebra. It could have been a lot worse, she might have been paralysed, but still she'd been in serious pain since. The way her family had handled it was infuriating. Taking complete charge of the private medical bills, yes, but also treating Suki like a child. Petra wouldn't understand the full dynamics of the Barlow family, but she could recognise the mean mix of punitive control they applied to her. They clearly didn't like that she'd opted out of her family's questionable activities, but instead of disowning her or simply letting her go her own way, it seemed to Petra that they used every opportunity to keep her under their thumb, reliant and compliant. She didn't know why Suki just went along with it, asking cap-in-hand for her medicine every month. She would never understand: here in the old world, old money and old malice was rooted far deeper than she could ever fathom in her colonial naivety.

'Don't look at me that way. These are special medicaments, Pet. They're not easily available on the high street.' She shrugged. 'You're probably right I should try for my own supply, but they're expensive and it's not easy to get a prescription. And if I did, I couldn't afford them.'

Suki's money was all tied up in the family. She received an allowance on a handful of debit cards, and simply directed all her bills to the family accountants. It never really seemed to bother her that she had no savings of her own. A few years after Petra had come to study in the then United Kingdom, just after Helena had come to join her, the newly independent England had privatised the National Health Service, so now it operated on two tiers. A creaking, delay-ridden basic service, and everything else covered to various extents by expensive private health insurance.

'Jeez. Tell me about it,' Petra said.

'Speaking of which, how's your mum?' Suki said as she pushed up and slinked her black-clad frame towards the shop floor; the stiffness of her movements somehow adding to the elegant effect. Petra followed her, regarding the perfect purple-tinted black dye job and the impeccably shaped and knife-keen fall of her hair down her back: the well-bred kid could try to escape her family but somehow she would always remember her breeding. It was as if she'd gone to walking school, for God's sake.

Petra hesitated. 'I didn't actually get to her.'

Suki turned and smiled quizzically. 'You didn't go and see your mum, then?'

'Well, it was a very minor thing and I doubt she even wanted me there. Anyhow, I'm going to pick her up later, so…' Her guilty prattling ran out of steam.

'What did you do instead, Pet? You look like the cat who got the cream.'

Petra waved her phone with its precious cargo: *Vincent Rice, Falling Guy*. 'I met someone interesting.'

'Really?'

'Yeah, I know I have a track record of dubious attachments…'

Suki smirked – she'd helped Petra mop up after a handful of her embarrassing forays up the wrong tree.

'But this is different, I can feel it.'

3   Yes, Petra had chosen to chase Vincent instead of check in on Helena before the procedure, so she was anxious to collect her on time at least. It was a really short drive, but there was a broken-down bus on Dormer Place and she hurried into the MyHealth Clarendon Hospital's waiting room ten minutes after the agreed time.

'I'm sorry I'm late, Mum,' Petra said as she hurried into the waiting room.

'No problem, love. I've been enjoying these adverts on the screen here.' Helena's full-chested voice and unmodified West Rand accent reverberated through the little space – an old parlour of a Victorian house subsumed into a modern conglomerate, now lined with veneer flooring and white paintwork and a cabinet that might have held free tea or water back in the day but now only supported racks of brochures. The room was fitted with three large flatscreens showing frames of public health advice between adverts. About ten waiting patients sitting evenly spaced from one another on once-plush scandinomic chairs, bought before bankers' wages were prioritised over public services. 'And who's this *Mum* you're talking about?' It was something of a running joke, Helena calling out Petra's attempts to blend in to her new home still, after years in immigrant limbo. Petra had never referred to Helena as 'Mum' before they came to England;

in private she still defaulted to 'Mom', and Helena saw this as a lack of authenticity. Petra used to counter that trying to blend in showed consideration for your hosts, a respect for their hospitality, a willingness to get to know them, but she'd given up arguing. She knew Helena understood and was just needling her for fun.

Helena's loudness could be read as the hearty jollity of an arty woman launching into her sixties, the way she intended it. But Petra knew that it might just as easily be seen as arrogance or aggression, a form of attention-seeking, deliberately designed to upset the delicate social order in awkward public spaces like this. Already an old man in the corner by the window, woollen coat and scarf still protectively wound about him despite the overheated air, coughed and murmured, and Helena, awkwardometer operating on high, turned to face him.

'You're from here, aren't you? I mean, you're English born and bred?'

The man said nothing.

'Could you tell me, sir – would you like it better if she started calling me "Mum" to pretend to be English, or do you think she should share her wondrous and exotic uniqueness with her new compatriots? Bring them some of the warmth and spice she carries from Africa?'

The man stared fixedly ahead of him. Petra was about to say something to her mother, but her glance was drawn to the woman sitting two seats over from them in a slant of transient sunlight from the window. A shock of orange curls, half a face. The other masked in shadow. The woman turned, and for a moment she was out of the shadow, in complete sunlight.

But she still only had half a face. It wasn't a mask or a bandage. The lower half of her jaw was just... not there. As if it had been eaten away by small teeth. That's how it seemed for the second the woman turned. But she settled back into the slant of light and her face looked natural again. Just a weird optical illusion. The shift in light and contrast. The woman was looking back towards her, but not really focused on her. Petra thought she should stop staring. Besides, Helena was still talking.

'I always tell her she's too old to be learning new ways to fit in. That's what a kid does at school, hey?'

'Stop it,' Petra hissed, turning her attention back to her mother as she felt the spite coming from the old guy. She physically rotated her mother towards the door.

'I think people should be themselves, don't you?' This was directed more at the air than at anyone specific. Helena was winding down, her voice mercifully becoming less public. 'The rest of the world can like it or lump it. Hey, love?'

'Yes, Mum. Shush, Mum,' Petra said.

'You're too right, love,' the man said, clearing his hoarse throat and offering a smile to Petra's great surprise and relief. She'd been envisioning Helena stoking an ugly scene, an episode of go-back-home apoplexy. 'My daughter's the same. They worry a lot, don't they? Too many people telling them how to behave.'

Helena turned to face him. 'My point exactly, sir,' she laughed. 'It's a pleasure to know you.'

Petra kept her arm around Helena's shoulders and directed her towards the exit. 'Let's go, Mom.'

'Far as I'm concerned, you're welcome here, love. Just be

yourself,' the man advised. 'And remember to have fun. Life is short.'

Once they'd signed the paperwork at the reception desk, Petra hustled Helena through to the cashier's room, remembering not to drag her mother too fast. Helena was giving no indication that she'd had her side sliced open a few hours before and a vacuum tube stuck into her organs… 'Is a gallbladder even an organ?' she asked Helena. They were like that – Petra fully expected Helena to slot into the gap in her thoughts, and often she did. As an only child with nobody else to compare with, Petra thought she had a close bond with her mother. Sometimes she imagined them like the sort of sisters you'd see on TV; Helena had always been on the same wavelength as Petra. She could follow the unspoken trail of logic that had led from one utterance to the next.

'I think so, ja. It stores bile. For later use.' She handed her discharge forms to the woman behind the reception desk. 'I'd prefer not to store my bile,' she told the receptionist.

The woman nodded noncommittally. 'Could I see your medical insurance card? We don't seem to have it on the system.'

'You guys photocopied it when I came in,' Helena said.

'They must not have entered it. Do you mind?' She stuck her hand out.

'Not at all.' Helena fished in her backpack – she didn't do handbags – and finally retrieved her wallet containing the card. The woman generated a bill and Helena paid the shortfall amount that went over the deposit she'd already paid. Trying not to wince, Petra bit her tongue. This wasn't the place or time to discuss her mother's finances.

'Wasn't that a nice old man?' Helena said as they stepped out to the road. 'I hope he's going to get better.'

'I thought you were embarrassing him. I thought he was going to get angry.'

'I know you did, love.'

The full set of assumptions and prejudices Petra had learned growing up in South Africa didn't translate here, so she'd got used to being wrong about people. Chalk it up to affirmative experience. She changed the subject. 'How do you feel? Was it sore?'

'Fine. Really. It was just like a dentist appointment.'

'Yeah, except with abdominal surgery. We're over here. Suki lent me her car.'

'I could have taken the bus home, you know,' Helena said. 'Or walked.'

'I'm not that bad a daughter. I wouldn't expect you to walk home after surgery,' Petra said, fishing for affirmation she knew she'd get.

'You're a lovely daughter. The best daughter I could ever have.' Despite all the changes in her life – her father first walking out on them, and then shacking up with Helena again once Petra had left, then dying on her; Helena's teaching studio burning down; the insurance failure; moving here at her advanced age – Helena's love remained constant, and it was in these ritual exchanges that she proved it. As much as Helena prided herself on being free-thinking and unconventional, she knew the importance of saying the right thing at the right time. Petra was twenty-nine years old, but her mother's trusty refrain felt as comforting as if she was eight years old and having Vicks rubbed on her chest.

Helena winced when she bent to get in the car – Suki's little racing-striped mint-green Abarth was particularly low to the ground, and Petra remembered who she was here for. She drove carefully through Leamington and out towards Warwick. It was a short way, no more than a half-hour stroll on a better day.

'Did you get to see them doing it?' Petra asked. The gallstone drainage had been performed under local anaesthetic. Petra had looked it up – acute cholecystoenterostomy was meant to be a quick in-and-out. A small incision, a stent, drain the stones and any infected fluid – Helena's gallstones were small enough to drain, but plentiful enough to be extremely painful – bung up with painkillers and antibiotics, and away you go. Next customer, please.

'I didn't try, love.'

Over the river (Shakespeare's Avon!) and on to the MyPharm at the big supermarket to collect Helena's meds. On the NHS, medicines used to be free with a small prescription fee, but now the system was pretty much like it had been in South Africa. You could queue for eight hours on your specified appointment day at the government depot for your generics, or you could buy your meds full price at the pharmacy and, depending on your medical scheme, you could claim some or most of the cost back. Petra knew what she wanted for Helena. The full course of medicines now, and no queueing.

When they'd discussed getting onto the MyHealth scheme, and Petra had pushed for the comprehensive cover for Helena, she hadn't argued, even though it would cost precisely half her housing budget. The fact that she'd accepted the trade-off –

full medical cover and a tiny, sunless ex-council flat in exchange for space, greenery and a future of *essential services only* – showed Petra that Helena was worried for the future, although she'd never admit it. That Helena had given up her light, her view of birds in a little garden, was privately devastating to Petra. If only Petra had made more of herself. Instead of fucking around trying to be an 'artist' all those years, Petra could have got a real job and be on a career path; she could have been renting a place with more than one bedroom and Helena wouldn't have to stay here. God, if they'd stayed in South Africa and she'd been a lawyer or something, she could have owned a house with a separate cottage. But her father had screwed them both over. Apart from the fact that they could only spend his money here because of pension rules and exchange controls, his death had hit Helena harder than his disloyalty and she still hadn't quite got over it, even though he had died more than ten years ago. Helena liked to pretend she was a free spirit, but she was supernaturally loyal – to her loves, to her vision, to her idea of what love and life should be – and Petra realised she'd inherited the same bull-headed idealism.

Then back towards the river and right at the Indian restaurant, she found a parking spot near enough to the door of Helena's building. Next to a trio of men leaning against the wall, working on rolling a cigarette, long toms of Stella inserted in their coat pockets as if they were cupholders, the big billboard on the side of the convenience store was advertising three shows the Emscote Road commuters could watch on TV. The vast image was split into three – one with the leering skull face of a glacial zombie, one with a devil-horned witch, and one with the hideous, menacing face of the American president. Up close, the effect was quite overwhelming, and often Petra wondered if it was fair to show that to the children passing by to school every morning or the innocent folk nipping into the shop for a pint of milk.

Petra walked close to Helena along the pavement across the road from the three men. When she'd first come here, she'd been fearless – she'd grown up in Joburg, for God's sake, and Leamington drunks and dealers hadn't frightened her. It had all been a bit like a holiday. At first, the conjoined towns of Leamington and Warwick had felt like a living theme park. Leamington's Regency World counterpointed by Warwick's grand Tudor Land and Fun Castle. Down the road, there were pubs older than Shakespeare! So the parts in between – Economically Depressed Midlands Nightlife World – had also seemed a bit unreal, but the gloss eventually wore off. She'd suffered years of overlong nights and humourless, blank-eyed and grimy catcalls and while, thank the Lord, people weren't allowed to carry guns here, she'd seen enough pictures of the grotesque, crenelated Rambo things used in knife attacks, read enough news stories of women murdered on their way home, to stop being complacent. All in all, it was safer not to be fearless.

So a pop over to the other side of the road it was, until safely past the men, who in the event hadn't even looked up at them but had laughed in a lively way when the short one had got the blunt lit. Helena had winced again as she'd leaned over to enter her code into the pad at the lobby's reinforced glass door.

'We'd better get you upstairs,' Petra said as they pushed through the door. 'Will you be able to have a bath? I'll start up a soup or—'

She stopped talking when she realised they weren't alone in the lobby. A woman was standing in the dead-end corner among bikes and forgotten boxes under a flickering downlight. Petra had to look twice, but she was sure of what she saw. The woman was young, probably mid-twenties, and had a trim body, somehow elegant in her coat, not dumpy and overquilted like Petra always felt in winter. The mouth and jaw were alright – she would have been pretty, even, Petra thought, if it weren't for the eyes.

Her jet-black hair was held back in a rose velvet barrette. It might have been elegantly styled in the morning, but by this time in the evening it was lank, looked a little damp or greasy, and strands of it hung loose. Her mouth hung open, as if something forgotten was on her lips. Thoughtful, hesitant, not like Petra's mouth would look if her eyes were like that.

Because Petra's stare was drawn back to the woman's eyes.

They were empty. Not just dull, or tired, or lifeless. The irises were all pupil and the void inside them was sucking the world into them. That's how it appeared for a moment, before she realised that the woman's eyes were just red, painfully red; puffy and swollen from sobbing.

'My God,' Petra said, hurrying over once she'd got her limbs to work. 'Are you alright? What happened? Can I...'

But a trick of the light, a flick and a flash.

'I'm alright, love. You don't need to fuss. It's only three floors.'

Petra turned to where Helena was watching her. 'No, Mom, not you... I...' She turned back to the bicycles and boxes. 'Where...' Petra pushed between the bikes in case the woman had collapsed there while she'd turned to Helena. But she was gone – she was probably embarrassed or self-conscious; she must have hurried out the front door while Petra's back was turned.

'God, I hope she'll be alright,' Petra said.

'Who's this now?' Helena said.

'The woman who was standing here, Mom. Jeez, did you see her face?'

Helena stared at her. 'Nah, love. I didn't see anyone.'

4 Petra left Suki's car in the bay behind Needful Things before walking home. Usually when she borrowed it she'd keep it until the morning, but tonight Suki was heading to the Leisure Dome events venue at Birmingham airport for a night of queue fieldwork at a Reprise Girls concert.

One of Suki's side hustles was a freelance queue-research collective she'd formed called Line Logic Limited, whose services were commissioned by a range of events promoters, shopping malls, casinos, transport franchises and the like. Their methods were based on a mixture of social psychology and mind-control techniques. At a concert like tonight's, Suki and her colleagues would use a variety of diagnostic tools to record customer behaviour as they queued for entrance, for snacks, for the toilets, and at the parking lots and train stations afterwards. In this case, the aim was to try to balance customer experience with cost-effectiveness, but everyone knew that at concerts, customer experience was by far the lighter end of that balance. As evidenced every summer, music fans of a certain age and deprived of regular sunlight would pay hundreds of pounds to crawl through piss-and-beer-saturated mud to be in the general vicinity of a band they liked. You had to be more careful of customer experience where attendance was voluntary, or if a conference could be moved to another venue next year.

The work had originated at a psychology student club at university but Petra had no idea why Suki still did it. She certainly didn't need the money, and it wasn't that she needed to get out of the house. Suki went out a lot, had a wide circle of what she called her 'frenemies'. Maybe it was just stimulating fun, and more so because it was something the Barlow clan hadn't laid out for her.

Other times, and for other clients, she'd played a more insidious role. She'd be tasked with deliberately cutting queues at banks, pushing down the up escalator at the Bullring shopping centre, farting in lifts, singing loudly on trains. It was clear she enjoyed these jobs more, and Suki would regale Petra with preparatory talk on the Milgram experiments, the pros and cons of serpentine queues, queuer distraction, misdirection and redirection, and the polite flesh-eating zombie sheep effect (Suki had probably made this term up for Petra's benefit). She thought back on Helena's performance at the hospital earlier – she'd be a great fit if Suki ever needed any more fieldworkers. She could earn some pocket money being her embarrassing self.

Suki had her phone pressed to her ear when Petra unlocked the shop's rear door, so she handed over the keys and mimed that she'd see her sometime tomorrow.

Walking home, Petra texted Helena. *<Everything okay? Was the soup nice?>*

She knew her mother would be fine – she was just overcompensating, still feeling guilty for earlier. Sick mother blown off for random strange man. She toyed with the idea that she had just been carried away by a moment, the surprise of him appearing in mid-air, crashing to her feet like that. But even now, hours later, the thought of Vincent, his gentle eyes, his perfectly imperfect features, the sprig of grey through his beard that sang of life and love and laughter and tears and experience, sent a little jolt through her. Yes, she knew this was an overreaction, and yes, she knew that she was prone to them, but it was fun to feel in love. It lightened the gloomy days. Wasn't it better to delude yourself into feeling love than feeling hate?

Vincent had been cool and relaxed, but not too cool. She could swear she felt an intense something – *recognition* – from him too. When he'd handed over her phone, his fingers had been trembling just a little.

<*I'm fine love. Stop stalking me*>

And a few seconds later.

<*thanks <3*>

<*I'll stalk you again tomorrow then. Call if you need anything, okay?*>

It was only a little after seven when Petra got home. It had seemed later – it had been a long, busy day. Somehow, seeing that poor woman in Helena's lobby made her think it was far later than it was, as if you shouldn't be able to see awfulness like that until after ten. She'd replayed the incident in her mind as she walked. Should she have run out into the road, chased the woman down, demanded that she accept some help or go to the clinic across the street? She could have asked her what happened, who hit her like that… but what could Petra do? It wasn't any of her business. The woman had just been standing there, not asking her for anything. You can't force someone to accept help.

What also troubled her was just how fast she'd disappeared. She'd only turned to her mother for a second, spoken a couple of words, and when she'd túrned back the woman was gone. Maybe there was another door behind the lobby storage space that she wasn't aware of. Or maybe she'd been talking to her mom for a little longer than it seemed and she'd just walked out the front door. The lobby was small; you could cross it in five steps. The woman was just on her way out, there was nothing weird about it. It was like a magic trick – the flickering light, distraction, misdirection. That's the only way people disappeared in real life.

Her flat stared blankly back at her as she pushed inside and dropped her bags by the door. The too-expensive fourth-floor studio at the corner of Dale Street had probably been a laundry or utility room for this building that had now been split up and converted for student rents. But it was home. The neighbours were a blend of studious, anonymous and quiet – none of the all-night parties Helena had warned her about when she'd been considering this flat. And since she was on the top level, she didn't suffer from ceiling percussion or much road noise. The benefit of the recent conversion was that the windows were double-glazed and well insulated and the furnishings were clean and new, even if utterly characterless. Quite frankly, after spending the day in Suki's trove of weird whims, coming back to a bit of neutrality and blandness always suited her.

The more concerning blank stare was from the fridge when she opened it. She'd have to go out again and get something to eat. That was one aspect of self-sufficiency she'd never wrapped her head around. And things were so convenient here. She lived so centrally, she could literally put her coat and Uggs over her PJs and stump a couple of very narrow blocks to an all-night supermarket – it really wasn't hard, but yet her fridge was empty.

Before thinking too much, she picked up her phone and called Vincent.

'I didn't know if I should bother you twice in one day but I'm really hungry.'

'Shouldn't you eat, then?'

'Tell me… do you eat too?'

He paused, laughed briefly. 'I do. Yeah, I've been known to.'

'What do you like to eat?'

'Um, a variety of things. In fact, I'm looking at some foodstuff right now.'

'Really? Where is this foodstuff to be found? And can I come and look at it too?' Oh shit. Too late, she imagined where he might be talking from; she'd been so carried away by the rhythm of the conversation and his easy, easy voice in her ear – but what if he's at home? With his wife. God, Petra, you know nothing about him.

Another pause. 'I'm not sure.'

Petra could've, would've, should've just put down the phone. But she didn't want to let this go, and she didn't know if she was just kidding herself, but she was certain he didn't want to either. 'I mean, we need to eat.'

'You know, you're right,' he said, as if settling an argument with himself. 'We do. That's why I'm stood here.'

'Where?'

'The Express.'

'The one on the Parade?'

'Yeah.'

'So can I come see you? We can eat.'

'Yeah, that'll be good.'

'Give me fifteen.'

She disconnected and cursed herself. Fifteen minutes? What was she thinking? That wasn't enough time to make herself look or smell nice. But she couldn't expect him to wait in a supermarket all night. It seemed a good idea at the time, to take his banter to its logical extension, instead of suggesting they meet at a bar or restaurant like a normal person would. That would have felt too forced somehow, too formal.

Screw it, it would have to be pits, ponytail and a new shirt. He'd seen her like this at lunchtime and hadn't minded, so let this be a test of whether what she was feeling meant anything. If not, if he was disappointed in her, it would be good to know early. But somehow, she felt confident. That voice, those eyes – they resonated with her vibe. Or however Helena's favoured eighties funk-fusion put it.

When Petra got to the supermarket three minutes late, Vincent was holding a melon and a cucumber like Hamlet facing a particularly difficult choice. Surely he'd noticed her coming up the street and posed like that for her. The idea of being watched, waited for, sent a complex flurry of fear and excitement shooting down her spine.

'I'm glad you came,' he said, putting the produce back in their bins. 'I was about to be picked up by security.'

Petra played along, glancing at the security guard at the door, a large man she'd seen here often and who seemed friendly enough, but who was actually training his gaze her way.

'Nice though Leamington is,' he continued, 'they don't like people like me loitering in the fresh produce aisle.'

'I'm sorry,' she said, remembering that rude idiot at the studio. He spoke like that simply because he could. 'Sorry to make you stand here. I could have made a less awkward plan, hey.' She deliberately let the South African inflection slip off her lips. She didn't want to try to blend into the background, act like anyone else to impress him; she wanted him to get to know her as she was.

'It's alright,' he said, making his way towards the exit, where he nodded at the guard. 'Cheers, Zim.'

'Where's your shopping?' she asked.

'I didn't want to carry loads of bags around. I'll pick them up later.'

They settled on pizza and headed over to Basement Barry, ordering before finding a nook in the arched cellar downstairs, next to a rusted nautical artefact with a thick steel frame and a glass lens, and a Basquiat-style painting of a banana on a bicycle. Vincent snapped open his can of apple juice and Petra pretended to savour her sparkling water. She could have done with a glass of wine, but didn't want to booze alone.

'I still can't get over the fact that I made you wait twenty minutes in the bloody Express and you didn't even get to do your groceries. I'm so sorry!'

'It's alright.'

Now that she had the chance to sit across from him and really look at him, she still couldn't place his age – the grey strands in his trim beard meant probably over thirty, but he could be a fresh-looking thirty-five or even forty-five. Would it be rude to ask? Yes. 'So, were you holding that melon and cucumber the whole time? It was a good look.'

'No. I was just trying something. I also checked out the local history books, which I'd never noticed before. It was quite interesting, actually. I thought I knew all there was to know about Leamington.'

'Have you been here all your life?'

'Yeah. My grandfather came here in the seventies.'

'The Windrush generation?'

'No. That was earlier. The fifties, after the war. My granddad came from Malawi, not the Caribbean.'

Petra was blushing, she could feel it. 'Christ, what an idiot. I'm sorry.'

Vincent shrugged. 'For what?'

'I was only half the world out. Making stupid generalisations.'

'It's fine. You asked. More than most people do. Plus, my nan's Jamaican, so you're half right.'

She smiled her thanks to him.

'Anyway,' he said. 'I try not to bother about identity politics wherever I can avoid it. Sometimes it gets in your face but most of the time you can ignore it. It's much better here than what my granddad went through in Malawi, what his family experienced when they first moved here.'

'That's a generous way of looking at it, I suppose,' she said, taking a sip of her water. 'Still, don't you get sick of it?'

'What?'

'Trying to be good. For them.' The watchers, the judges, the racists, the nationalists, the xenophobes.

Vincent sighed, nodded once.

'I mean,' Petra went on, 'I've got so much less to complain about than so many people have, and still I sometimes feel targeted. I feel watched, like the big *They* are just waiting for me to do something wrong and confirm their suspicions.'

Vincent puffed his cheeks out. 'Try being black. You can be twentieth-generation British, and they'll always see you as a criminal straight off the boat.'

'Exactly. That's what I'm saying. Don't you get sick of it?'

Vincent shrugged.

When Petra saw he wasn't going to say more, she pulled herself together. She shouldn't be haranguing him ten minutes into their date. She changed tack. 'What did your grandparents do here when they arrived?'

'My Nan Gloria was a nurse – worked her way up to matron at the rehab hospital. She met my Granddad Max there, who was also here to train as an RN.'

'This was your grandfather who… from the studio?' Vincent nodded. 'How did he get involved in that?'

'Max was a musician in Malawi. Jazz, pop. The hospital work was a job, but music was always his first love. He could play everything – keyboards, bass, guitar, sax. He used to tour a lot, across to Zambia and down to South Africa. Banda took against artists like him – the whole scene was too liberal for his national programme – and Max stayed on after his training.'

Took against him. That was a laden euphemism if ever she'd heard one. It echoed with the agony of beatings, arbitrary imprisonment, torture. 'There's so much I don't know about the region that I should,' Petra said, regretting the heavy direction of the conversation. 'My dad was English, my mom's deeply South African. So in a way we're sort of transient semi–sub–Saharan neighbours, right?'

Vincent smiled, but warily. These things were complicated, and Petra knew that. 'Well, I'm English. Never been anywhere in Africa.' Petra bit her tongue and just nodded. If she said sorry one more time… 'But I know what you're saying,' he said, generously rescuing her from her hole again. 'Our families have come from a long way and we've both wound up here, now,' he said, indicating the space between them on the table. 'That's okay, isn't it?'

'Yeah,' she said. 'That's the important part.' She hastily rewound the conversation. 'You were saying how your granddad got to own the studio?'

'Oh, yeah, medical jobs started to be outsourced and became a bit of an unrewarding slog. Max had been gigging and doing sound tech at Brook Street on the side and they offered him a full-time job, and then he became a partner, and then he sorta became the last survivor.'

'And now that guy from earlier, Francis, he's buying the place?'

'His boss, yeah. Guy called Curtis Worthing – he's a—' He swallowed what he was going to say and looked over his shoulder as if Curtis Worthing might be right in this basement with them. 'The property's worth a lot. They're keeping half of it and converting the rest into flats.'

'Was there no way you could keep running the business? Keep it intact and rent it from this Curtis guy?'

'I guess they can make more money from flats. Besides,' Vincent shrugged, 'there's only Gloria left who knows anything about music, and she doesn't want to run the business alone.'

'Why don't you help her?'

He snorted a derisive laugh. 'I don't know enough about it. Don't have a musical bone in my body. Anyway, I'm not planning to…' He stopped talking.

'You sounded convincing when I heard you talking about the equipment.' *When I'd been spying on you, that is.*

'Yeah, that's tech stuff, not music.'

Petra guessed that the tech stuff and the music would go hand in hand in a studio, but didn't know enough about it to say anything. Besides, it seemed to be a sore spot. Gouts of historical sadness and disappointment were loaded into the sale, that much she could see.

'Besides,' he continued, 'the business was running at a loss even when Max was alive. We'd never even afford the utilities.'

'So you've thought about it, at least.'

'Yeah, for sure.' He trained a look on her, deciding whether to add something else. Finally he opened his mouth again. 'You know, my daugh—'

Their electronic order buzzer sprang into life, cutting him off, and Vincent went up the narrow, creaking stairs to collect their food. Whatever he was going to mention seemed important and Petra wished he'd been able to finish.

She watched his wake settle behind him as he left and pondered their meeting so far. Call it a date. It did feel like a date; it certainly was the most date-like hangout she'd had for a while. Why had she allowed it to take such a serious turn?

Normally, she'd never talk politics or probe into someone's family history a minute after meeting them, but even though it was spoiling his mood and she was probably busy crashing and burning, she still felt there was something not normal, something better than normal, about Vincent and their serendipitous meeting.

Deep down, she couldn't shake the feeling that he had fallen into her life for a reason, no matter how she tried to write it off as the fanciful yearnings of a lonely person. Maybe the reason wasn't love, as she'd assumed and hoped when it had happened, but there was definitely some reason. She was being real with him, feeling entirely natural, asking him questions simply because she was interested in the answers, not because they were the polite or optimal thing to ask; she was revealing her own unformed and vulnerable worldview rather than presenting a curated, polished picture of herself. No matter how badly it was going, she couldn't bring herself to regret it. When she felt her best, in her most confident moments, she was messy, interesting, decidedly uncurated – and something about Vincent encouraged that. This evening and its muddled imperfection was a moment of authenticity like she hadn't felt in... forever. No posturing tonight, no trying to fit in, no acting the good immigrant – just failing authentically.

She laughed to herself and looked up, focusing on the people around her. There were just four tables crammed into this chamber of the basement, two slightly larger tables with students squished around them, and across the room another small table, where a man in a cream suit and a white-banded black fedora sat facing her. He lounged on his chair like a colonial throwback, smoking a cigarette. His eyes and most of his face were shaded under the brim of the hat, but Petra could tell he was staring at her. She tried to make contact with the dark void for a second before the man brought his cigarette up to his mouth and she flinched away. Self-conscious, she concentrated on unscrewing the cap of her bottle and pouring more water into her glass. Her hand twitched and she spilled a little on the table. She took a napkin and blotted it before looking up at the man again.

He was gone.

She looked again, just to make sure, craning to see past the kids at the table in front of her in case he'd just moved out of her eyeline. But he was gone.

She replayed her actions in her mind. Pouring, spilling, wiping. It couldn't have taken more than ten seconds. But maybe that was enough for the guy to get up and leave through the archway right next to her without her noticing, while she was distracted. Maybe what she had taken for a deep slouch was actually him in the process of standing up; maybe what she had taken as a slow, static stare was really the man surveying the room as he left.

The cigarette was odd, though; she'd surely smell tobacco smoke in this small space. But maybe it was a vape, or maybe the cigarette wasn't lit. Maybe he'd just put it to his lips as he made to leave. That was feasible. She could have sworn she'd seen smoke, though, trailing upwards, and then a slow exhalation as he watched her. But maybe that was just conditioning – you expect to see smoke when you see a cigarette; the two go hand in hand, you don't even need to think about it.

It had been a day of disappearing people. She couldn't quite shove their contorted faces out of her mind. It didn't mean anything; she was just tired.

Vincent was coming down the stairs with their jumbo half-and-half pizza on a wooden pallet in one hand, and beer and a small bottle of wine in the other.

'Did I say it out loud?' she asked.

'What?'

'That I wanted some wine?'

'Nah, but I felt like a beer, so I took a flyer. Can I get you something else instead?'

He set the food and drinks on the table. He'd chosen a pink wine for her, a brave choice for someone he didn't know. It was exactly what she wanted.

'No. This is perfect.' She cracked open the wine bottle, filled her glass, took a long glug, and refilled with a sigh.

'Long day?' he asked.

'Yeah, a bit,' even though it's not the sort of thing you should normally admit on a first date. 'More weird than long.'

'How so?'

Petra didn't want to invite the spectre of that poor woman with her swollen eyes to this table right now – the weight of that reality was too much of a downer. 'Oh, no real reason. I think I've started to lose my mind. I've started to hallucinate.' She said it like a joke, which she supposed it was.

'I'm having the mushrooms next time,' he said. When he saw she wasn't going to say any more, he said, 'I had some weirdness today, too.'

'Tell me.'

'I won a prize for a contest I don't remember entering.'

Petra laughed. 'Yeah, and I bet you have to email your bank account details and PIN to claim it, right? I've won that prize a few times myself.'

'That's what I thought, but this one's legit.'

'Seriously? Don't tell me you clicked through.'

'No clicking involved. It was in a letter, hand-addressed, to my door.'

Petra took a sip, leaned forward. 'Really? What was inside?'

'Tickets. For a show.'

'What, like cinema tickets? A concert?'

'It's three shows, actually. I've got no idea what it is, but it's something called Metamuse.'

'*Metamuse*? Are you *kidding* me?'

5   There is no queue outside La Rustica at 7:30, no evidence that a show is happening in the somewhat upmarket Italian restaurant on Regent Street. You've eaten here once before, a special-occasion meal to celebrate a graduation or a promotion, and when you are ushered inside, the decor is familiar – overbrushed velvet on the banquettes and drapes and hand-painted scenes of Umbria on the walls, dents of plaster and scratches of previous diners' love-declaring graffiti. It's a comforting familiarity because you're suddenly nervous of being out with this person. This show is a stupid choice for an official first date – so many potential traps, so many possible ways to make a fool of yourself.

The man at the front desk checks your names on the guest list, nods and smiles and then asks you for your phones. The invitation detailed the strict no-phone, no-recording, no-uploading, no-nothing policy, and you've been prepared to cede your phone, but still it feels like an invasive and risky demand.

Your table is in an alcove towards the back of the restaurant and you glance at the other paired-up guests as you pass – mothers and daughters, friends, colleagues, and a scattering of more established couples than you.

The trappings of a perfectly ordinary dinner date to start with. Mood music, soft temperature, a martini as an aperitif.

The only glaring indicator that this is a Metamuse fabrication are the headphones you're instructed to put on.

Set up on the table between you is a board game of sorts, like chess with fewer squares and large abstract pieces made of scented wax. The voice in your ears instructs you how to move your pieces as you drink your cocktail. You get the feeling that you're being calibrated – monitored. You figure out the cat-and-mouse pattern of the game that consists of about fifteen minutes of intense, flirtatious avoidance, eventually culminating in you and your date touching fingers over the last piece. The little action is charged after all the evasion, and the wax piece is beginning to soften, the combined heat of your hands moulding it and turning it into an imprint of the space between you, the notches where your bodies might fit.

Then you eat. Perfectly tender pasta and garlic bread oozing with butter – again, probably not a good first-date choice, but it's a choice you believe you've decided from the menu, not preordained by the voice, and it's cut pleasantly by the bottles of red wine.

After the meal, you are given parts to repeat in a dovetailed story, and then gradually given space to improvise. You can't remember what your lines were now, because you were also instructed to keep looking into each other's eyes as the story unwinds. The first minute is funny; the second and third uncomfortable and awkward; by the fourth, you are seeing rainbows around your partner's head. By the tenth, their face is your own.

• • •

The tantalising foreplay of the show had reached an excruciating pitch by the last course. The game was over, and Petra had been left staring across at Vincent, her toes riding under his trousers and up his ankles under the table as she worked tiramisu between her lips. By the glazed look in his eyes, she guessed he was sharing her vision of her skin smeared with the stuff, lying back and waiting for Vincent to clean her.

But when they'd got to her flat, they hadn't managed to act on that vision. They hadn't even got the lights on in the kitchenette, just struggled out of their clothes by the doorway. The next time was slower and more comfortable, and by then Petra was kinda relieved they hadn't gone the full sticky kink, because she could rest in his strong arms and trace his skin against hers, map hairs and the spots and the scars that made up his life as he talked and moved against her, his ridged solidity pressing indelibly into her.

Eventually, she had to get up for a pee and a glass of water. Vincent stood up and stretched, making for her shelves and plugging some smooth groove into her dock. Falling Man's Post-Mindblow Comedown Playlist.

'What do you want?' she asked from the kitchenette.

'That's a big question for three in the morning,' he said. 'What do *you* want?'

'Besides rooibos tea?'

When he started riffling through a pile of her drawings, she let him – like letting someone scratch through her underwear drawer, skim through her diary – fighting the urge to hurry over and snatch his hands away as she steeped the tea and laid out biscuits on a plate. She avoided looking at him, afraid of one wrong reaction, but the noises were good, a muttering, a 'hmm', a gasp. 'Jesus, these are good.'

When the tea was done, and only then, she placed them on the coffee-table crate and went to him and took his hand away, turning him and leading him back to the couch.

'Show me some of your stuff. I loved what I saw in the studio. That was you, right?' He allowed himself to be diverted and flicked onto a site on her tablet as she brought the tea. She settled herself into a twisted knot between his limbs and rested her head against his shoulder as he skimmed through the photos.

'Ooh, this is gorgeous,' she said when she got to an image of the fog-shrouded late-night Metro takeaway, its green and yellow neon blurring into a sickly hue that swirled over the hooded silhouettes of the smoking boys outside.

'Yeah, I like it too. It's our claim to fame,' Vincent said, twirling a strand of her hair between his fingers.

'What is?'

He pointed at the hand-lettered caption in the bottom-right corner. '"Ghost Town." Haven't you heard of it?'

'I don't think so.'

'Surely?' He went into an eerie falsetto: '"This to–own, yaa, yaya yaya."'

'Um.'

'The Specials recorded it at the Brook Street studios, released it in June 1981. It was big that year – it was like the theme tune to a few months of serious discontent. People in the cities felt like they were being neglected by Thatcher, the unions were being crushed, the owners getting richer, the workers getting screwed. You know, the usual. There were a few riots, stamped out of course. Some of the papers even called it Ghost Town Summer.'

'1981, you say? I have to ask, but how old are you? There's no way you could have been there.'

'I was. Just about. A baby.'

Okay, she was getting somewhere. He must be about forty. That seemed about right. 'So not rioting, then?'

'Not on the streets, no.' He smiled and Petra was glad for the light tone, the opportunity to steer away from politics. 'You'll hear my granddad on that track if you listen carefully. He re-ran some of the bass tracks on the master in post-production.'

'That's cool,' she said, and the magic of recording struck her for a moment like it must have struck the first people to hear a voice playing off a wax cylinder. Here was the ghostly imprint of a man who'd just died, still being heard every time the song was played. Of course, anyone who was filmed or recorded or photographed was immortalised in the same way, but the fact that Vincent's granddad's imprint was almost invisible, just a flicker of the imagination, like a shadow flitting in the peripheral vision, an arcane secret known only to a few people, made it seem somehow more charmed.

Then Vincent stared at the dark square of the uncurtained sky, resettling into a thoughtful mood as if remembering where he was, who he was.

'You look sad,' she said, knowing it was probably a stupid, presumptuous thing to say. You don't probe too deeply into a guy's personal life when you've seen him like three times.

'Yeah?' he said, looking up at her and smiling thinly. 'Sorry. Just lots on my mind.'

'None of my business, really,' she said. 'I know this will sound stupid and presumptuous, but I don't think you're a sad person. You feel like a really positive, optimistic guy to me, and I think you're hurting.' *Where the hell did that come from?*

He nodded, looked into her eyes and linked his fingers with hers, deliberately recalling their intimacy from a few hours ago. 'True, I guess. They say people's brain chemistry determines their happiness baseline – the level you run at when everything's going fine. I think I used to be quite happy... but things have been pretty rough lately.'

'Can you tell me about it?'

He looked from her eyes to her lips, away to the wall, opened his mouth, took a long breath in. 'I'd rather not. Sorry.'

She tried not to feel stung. 'It's honestly none of my business. But I genuinely hope you feel better soon. And I'll help if I can. Okay?' He smiled, a little patronisingly, but she pressed on, dogged as Helena when she'd found a mission to be on. 'If you want to talk about it, I'm here.'

'Sure.'

To deflate the tension, she proceeded to whitter on about the gap in British pop culture that kept on tripping her up at pub quizzes and game shows because she hadn't grown up here, and who the hell were Squidgy and Flumpy and Mr Dick anyway? Some time while they were talking, they went back to bed and she passed out wrapped around him.

6 'He had *Metamuse tickets?*' Suki's voice rose a couple of octaves from its usual smoky undertone and she sounded, for a moment, like a teen discussing a Cinnamon Dolls reunion tour. 'How?'

The lone browser – Freddie from Gravity's End, the sci-fi bar across the road, who hung out here every Monday before opening time, mainly to observe Suki and never to buy – looked up from the magazine rack. He had a mop of curly black hair over a thin frame that might have been quite a sexy hip-dishevelled look if he had a dash more self-confidence to go with it. As it was, though, he was more annoyingly furtive than intriguingly aloof. His glance darted back to Wonder Woman when Petra's glance crossed his.

'Won them, apparently. But he says he doesn't even remember entering the contest.' Petra tried to arch back in her stool behind the counter – she was stiff and sore and replete and dozy after the weekend – but it was hard to do since the designer stool's seat was a minuscule scooped disc of white plastic.

'I couldn't believe it when I heard they were even running a season here,' Suki said.

'Wait – you *knew* and you didn't tell me?'

'I only read about it on Art Forum about six months ago. Tickets were long gone. But why here? That's the weird thing. I mean, Paris, Tokyo, Oslo, Boston... and Leamington Spa.'

'Maybe Jouval and Barnes have some connection here? Maybe Olivia said, "Hey, why don't we tour in Leamington instead of London this time? I can work in a visit to my nan."' Olivia Jouval and Rashida Barnes were Metamuse's founders, who faced their publicity with tightly guarded and highly curated personae – as far as the doting art press could see, they had no past and no personal life beyond their slick masks.

Suki laughed, a deep throaty sound that turned into a raking cough. 'As if.'

Petra shrugged. 'I don't know. Anyway, why not Leam? It's a cool town. Hip and happening. I only just learned that Stormzy used to live here.'

'Who?'

Petra ignored her. The grime artist had become so popular that white middle-aged, middle-class shirefolk were dropping his name and lyrics. There was no doubt Suki knew of him; she was being deliberately obtuse. 'Admittedly it was just a course or something. Wasn't compelling enough to make him want to give up the bright lights of London for good. I also read Nathaniel Hawthorne lived here for a while.'

'*Scarlet Letter* Hawthorne? Is that so?' This piqued Suki's interest, as Petra thought it might. But she was surprised Suki didn't know this already; she wasn't one to pass up any new bit of local witchery-related arcanum.

'Our town didn't seem to impress Hawthorne all that much.'

'Well, he's an insensate plodder then,' Suki said. She liked to put on the heiress-in-forced-exile-in-the-salt-mines-of-the-provinces act, but she'd snap to Leamington's defence if it was criticised. In her less guarded moments she'd pronounce that Leamington was an island of creativity and liberal sensibility in a wasteland of petty conservatism. 'But I must add that factoid to my list. It's up there with Crowley.'

'What about Crowley?'

'Don't tell me you don't know that? Aleister Crowley was born here. Right on Clarendon Square.'

'Huh, that's something.' Despite herself, Petra was impressed. Crowley – whack-job spiritualist, Satanist honcho, proto-hippie free spirit, call him what you will – was someone people would have heard of. She hadn't heard that name for ages, but she'd had some high-school friends who'd fancied themselves occultists. It was what kids did back then, before flaying yourself in public under the bright lights of social media became the enforced global teen pastime. She used to go up to the Melville Koppies with her friends and play at Wicca. The kids pretended it was just a joke when they went up there, but they performed the rituals with dead seriousness, both thrilled to access their personal power and terrified of letting it out. Tania, Lyon, Kath – what had happened to them?

She hadn't thought of those days for ages – it seemed so long ago; another life, a world away. She'd really allowed herself to become mundane, secular. Even though she'd never been religious, she'd had a sense of the spiritual back then. Later, as an older teen, she'd recoiled from her own embarrassing credulity and left all that behind. It was stupid, and Crowley was just a psychotic egoist. But right now, that vast distance between here and that thirteen-year-old girl in the candlelit hills on the other end of the world collapsed, and a connection between those two lives clicked into place. They were the same life after all; Petra was still the same girl.

'His parents were brewers,' Suki said.

'Ah, that explains it,' Petra said, quickly stuffing the ghosts back into their box. 'He was a bit of a dick, though, wasn't he? A poser, a fake. Like a two-bit cult leader.' She was being deliberately provocative, wanting to gauge Suki's reaction. Suki may style herself as a goth, but if she seriously was a follower of Crowley, Petra might have to reassess their friendship. 'I picture him like an Edwardian Charlie Manson.'

'Yah, probably. You'll find that all those boys in their pharaoh garb and wing suits are only in it for the cupcake.'

Petra laughed. 'Do you often hang out with boys like that?'

Before Petra could respond, Freddie, who'd been edging closer, chipped in, 'Sansa Stark, too.'

'Excuse me?' Petra said. The title of a top-shelf movie?

'Sansa Stark is also from Leamington.'

'Sansa Stark's from Winterfell, Freddie,' Suki said, and Freddie flushed at the intimate fact of his name on Suki's lips. 'And she's a fictional character, love, and that means even you don't stand a chance.'

'You know what I mean. Sophie. Sophie Turner's from Leamington. I just thought I'd suggest that for your list.' He clearly didn't mind admitting he'd been listening in to every detail of their conversation.

'Already got that. Filed under moderate-to-rad provincial claims to fame.' Petra knew that, despite her nonchalance,

Suki would geek out if Sophie Turner ever came drifting into her shop. 'Have you got Ben Foster?' Suki asked.

'Ben who?'

'The goalkeeper and one-time Nicest Man in the Premier League, love?'

'Nah,' said Freddie. 'I don't watch rugby.'

Suki shrugged and Petra gaped at her. 'Sometimes, Sook, you honestly surprise me.'

'What?'

Petra leaned back carefully. 'Well, that's quite a few celebs. The birthplace of lawn tennis, the jet engine, the Jaguar XT, and Crowley. It's an economic and cultural nexus after all.'

Suki pursed her lips and gazed out of the window at the shopfronts across the road. But for the rough sleepers in their doorways, both shops were vacant now. One of them used to be an express language school from back in England's more internationalist days, and next to it another interior design shop, more focused than Needful Things but not as comfortably backed. 'So, anyway, this husband of yours – cos if you don't marry him, I'm going to – there're still, what? Three more shows left?'

'Two.'

'Two more shows. That's alright. Nip-in marriage, pre-nup, quickie divorce after the finale. Unless his streak of mysterious luck continues…' Freddie swapped magazines, *Habitat* for *Living Fossils*, pretending not to drop eaves.

'Hey, hey. Back off. Those tickets are *mine*.'

'This *chap*. He did get tickets to all three, didn't he?'

'Yep.'

'And are you sure he's planning to take you to the next one?'

Petra flashed back on what she and Vincent had done on Friday night after *Intimacy*, and Saturday night, and Sunday morning. It was cool of him to ask her in the first place, but it had gone well – very well. Whether it was truly love and lust at first sight as she believed when he fell at her feet, or whether it was the manipulation of the immersion itself, they'd ended up holed up in her flat all weekend, only getting dressed to answer the door for the delivery guy. She couldn't prevent the smarmy, horny little grin that rose on her face. 'I presume so.'

'Have I mentioned that I'm jealous?'

It shamed Petra just how good this made her feel. That she, poor little Commonwealth girl, could make Old Money Suki Barlow jealous of anything was a personal achievement. Even though, of course, the achievement had nothing to do with her own endeavour. 'No,' she said, 'tell me again.'

Suki scowled. 'So you did part one on Friday night – *Intimacy*, was it? What was it like?'

'Essentially, it's a hyperreal dinner date – you sit in a real restaurant and follow commands piped into your ears. I don't know – the production somehow got us to hear things on the inside of our skulls—'

'They're called headphones, love,' Suki chipped in.

'Ha ha. It was more than that. Like they'd taken control of my nerves and my brain chemicals.' Suki was still looking sceptical. 'Ag, never mind. It's hard to explain. I shouldn't be trying anyway.'

'Ah, already part of the Metamuse cult. What, do they make you sign an NDA?'

'No,' Petra said. 'It's not that. It's just…'

'*You have to experience it for yourself.* That's what all the bloody reviewers say. Lazy hacks.'

'It's because it's audio and motion, dynamic. The experience is tailored to each participant. I guess it's hard to encapsulate in a review.' Suki rolled her eyes. 'But I can tell you it had an effect. They encourage you to do it if you know each other, and I think there must be different grades or narratives, because you wouldn't want to do this one with your mother, or brother, say…'

'God forbid,' Suki said.

'The one Falling Man and I did… Jesus.' She liked referring to Vincent as 'Falling Man' – it was her own private code shared only with Suki, and encapsulated all the romance and the physical longing she couldn't broach with anyone else. 'We were asked to stare into each other's eyes while this track played, and, God, I felt it in—'

'Oi, Freddie,' Suki called across, tapping her wrist. 'Opening time. Murphy's calling.'

Freddie put the magazine back on the rack, and did his best attempt at a confident saunter out of the shop. Two interchanges with Suki in one morning. As good as second base.

'So all this mind-blowing artificial intimacy is why you pulled a sickie on Saturday morning?'

'You don't mind, do you?'

'Of course not, darling. In these stolid times, the pursuit of passion is the highest calling. What else would I be doing on a Saturday morning?'

Petra could imagine all manner of answers to that question. The woman might be some sort of vampire; she never seemed to sleep. She seemed to go places and be back without travelling. The Abarth might simply be a prop to help her blend in, when she actually transmogrified and translocated and transformed her way around the country.

'You knew I wasn't really sick, didn't you? I used our emergency code.'

Suki picked up her phone and pretended to read a text message off it. '*Dear Suki – something's come up. Running a temperature. Your darling Pet.*'

'That sounds about right.'

'But you do know you're not in love, don't you?'

Petra, who'd been primping the stock on the countertop, froze as if caught in the act of something. 'What?'

Suki glanced through the front window to make sure Freddie was well away. 'It's all mind tricks. The Troxler effect. Stare into someone's eyes for ten minutes and you'll start to see monsters, angels. The man you want to marry and spend the rest of your life with and have a litter of babies with.'

Petra sighed. 'I didn't say I was in love.'

A New Show Gets Under the Skin

Idiopathy, Metamuse, rue Clauzel, SoPi,
Paris, 5–12 May

Dozens of adverts and invitations trumpeting the newest,
hottest shit in theatre clog my inbox daily. Always on the
lookout for the newest, hottest shit to tell you about, I
dutifully trek out to cover the most interesting-sounding
shows, and most of the time they're disappointing – poorly
conceived, badly written, and barely designed.

It's no wonder they find no investors and have the
production values of a bored and uninspired child's rainy-day
puppet show. I come out of the dusty loft feeling like I've just
watched some egotistical art student's sloppy wank, and most
of the time I don't even bother filing a review. Instead, I go
home and drink and wonder what the fuck I'm doing in this
moribund industry.

That was the first difference about Metamuse. They didn't
approach me. They didn't advertise. And from what I know,
they didn't send out the usual scattershot PR mailer to anyone.
They seemed to want to stay below the radar. I heard about
Metamuse on the street – remember, where guerrilla art used
to live and breathe before we all took up residence behind
our screens?

I can't even remember where I first heard about them –
not Instagram, Art Forum, Deviant, but in conversations:

the bookshop guy, the chick talking to her girlfriend at the grocery, fellow underemployed hacks gathered in the tabac – and since then, there was a little background hum growing that I didn't even recognise at first.

But I remember the look of the couple coming into the Coupe de Miel on place Gustave Toudouze the night I happened to be finding my solace there. They looked like they were floating a few inches above the floor, haunted, connected. They looked like they were ready to pull each other's clothes off and perhaps eat each other in a Cronenbergy way, but that they didn't need to because they were already *inside* each other, if you know what I mean.

They sat down at the table next to me and I turned my attention to them. 'Where have *you* been?' their friends teased, recognising the same enviable otherworldliness I had seen. They cleared their throats, glanced at each other, and I *heard the words* they looked at each other. Do we tell them, or do we keep this our dirty little secret? Do we share the love or do we hold it to ourselves, keep it burning between us forever? That's what they said in that glance, I fucking promise you.

They decided to share the love, telling their friends they'd been to an 'experience' at a pop-up gallery space right here on rue Clauzel. A show called *Idiopathy*, apparently the first in a series of three short-run pieces that they're rather loftily calling a 'season'.

So I immediately scuttled off to see if I could get tickets for this show. Long story short, you can't. The fact that I got in feels like some sort of miracle. It just so happens that as I stepped forward, after queueing behind seven other people who I watched getting turned away one by one, the woman at the door got a call. Someone had been eaten by a purple hippopotamus (that's what she said) and there was one slot freed up, first come first served. I was there first.

That was the last night of the show, I found out; it had run for just a week. Under 'Coming Up', the Metamuse website only says 'watch this space', so you may think it's a bit pointless for me to be telling you all this, but I'm telling you about it because it's the first show I've seen, maybe ever, that didn't disappoint me. I didn't have any expectations going in, but even if I had, the show would have not only met them, but exceeded them, and if you read my reviews regularly, you know what a rare statement that is.

Well-conceived, meticulously planned, and incredibly produced, which raises questions. Whoever's paying for this isn't going to make their money back with ticket sales.

Let's get it out of the way. I don't like sharing headphones. Even though the woman at the entrance made a show of unwrapping the (biodegradable potato starch) plastic wrap off the headphones in front of me, I had visions of those airline sets simply being collected in a trash bag along with discarded tissues and puke bags and sneezed-on menus and twenty-seven-day-old in-flight magazines that are soft from desperate fingering, then being perfunctorily sprayed with an empty aerosol before being sealed up again for the next flight. I returned the doorperson's favour of transparency and fished my sanitising gel out of my bag, and gave the headphones a performative rub before proceeding.

The man at the next counter passed me a blindfold, similarly wrapped in plastic.

So who are Olivia Jouval and Rashida Barnes?

(And do you notice that I'm deliberately avoiding telling you about the show? For one thing, it's bloody hard to describe to you without, you know, experiencing it yourself. And for another, I want to hold it to myself – I've searched longer and harder for this moment than that floaty couple at Coupe de Miel, and am less generous about sharing. My editor tells me it's my job, but since I'm being paid per word, let's see how long I can leave you in suspense.)

The Metamuse website and Instagram account is all one can easily find about Jouval and Barnes. The bio goes something like, 'Olivia Jouval and Rashida Barnes are the founders and creative directors of Metamuse.' That's it. And of course, the only images we get to see of these mysterious creative directors are the heavily disguised portraits of Jouval that have become something of a trademark. Rashida Barnes always remains behind the scenes, unexposed.

I wasn't satisfied and did a little digging, and found scans of a few fringe theatre programmes from the late eighties. Olivia Jouval trained at England's prestigious Beauchamp University performing arts department from 1978 to 1981, but there's no record of her graduating. Rashida Barnes was there at the same time and I could uncover a little more about her. She attended Beauchamp on highly competitive full scholarships for dancing and theatre practice. Unlike Olivia Jouval, she did graduate, but she seems to have had a quiet career until the Metamuse breakthrough. The only pre-Metamuse records of her name I could find were in the credits of a dance production called *Ex-stasis: The World in Six Discrete Movements* which toured Coventry, Bristol, Den Haag, Rotterdam, Lille and Lyon in 1988 as part of an educational collective, giving theatre experience to kids from state schools, and in the acknowledgements of a programme for an 'expressive reaction piece' from 1989 funded by the now defunct Artists' Support Network based in Birmingham, England, that played during the Midlands Art Festival. After that, she seems to have gone as dark as Jouval.

There's a lot of rumour and false information, of course, the sort of digital crap that fills any quiet space on the internet. Hints about murder and steamy affairs, a particularly pernicious strand on the more obsessive fan boards about a tragic love affair, or triangle, or quadrangle, but nothing substantiated or worth delving into, unless you want to emerge hours later with a headache and feeling very dirty. Real facts about Jouval and Barnes are thin on the ground.

So the fact that they've turned up again decades later, presenting highly technical and extremely confident bleeding-edge work that's creating a querulous buzz, is quite a surprise. Where have they been hiding all these years? I asked myself if they were even the same people who were at the Beauchamp Drama Society in 1981, but it's clear enough from comparing the photos in the college yearbooks with the new material on the website and the Metamuse Instagram that it's them. In her pictures, Jouval reminds me a lot of Cindy Sherman – that chameleonic face that can be contorted in a hundred ways, but still remains distinctly herself. Rashida Barnes has more of a classic, raven beauty, but with the right hair, make-up and couture could also be confused with any of two dozen current pop stars or A-list actors. But I'm diverging from my point. Jouval and Barnes aren't in this show – it's not about them. Along with the invisible magical pixies of their Metamuse company, they made it, and *Idiopathy* is about *you*.

I'd better try to talk you through it now, hadn't I?

Sorry, just one more aside while I remember it – I don't think Jouval is even Olivia's real name. It's not a common name, and it's suspiciously close to the birth name of the nineteenth-century French feminist, Olympe Audouard, who was born Félicité-Olympe de Jouval. Change Olympe to Olivia to be more palatable to a contemporary English audience? But if it is a pseudonym, she was using it back when she was registered as a student at Beauchamp, which would imply quite a long-term commitment to fakery. Which would be perfectly appropriate for an actor, you might say.

I move through a double layer of heavy blackout curtains into the holding room beyond the reception hall. The building we're in could have been the back store of one of the large groceries or pharmacies on rue des Martyrs around the corner, but now it's vacant, the typical spot for a pop-up. But Metamuse has put lush red carpeting in the lobby and painted the temporary walling a lacquered oxblood and black, so it looks more like an upmarket Asian restaurant than a temporary art space. But there's no smell of food. No acrylic smell of glue or paint either, as you might expect – there's a surprising lack of smell altogether.

There are seven other people in the room with their headphones on, waiting. The two couples who came together cast glances at each other.

'Put on the blindfold,' says the silky voice in my ears. Immediately I'm confronted with the first signs of expensive production quality in this show. The prompts are delivered automatically, using pinpoint location tracking, most likely from a chip embedded in the headphones – that's why we germophobes can't just plug in our own pods. There's none of the normal mood-killing 'Type in 17 on your devices now' and the audience fumbling and clattering and trying to ignore each other, desperately trying to stay in the bubble that you get in this sort of show.

And that voice. This is not a bot or a student actor flatly delivering scripted lines. Somehow Metamuse has chosen the precise voice I want to hear whispering in my ear as she fucks me. How does Metamuse know the voice of my composite dream lover? Even if they somehow profiled their guests from Fakebook dumps or something to find the perfect match, I just turned up at their show randomly. I feel a little invaded and more enticed than I want to be. I'm meant to be a critic.

Maybe I'm making too much of it. Maybe everyone gets this voice and I'm just in a receptive mood. I've had a few drinks, I wasn't expecting to work tonight, don't have my armour on; the couple who came into the Coupe were hot. I've been primed to comply, haven't I?

I do as the voice says, unsheathe the blindfold and put it on. The cloth is soft and smells of a scent I know from somewhere.

'Good,' says the voice. 'You're obedient.'

A tape loop wouldn't know if I'd complied. My movements are being tracked electronically, or maybe each audience member is being individually guided – that's unlikely, isn't it? Shows like this usually have a budget stretching little beyond the director's coffee and whisky. Either way, I'm being watched. It's an unsettling feeling.

'Walk for me, will you?' the voice now says. 'Walk towards the sound.'

Which sound? I think – there are lots of sounds. I'm becoming attuned to the shuffling feet of people around me, the low, murmured conversations. Someone brushes against me, mutters an apology. Someone coughs – too close to me, and suddenly I'm stifled. Aware that I'm being watched, not wanting to get in trouble with *her*, I lift the blindfold anyway, just a little bit, for an orienting peek – but beyond the blindfold, the room is as dark as inside. The lights are off, and it takes me ten or twenty seconds to locate the low red eye of the single emergency light above the exit curtain. The public safety committee would shut this place down in a second.

I can't see the other audience members, only hear one or two scuffles more distant than they should be in this small room. To their credit, nobody has pulled out their phone to ruin the effect, but I've already lost my mental map of them. Then I realise we're probably not even following the same commands. I glance at the red dot once more, but I'm not going that way – I'm going deeper inside. I'm going to walk towards the sound. Because now it's clear where I should go – there's a mechanical grinding sound coming from a little way away. Painstakingly, I whisper-walk my way towards it, feeling the air in front of me.

So far, all they've done is turned off the lights, just a childhood game, and I'm terrified, my heart is hammering, and when the voice comes into my head – 'Good. You're doing well.' – she's so warm and comforting, I anchor myself to her. In less than five minutes (I realise afterwards, after analysing the experience) Metamuse has effectively stripped my natural defences and made me an acolyte. I will do anything she says.

And that, I think, is the point here. You don't think you are the sort of person who will follow arbitrary instructions from a faceless stranger, but you are. You do it every day. You follow commands to blend in. You do what's expected of you to stay out of trouble.

I'm not going to tell you everything about what happened in there, because you should experience it yourself if Metamuse runs this show again. And discussing it with the others who came out, it seems that either the journey is completely new for each participant, or there are several different strands, so what I experienced will probably not be what you experience. And of course, even if the script was exactly the same for everyone, the way everyone plays it would be different.

At one stage, the voice told me I'd feel a hand on my back, and I felt the hand on my back, even though there was nobody in the room. I have to admit, I was a bit terrified, but also I wanted to know where else she could touch me idiopathically.

At one stage, I sat in a sightless room, hearing perfect strangers confess their deepest shame and desire. We want to confess. We want to be judged. It takes very little to strip us down and spreadeagle us before authority. In *Idiopathy* the authority was benign and seductive, but I realise I would have followed orders just as docilely if they were barked as threats. I told secrets to *her* and to *them* that I thought were walled up inside me forever.

Psychotherapy gets it wrong. It's too conscious. Instead, lock your patients in a darkened room for fifty minutes and they will dissolve.

7

'I even showed him my pictures,' Petra told Helena, sliding the pie onto side plates.

This made Helena look back across at Petra from where she'd been staring out the window at a pair of cats squabbling in the block's mudhole of a garden. It was Tuesday morning; Needful Things only opened at noon on Tuesdays to Thursdays, and Petra had brought the slices of pecan pie from the Three Elephants partly in guilt for not having her mind fully on her mother for the past few days: she was in recovery from a procedure, after all. A good daughter should have been hovering around her all weekend, not fantasising about a kind, sad stranger she'd just met and shagged on the weekend.

But now Helena raised her eyebrows and Petra half regretted mentioning her art to her. It might set off another round in the *Petra, you really need to do what you love in life* lecture series. There hadn't been a session of that for a while, and Petra had hoped the topic was finally dead.

'That's great, darling,' Helena said tentatively. Petra knew Helena harboured lofty hopes for her Creative Becoming, but she'd become defensive whenever it came up. It wasn't that Petra felt Helena wanted her to fulfil the creative dreams she had failed to achieve. A regular mother-and-daughter dynamic like that would be secretly affirming, a bit of inter-generational jealousy would make Petra feel good about herself – but Helena was creatively self-fulfilled, admirably so. The simple fact was that Petra never thought herself or her art worthy of those ambitions. Objectively, there were so many better artists out there, flashing up all over her timelines, ones who seemed naturally productive and joyous while they did it. They were the ones who should do art for a living, not her. Petra knew Helena wanted the best for her, but how could she admit to her deep-living, lee-draining personality whirlwind of a mother that compared to all the geniuses out there, her daughter was nothing special, and was trying to be okay with that? That's why she'd become defensive. Helena had recognised this and learned to tone down her enthusiasm. 'Are you still drawing?'

She'd given up for a while – almost three years – but in the last six months had taken it up again. She'd been inspired by a documentary she'd come across about new digital artists, and had followed some mind-blowing social media accounts of some insanely talented people. She made the decision to stop feeling she had to compete with these clever people for a slice of the pie, because she'd never win – they were simply better than she was... but she could still do it for fun, couldn't she? She'd taken the plunge and bought herself a new top-of-the-range tablet and stylus and started up again.

It was all thanks to Suki and her charity – because that's what the job was; she was underworked and overpaid compared to anyone else in retail – that she could afford the new equipment. But she'd never even told her that she tried to do art. She'd never show her pictures to Suki. It was possible she'd like them, but there was also a good chance she'd scythe them down in an unthinking act of irony, and that would be devastating. As nice as Suki was, she'd struggle to understand how hard the rest of the world clung on to their hopes and dreams. They were tiny pieces of flotsam keeping them from drowning – they clung on to them because second chances don't come easily. Giving up and starting something new; 'failing better', 'pivoting', 'reinventing yourself' – all those motivational buzzwords required a financial safety net that most people didn't have. That's why working-class artists couldn't 'fail better'; they were just set up to fail.

Anyway, the new pictures felt too intimate, too dangerous, to show to Helena. 'A bit,' Petra said noncommittally, and escaped the conversation by wandering off to the kitchen to make coffee.

Evidently a lot had changed inside her in the past three years. She'd done a lot of fantasy portraiture in the past – hyperreal glossy beauty that maybe teen girls would like. Once upon a time she'd imagined illustrating her own books with them and selling a bazillion copies. When she'd taken up her new tablet with that flush of new-start energy, she hadn't had any product in mind, but maybe it'd be nice to do a comic or story featuring her strawberry-gloss girls – not for publication, just for her own enjoyment, she didn't really know – but instead of pretty, her mind and her hand started to deliver damaged faces and scarred bodies. She'd had no idea where they were coming from, but that memory of long-gone witch-Petra lighting candles on the Melville hilltops made her realise: maybe they had been inside her all along.

She'd shown Vincent the pretty ones first, the ones she'd done before; the ones she'd collected in her portfolio that had been roundly rejected – well, she'd given up after four firm and fulsome 'no's, so she couldn't really class the rejection as round. The cherry-lipped zodiac girls, their blush and limpid eyes and the sunlight effects playing over their sexy-cute freckles; their teen-dream bodies and lustrous fantasy hair. They were you, imperfect and shy, but perfectly turned out, like in the final scene of a cheesy, unironic romance movie. But cocooned with him in her bed, his nakedness and his utter acceptance of her nakedness making her feel safe, she'd scrolled across to some of the newer stuff. Beautiful Poppy drowning in a pool of pills; Clara, bruised and cut and still defiant; Elise with her corporate tattoos gone wrong, infected and seeping; and especially Tatia, with the demons in her eyes. She wasn't sure what was compelling her to channel these feelings, run septic nails across the idealised portraits, but it was almost as if just making pretty pictures wasn't enough anymore – she was compelled to gouge deep and find the blood beneath the surface.

'Jesus,' he'd said. 'These are insane.'

'I'm sorry,' she'd flinched, sweeping them away. 'It's just something—'

But he'd caught her hand and stayed it. 'No, I mean they're incredible. Hot, to be honest,' he said, running his foot up her calf, shifting it up past her knee. 'They're dirty. Hardcore. Where do they come from?' He didn't have to say, *I never imagined pictures like this coming from someone like you*. The way he'd scanned her with his eyes, reassessing her, said it all. That's what she'd made herself into – neutral, depthless, normal, trying to fit in, trying to blend. It was a process that had started years ago, that sensitive young girl's first flinch away from personality, and continued still today, the process of normalisation and homogenisation exacerbated by the searing self-consciousness of being a migrant.

'Do you think I'm soft? I'll have you know I was born and raised in Gauteng, china,' she'd teased in a rough Joburg accent.

He'd held up his hands. 'No, no. It's just that… you just didn't seem… troubled.'

She'd smirked. It was invigorating, a new relationship. Vincent knew nothing about her – she could paint herself in any way she wanted.

'So do you know what he does?' Helena called through to the kitchen, where Petra was spooning coffee into the cheap plunger. The mesh filter was bent and it let half the grounds through, no matter how slowly you pressed it. As always, she spent some time trying to straighten it, made it worse and pricked her thumb. Next time, she promised herself – as always – she'd go to the supermarket and get a new one for six quid. Surprise her mother.

'*Does*? What do you mean? As a job? Are you checking if he's marriage potential?'

'The day will come, darling, when you'll ask me that and I won't laugh it off.' Helena came to lurk at the kitchen jamb. 'I'm not going to be around forever.'

'*Jee-zuz*, Mom. So I need to get a man in place to look after me after you've shuffled off, is that right?' She immediately regretted it, even though this was a tone they could take with each other.

Helena shrugged.

'It worked well for you, hey?'

Helena smirked. 'Fair point.'

'Besides...' Petra was going to say something jokey, like *You're going to be around forever*, but it seemed inauspicious, somehow, in the week her mother had had surgery, no matter how minor. She poured the boiled water, giving the sentence enough time to die a natural death. 'How're you feeling?'

'Fine. So?'

'So what?'

'What does he do? This lovely man of yours?'

'Is that a tone I detect, Mom?'

'Tone? Me? What would I intone about?'

'I know what you're thinking.'

Helena laughed. 'Tell me.'

'"You always think you're in love and you never are. Remember Martin, remember Clint, remember Devin..." Blah blah blah.'

Helena squeezed Petra's forearm. 'I'd never think such a mean thing about you, my love.'

Petra spun around and folded her arms with an exasperated puff. 'I've heard it all already from Suki. I don't see the need to justify my feelings.'

'Okay, my darling. I didn't ask you to.'

'I feel what I feel and I'd rather give good emotions the benefit of the doubt that be an untrusting, closed-hearted... *hermit* all my life. Okay?' Just because relationships hadn't worked out in the past, didn't mean she should stop hoping, stop seeing the potential in other people, trusting her gut. Come to it, she was bloody proud of herself for still being able to feel, with Rod and Helena as her relationship role models and her disappointing track record. She'd got that off her chest.

'Good, Petra. Tell me: what does he do?'

She breathed it out and turned back to her mother. 'A lot of things. He's an artist at heart – he takes beautiful photos. All night-light and dank puddles and raindrops and reflections. But needless to say, his art doesn't pay the rent. He used to work as a sound engineer at his granddad's studio, but he died and they've just sold up. Now he does whatever. At the moment, he's helping dismantle the studio. He said he got close to a level II electrical certification.'

'But?' Helena said.

'I didn't say *but*.'

'I heard a but.'

'Ja, I did too when he told me. But he never said what happened. The conversation kinda went elsewhere. We started talking about our families…'

'Oh.' Helena nodded. 'Like *family* family? He's not married, is he?'

'Ha ha. No. But I think he's got a daughter.'

'You *think*?'

'Yeah. He started saying so, but he didn't say much else. The conversation moved away.' Looking back now, it was funny how that conversation did seem to swerve back to her every time they veered into certain details. Like about his personal life. The only family member he seemed happy to talk about was his grandfather. She started pushing the plunger down.

'Oh. How old is she?'

'I don't know. He didn't say.' She was pushing too forcefully. The filter was clogging and the pressure was pushing back at her. She should just ease up a little.

'Where does he live? Here in town?'

'Jesus, Mom. The real third degree.' It was unlike her mother to grill her like this – maybe she really had been spooked by the operation. Maybe she was feeling mortal after all. Realising this, Petra knew she could just be kind and let it go, but she was needled on Vincent's behalf. It was probably the sort of coded grilling he'd get daily. *Do you live here in town?* really means *Are you financially stable and reliable and bourgeois and obedient? Do you fit in?* Leamington was expensive, and 'living in town' involved unspoken implications. 'What are you actually asking here? Has anything I've told you given you any reason to mistrust him?' She was asking herself, wasn't she? Looking for confirmation. She had fallen deeply and heavily for Vincent, without her usual passion-stifling period of due diligence. Now the coffee spurted up and splashed out of the spout. 'Shit. Dammit.'

Helena stepped over, grabbed a washcloth, and rinsed it in cold water and wiped the spillage. 'I don't mean anything. I'm just interested. You know me: I don't judge you.' She pressed her cool, damp hand onto Petra's.

'I know, Mom. I'm sorry.'

Petra poured her milk and stirred half a spoon of brown sugar into her coffee – Helena took hers unadorned, like a real frontierswoman – and they went back into the living room.

'I don't want to set you off again, but if you're serious about Vincent – and it looks like you are – you should find a chance to go and see his house, get to meet his daughter. You can tell a lot about a man by the way he speaks to his children.'

'Hm. If that's true, I wonder what meeting Dad at home would have told anyone.'

'I think you know, darling.'

'Yup,' Petra sighed.

8 Back home after work, Petra shucked off her boots and her coat and sprawled out on the couch. The flat still smelled of sweat and food and cologne, even though she'd washed the sheets and dishes on Saturday night. It wasn't bad, this sensory reminder of the very pleasant night, but she wasn't a teenager anymore and probably wouldn't be crushing the towel Vincent had used to her face anytime soon.

But his photographs – those she could dreamily get lost in. She called up his Photogram and Deviant Art pages and drifted through his night-lit streetscapes for a while.

Funny to think he might not have even come back to her flat. *Intimacy* had been quite uncomfortable to start with, like being watched making love. It wouldn't have worked with anyone else – it was almost as if they'd measured the chemistry, the endorphins and pheromones slithering between Vincent and her. It was almost as if the activities on their date were deliberately chosen to match them. Thinking back, that's probably exactly what happened. There was probably a variety of set routines and they simply selected one for each participant when they saw them sitting down – it would have been easy to choose the sexiest routine for Petra and Vincent, pegged as randy first-flushers the moment they came through the door. Though it was a little awkward at the start, and she thought she'd totally blown it by the middle, messing up the instructions, by the end their fingers were threaded and their eyes were locked – according to the script, yes, but it felt like they could have sat there, intertwined, forever.

Alone in her room, she played 'Ghost Town' a few times. It was surprisingly mellow for a protest song, but it was catchy and she could see how it might go viral – she could imagine gangs of disaffected kids using that out-of-kilter singsong refrain as a taunt to police during the riots in 1981. Laid back, angry, resigned, the song was a bit of them all – a lot like her image of Vincent.

That memory refuelling her this evening, Petra picked up her phone and texted Vincent before thinking too much.

<Petra: Heya. How're you doing?>

<Vincent (two hours later): Not too bad. You?>

<Petra: Very well. I had fun on Friday. I'd like to get together again if you're keen.>

<Vincent: Sure>

<Petra: Okay. Great. When? Where? Any place you like to go?>

<Vincent: I'm easy.>

<Petra: Glad to hear it 😊 >

'It's so good to see you,' Petra said, opening her arms. Vincent rewarded her with an enveloping hug, his hand moving up her back and to the nape of her neck in a way that made her want to cancel drinks and go straight back home with him. When they broke it up he stepped back and assessed her with a sigh, and it was clear he was thinking the same thing.

Thursday evening was the new Friday evening by the looks of the Ragged Boar. The pub was heaving inside, full of workers denying there was still another day at the office this week, but they managed to squeeze inside and find a quieter side room upstairs.

'I hope I wasn't harassing you too much, being too forward.'

She wasn't sure if she'd been too forward or too uncool texting him on Monday night. The fact was she wanted to see him, and she liked to think of herself as far enough from teendom not to worry about being cool. Vincent's monosyllabic text style had been a little hard to read, but here he was, his warm smile and open face, and she'd give him the benefit of the doubt. Some people just were better at real-life conversations than texts.

'Yeah, of course. It's great to see you. Sorry I've been busy this week. Picton and Worthing have really been...' The sentence petered out and he took a sip of his beer.

'How's the clear-out? Have you managed to sell the console?'

'No. Picton's letting me keep everything there. He's charging me per week, but I wasn't going to flog it for nothing.'

'He's *charging* you?'

'Yeah. But not that much, less than storage. Do you know how expensive self-storage is? Jesus.'

Petra nodded. 'I know. Yeah. My mum and I brought way too much crap with us when we came here. Made the mistake for a couple of years of thinking we'd ever find a bigger place and unpack it. Ended up chucking most of it in the dump.'

'Oh.'

Seeing his expression, Petra gripped his hands for a second on the table between them. 'Not that that will happen to your console, though! You'll find the right buyer. Our stuff was rubbish.'

The tap had just turned on again – they were talking and touching like they'd known each other forever. That's how it had felt the minute he'd fallen at her feet; the way it had felt on Friday night. Again, she felt like she was talking to an old friend. Amazing how a few stupid lines on a phone and a couple of hours of silence could cause such anxiety.

Maybe he was married, maybe that was it. She imagined him ducking under the duvet when his wife went off for a pee late at night to send one word to her, like a prisoner waiting for the right moment to release a message tied to the leg of a carrier rat.

'What's funny?' he asked.

'Uh, nothing. So… uh, you live close by? Is this your local pub?' What next, Petra? *Do you come here often?* Or, *Do you live here in town?* Remembering the way she'd snapped at her mother for asking the same thing.

He shrugged. 'Dunno. Been here a few times – it's near the studio, isn't it? I don't do pubs that often, to be honest.'

'Yeah, me neither. I'd rather drink at home in front of the TV most of the time.'

A loud group of workers in high-street office wear – not wanky banker boys like you'd find in London, and probably not designers or advertisers or coders from Leamington's soft industries who would be wearing more expensive casualwear – came clumping up the stairs and requisitioned a few tables at the far end of the room, scraping and battering wood on wood as they rearranged the furnishing.

'You want to get out of here? We can take a walk, go sit in the dell?'

The little sunken park across the road may be nice enough during the day, when it was bright, but on a winter's evening? And she wasn't quite warmed up enough to invite him home with her just yet – that night had been special. 'Well, we've got our drinks, let's finish them. I like the fireplace here. That's something I don't have at home.' *Do you?* she wanted to ask. Why not? Why shouldn't she? She wanted to know about his life. So she did. 'Do you?'

'What?'

'Have a fireplace at home? I'm trying to picture you, Vincent. At home. Where do you live? Who do you live with?'

As she'd already learned to expect, he deflected the question with a small sigh and a twist of the lips.

The big group had just about settled their seating arrangements. They'd clearly been downstairs at the bar for a while, their conversations loud and full of laughter. Estate agents, maybe, or downmarket lawyers or accountants, but the room was dark, and their table was backlit by orange-shaded lights in sconces on the wall. They were moving around a lot too, gesticulating broadly, the shadowy backs of the people in front sliding across the faces of the people across the table – and they were loud, theatrically loud in this small room. They didn't *sound* like accountants or lawyers or people in cheap suits – they sounded like actors at a wrap party. Her eye was drawn by a flash of bright-orange curls, instantly obscured by a broad back, and the moment she got a look in again, she saw that the woman on that side of the table was wearing a hat, her hair pulled back in a ponytail. She couldn't make out the shade of the hair in the deep shadow there; probably just a trick of the dim lighting.

Petra had been able to study the woman in the hat surreptitiously because she was directly in her eyeline, but now a man stood up and shifted into the pool of light.

Jesus.

'I know that guy. I saw him the other night. At the pizza place.'

Because it was unmistakably the same man. His cream suit and white-banded fedora, the slicked-back hairstyle made him stand out like a zebra at a mule party. How could she not have noticed him coming in with the others? He was staring at them, and when Petra met his eyes, he nodded, a thin smile on his lips.

Petra was the first to draw away from the staring contest as Vincent turned in his chair. 'Which one?' Vincent asked.

Petra looked back at the table, but the fedora man wasn't there anymore. In his place was a man with slicked hair and a pockmarked face, but less striking, a blander expression – and no hat. He was wearing a white office shirt, his jacket hung over the back of his chair, and he was talking to the woman next to him. Amazing what your mind will let you believe.

'Wow, that was weird. I swear I thought I...' She stopped talking and took a sip of her wine. 'So, tell me about yourself, Mr Falling Man. Full disclosure is required if you want the full follow-up service.'

'What do you need to know, ma'am?'

'Personal life. Intimate habits. Relationship details. That sort of thing.'

He smiled. 'Well, for starters, I'm living with my grandmother, Nan Gloria. I moved in to help her after Max died.' He shrugged. 'It's a three-bedroom house. She doesn't ask for money but I pay her a little rent. No wife or girlfriend, if that's on your form.'

'Oh, right. So, you said you had a daughter?' He hadn't, exactly, but she cast the line anyway. 'She's grown up, then? Lives with her mum?'

He straightened, looked her in the eyes. 'She died.'

Petra put her hand over her mouth. 'Oh, Vincent. Oh, God.' Tentatively, she put out her hand, touched the tips of his fingers then withdrew. She waited for him to speak.

'She had a congenital kidney disease. She needed a transplant.'

How could he just say this, like it was natural to move from cheap banter to the death of a child in a breath? 'Oh,' she uttered.

He raised his glass and talked into it as he tipped it. 'There was one available. A donation, you know. I was ready to give her mine. We matched.'

'So, then…?'

He put down the glass, opened his mouth, closed it again. Then he said, 'It didn't work out. Let's just leave it at that.'

'I'm sorry, you don't need to talk about it.'

'It's fine. I wanted to tell you. I never want to treat her like a secret. I'm really proud of her. She'd never want me to use her as an excuse to be closed off or whatever.'

'You get to act however the hell you please. I'm so sorry.'

He smiled at her, nodded.

'When did this happen?' she asked.

'Last year. No, fifteen months ago. Just before Christmas.'

Petra winced. 'Oh. Oh, no. But… but how are you so nice? How can you be so… normal after that? I would… I'd be…'

'Beccie loved life. She had this… unquenchable joy. She'd want me to do the best I can to carry on. It's hard sometimes. It's really hard. And I get so angry. It could have been avoided.'

'How old was she? Beccie.' Petra tried the name on her lips, hoping it wasn't a presumption too far.

'She was sixteen.'

'God. Do you mind me asking: where's Beccie's mom? How is she handling it?'

'Cara left us when Beccie was three. She never wanted to live here, never wanted to have a family, didn't particularly like me. She did try for a couple of years, but fell in love with an Italian guy and went home. Then she died in a hit-and-run in Walsall when Beccie was six.'

'Oh. Jecz.'

'Yeah. So me and Gloria and Max were all Beccie had for family.'

'I'm so sorry, Vincent. It all sounds so incredibly hard.'

'It was, yeah. I worried about how it would affect Beccie as she grew up, but in the long run, though I still feel really horrible thinking it, I believe it was better for Beccie to have grown up without Cara. As she got older, I realised she's going to be fine.' He stopped, replaying his words in his mind. 'She *was* going to be fine.' He sighed heavily and shook his head. 'Anyway, I ought to tell you I was thinking of going away for a while.'

'Really? Where?'

He shrugged. 'Anywhere, I suppose. It didn't really matter. But now, I don't know. I really like being with you and I'm thinking I could stay on a little more.'

Petra waited for him to say more, but they only looked at each other – their eyes meeting and darting, evading and meeting up again. 'I'd be glad if you can. But you must do what you need to do.'

He sighed, a long exhale. 'Well, we've still got those Metamuse tickets, right? If you still want to go with me, it'd be a pity to miss the next show.'

She looked at him and he looked at her, and there was nothing left in the universe but the charged space between them. She shunted her chair closer to him and he cleared the glasses aside and took her hand. Then they kissed, right there in the pub, like kids, lost in the fantasy world they'd built.

9 The second show is different.

Cabinet is staged in a vacant four-storey Victorian office block, once Leamington's central post office and stores, right next to St Mary's Church in the middle of town. This time the queue snakes past the bus stop and around into Priory Terrace, the theatre audience waiting excited and trepidatious in the drizzle; you feel a little awkward and self-conscious alongside the long-haul workers going home and the rough sleepers bedding in in front of the church. Your frivolous interest in functionless art is too flippant for the moment.

Check-in is in the basement parking lot, temporary lockers erected to store coats and the forbidden phones. This time the invitation has advised the audience to wear comfortable footwear that you don't mind getting dirty. *Cabinet* is going to be one of those vast immersions Metamuse is famous for. You've read about similar immersions in the Tokyo and Boston runs. These are not plays to be watched passively from beginning to end – they've built an entire world for audiences to explore on their own, wandering the sets and scenes and picking up on any one of the complex, interconnected storylines playing out in loops across the venue. Main strands might play out over several floors of a building or swoop from room to room, while small secondary scenes will lure just a handful of guests in a tucked-away closet. Every audience member's version of the show will be different, depending on where you choose to walk, all within the producer's very carefully controlled manipulations, of course. You might think you have free choice, but you'll be nudged and herded. As you queue, you're trying to regulate your expectations. You want to balance your will to win the game, to find the best bits, with a more relaxed wish to just go with the flow.

The invitation has also warned you that you'll need to wear hard plastic masks. *Some guests may experience claustrophobic symptoms; staff will be on hand to guide any affected audience members to decompression zones.* You've seen the terrifying, crow-like things in reviews of previous Metamuse shows, but still, once you're through check-in and have slipped on the mask in the featureless holding room, you're not prepared for the overwhelmingly eerie effect of wandering into the installation along with hundreds of other anonymised watchers kitted out like Black Death serial killers.

You knew it was possible you might lose each other during the show, so you made plans to hook up in the lower bar area when it was over; as it happens, it takes you no longer than two minutes to get separated. Your friend stops to tie their shoe and you go on just five paces to inspect a backlit prop of an old typewriter, and when you look up, they're gone. You double back the way you thought you'd come, but somehow the path no longer leads to the entrance; the alcove with the typewriter has disappeared and you don't know which way you're facing. After a couple of minutes' back-and-forth along the trail, you decide to move on by yourself.

At one stage, you're watching a dance scene set in a laundromat. The audience is subtly directed to lean back on the thrumming machines as cast members fly through, performing an elaborately choreographed number with sheets before disappearing in a flicker of careful lighting. There are eight or ten ways out of there, but when you push through to an unadorned concrete stairwell, you think you've made a mistake. You try going back through the stairwell door, but it doesn't budge. The floors below are dark – up is the only option.

The door on the third floor leads into a scene so quiet you can imagine the sound of traffic outside, before you realise it's a soundtrack of hushing ocean waves overlaying a low-pitched burble. As the background sounds become deeper and more immersive, you follow your senses further into the level, towards a wood-sided chapel at the end of a village street where a flower-strewn pagan ceremony was taking place, perhaps a marriage or a dedication. Despite the activity apparently playing out behind the brightly glazed chapel windows, you feel like you're alone. You glance back the way you came, visions of pagan horror stories flickering through your mind, but the way you came has been erased into darkness so you press on, an urgent, primordial part of your brain making towards the light.

When you get into the chapel, the music and movement have stopped, pretending they never existed at all. It's not so much the creepy wheatsheaf sculptures or the decaying flower arrangements that terrify you, but the scarecrows sitting arrayed on pews. What if there's a cast member ready to spring out at you? You'd jump out of your skin. You try not to look too hard, try not to will one of these undead effigies alive as you trace your route to the next room; still, it takes three circuits of the chapel before you can find the door again.

You make your way down a ramp into a set made out like an enclosed sunken garden. A smash of glass and a belt of forced laughter. Three teenage boys wearing jeans and track jackets are sparring under a tree at the far side of the garden, no more than twenty metres away. One of them is banging on a rubbish bin with a stick. *Thump thump thump*.

You scan for another way out – do you really want to see where this scene is going? – but the entire space around you is dark. At least there are three other audience members watching on with you, their crow faces perversely bringing some comfort.

Now there is another laugh. No, not a laugh – a stifled cry.

A bright light has come on, lighting up the thickening fog like toxic plasma. *Thump thump thump*; the boy is still hitting the dustbin with his stick. The second boy is slumped on the middle swing, his languid rotations mirrored in the sway and the creak of the third boy, who is hanging by the neck from the thick branch of the tree. His hood is hanging half off, crumpled to one side by the rope, revealing his buzz-cut hairstyle and his straw-filled sack of a face. It's just a bloody scarecrow.

You laugh with the boy on the swing, prove you can take a joke – *yeah, you got me* – but the dead-eyed boy-actor just stares back at you.

10 Petra hadn't had nightmares like this since she was a child. It wasn't just the show's images, the terrible things they'd showed her and *the way they made her feel* cycling through her overstimulated mind – sure, there was enough of that, too – but genuine perverted imaginings she was scraping up from some murky recess of her mind. Sometimes, when she closed her eyes, she'd immediately sink into a hole where the terrors lived; she wouldn't even feel herself falling asleep and she'd be there, being shown things she'd never seen, couldn't believe she was imagining. And then she'd start awake, the hair raised on her arms, a ghostly crackle receding down her back, as if something had been *touching* her.

Yes, the second Metamuse show was dark as hell, a sucker punch after the intense romance of *Intimacy*, but there was no reason it should be affecting her like this. *Cabinet*. And she could imagine some crazed collector watching from above as the audience wandered directionless and lost between the exhibits, the rooms, the stages, what they rather wankily referred to as 'moral scenarios'. Caligari, Moreau – there was definitely a measure of social experiment about it. Which was why Suki was telling her about how Sheridan and King reframed Milgram's obedience experiments by shocking a puppy instead of a person, who subjects might think is faking. And then about all the pseudoscientific techniques marketers have developed to sell you stuff.

'You think you're in control of your decisions, but you're not. It can bend your mind, darling, when you realise just how easily you can be manipulated. There's so much in common between what Metamuse does and what we do at Line Logic.' Disturbingly, Suki seemed to offer no moral or ethical judgement on either the marketers' Machiavellian work or her own.

While Petra entered stock invoices, Suki was decorating a front display table with a new shipment of Korean pop and soap paraphernalia. More expensive stock nobody bought. Not for the first time, Petra found herself suspecting that Needful Things was more than a simple vanity project to keep Suki quiet and happy. It could well be a laundromat for some of the Barlows' iller-gotten gains. But she was no forensic accountant and there was absolutely no point in trying to upset a centuries-old apple cart pitched on an obscure foundation of caste and patronage. As long as the ruling classes were happy to have her here, she should just shut up and go along with it.

'It felt so... organic. I had total free choice about where I was going, but this, sort of, *story* started happening. A bloody nasty story. It was almost as if there was a narrative connection from one room to another, even though there was no way they could know which passage I'd choose.'

'They knew, love. There was no free choice. They were herding you.'

'No, I don't think so. Honestly. I thought about it.' She hadn't thought about much else all weekend. She could have done with Vincent's company, at least a chance to compare impressions, but without him, she was left to wander those passageways over and over. In her dreams she got more and more lost, peering into alcoves that didn't exist in the show, revealing things that didn't exist in the *Cabinet* warehouse – even Jouval and Barnes and Metamuse wouldn't be sick enough to present what was apparently lying deep in her psyche.

'Did you notice Metamuse minions subtly opening and closing doors around you?'

'No, not really.'

'It was dark, though, wasn't it?'

'Yes, mostly.'

'So the minions and the black-painted doorways in the black-painted set walls would be invisible. The paths you were meant to take were subtly lit.'

Now that Petra thought back, it was pretty obvious – you bump into a chipboard wall in the dark a few times, discover that the black doors don't open, and you subtly and quickly learn to stick to the dimly lit path and push through the coloured doors only. Of course they were herding her. The realisation of just how simply – and effectively – she'd been played made her feel foolish and gullible, but also a little bit relieved. If she was feeling weird, as if the show's effects had been just for her, it was because the show wanted her to feel that way. She wasn't going loopy. 'God. It was so… intimate. Like they were in my head.'

'There were voices, weren't there?' Suki continued. Petra nodded. 'And ice-cold chills, a slap of humid air, just at the right time. Just a suggestion, to make you feel like it was a reaction – the chill for a fright, the warm flush for shame or arousal.'

'Yup, I suppose so.' Petra smiled and shook her head. 'Are you sure you weren't there?'

'I wish. This one sounds a lot like *The Crying Tree* – I went to that in Tokyo. It's big-budget stuff. Amazing they can afford it on their limited runs. All the top-end directional speakers, mini air-treatment units. They even changed the floorboards in one of the sets, used hard sponges doused in syrup and animal blood. Jesus, I remember how my feet sucked at the sticky floor.'

'Did you buy it? I mean, did you get freaked out?'

Suki shrugged. 'Hmn. Nah, I kinda knew how they did it. I deconstructed it too much to enjoy it fully. It's a bit of a curse, I suppose, doing what I do. Oh, how I wish for a pure and innocent and shockable mind like yours, my pearl.'

'Bugger off, Sook.'

Petra finished receiving the invoice, double checked the totals, and submitted the form into the system. She stood up and stretched, her spine crackling. She'd twisted herself in knots trying to sleep the last three nights, and had even become afraid to catch up with a nap on Sunday afternoon. Her eyes were grainy now, stinging. She sighed, took a sip of her cold coffee, and checked the time on the computer screen.

'Strange that Freddie hasn't come in this morning. I wonder if he's sick.'

Suki looked up from the table, where her fan of K-pop sticker books was taking nice shape.

'Who?' Suki said.

'Freddie,' she repeated. 'Guy from Gravity's End.' And

when Suki's expression remained blank, she added, 'The pub? He's usually here like clockwork for his Monday perv session.' She was used to being asked to repeat herself; though she didn't think it was particularly broad, her accent still seemed to take people by surprise.

Suki was looking at her with a *huh?* expression.

Shit, was his name not Freddie? Had she got it wrong all this time? She scoured her memory banks for the last few occasions they'd talked. Had she said his name aloud? How embarrassing if she'd called him the wrong name. But she could have sworn it was Freddie. In her mind, she'd pegged the name to Freddie Krueger. Once lodged, she couldn't really forget that image. Once, he'd even come in wearing a striped jumper.

She was about to say so when two customers came in. The first woman asked where the vinyl was and Suki led her to the stairs, flashing a grin over her shoulder at Petra as she went. 'Just pulling your chain, Pet. Of course I know who our darling Freddie is. A little joke.'

It wasn't funny, not today.

Petra waited until lunchtime to try Vincent again. Usually, she wouldn't hesitate to find a quiet moment and give him a call from the back office – Suki wouldn't mind – but being ghosted by him was an embarrassment she didn't want to share.

Petra had lost Vincent pretty early into the show, and had waited for him for thirty minutes in the come-down bar afterwards. He hadn't phoned or texted, and after scanning the gloomy roads outside the post office depot and the church, she gave up and went home, texting him along the way. Delivered and received. No reply.

She'd sent him a few more messages over the weekend. Delivered and received. No reply. Petra wanted to give him the benefit of the doubt. Maybe he'd been waiting for her all that time around another corner. Maybe they'd just missed each other. Maybe he'd lost his phone. But he could have called her from another phone, couldn't he? Checked if she was okay.

He could have come to her flat. If she was out, he could have left a note. *Sorry, I lost my phone. Are you alright?*

Maybe *he* wasn't alright. God, what if something had happened to him, and here she was, being a cow. She could go to his house and find out if he was okay – but she had no idea where he lived. She knew she was overreacting; she'd done it before, put guys off by coming across weird and overly needy. That time she'd freaked Steve out when he was away on a team-building thing he said he'd told her about but definitely hadn't. She'd even tracked his mother down. Steve had shamed her then, but this was a different case. What if Vincent was in trouble, and she didn't do anything about it, afraid of being made to feel foolish? Once the concern had lodged, there was no other way to dislodge it than calling.

The phone went through to voicemail, after a suspiciously medium number of rings. If it was off or out of range, it would go straight through. If nobody was there it would ring ten, fifteen times. If someone was cutting her off, it would ring precisely six and a half.

'Hi, it's me again.' She didn't say her name, imagining some phone-stealing stranger listening in to all her previous voicemails, getting criminally fixated. Had she left any personal details? Was there any way the phone thief could find her? *Christ, get over yourself, Petra.* 'Dunno if you're hearing this, but if you're okay, please get in touch or come see me to prove it. I'd really like to know. Okay, bye.'

She got back to the shop with a sandwich and a coffee from the Greek deli, her phone stashed deep in her pocket. There were a few customers in, Petra saw through the windows, but Suki was smoking in the alleyway, clutching herself in the cold wind chasing up the alley. She hadn't bothered to put on a coat, even though she nursed her cigarettes. It needled her. Petra pushed through to the shop and slumped down on the stupid stool behind the counter.

<7 Panther Road>

The message came at six, just as Petra was locking the shop. Suki had left at around four, with strict instructions to 'bathe in the glory of the blacklight of the impending apocalypse and all the good music it's flushing out at the moment', which meant, in Suki-ese, that she should enjoy the playlist she'd devised for her after lunch, made up of the most obscure and mournful emo tracks that she thought would match her slumping mood.

What Petra needed was a pick-up, not a dark mirror to amplify this unaccustomed gloom. She wasn't used to feeling depressed and she wasn't one to nurse needless introspection, but Vincent's abandonment had hit her. She'd really believed they were on the same wavelength. She'd trusted that he felt the same way about her; she thought she'd seen it in his eyes, felt it in his body. There hadn't been any doubt about that. And the show still reverberated in her mind. No, more than her mind – an all-body hallucination, like being back there in reality, but worse. Twisted, warped. The flashbacks hit her sharply and without warning. She'd never taken acid, but this was exactly how bad trips were described. Could Metamuse have spiked the drinks with hallucinogens to enhance their effect? They couldn't get away with that, surely. Would they want to?

Whatever the case, Petra was just trying to calm her breathing after a fragment of a very convincing waking dream – she'd been lying on her stomach on the floor, looking into a small door built into the skirting of a dark room in a grimy old house. Though it was bitterly cold, she seemed to be wearing just a T-shirt, and maybe she'd been dragged there because the T-shirt was rucked up and the skin of her bare stomach was grazed and stinging. She could feel the grit of the dust and jags of splintered wood, but worse were the balled pads of something the drag across the floor had dredged up – fur or mould or something soft and organic, a little bit sticky.

But the abject sensations on her naked, freezing skin weren't the first thing on her mind – it was that little doorway, what lay beyond. She had to be this low, at floor level, to see through it. It was a small door of children's nightmares. The sort made by anthropomorphic rats and mice, the sort who bundle curious kittens into roly-poly puddings, or by little folklore hominids who watch you and steal your stuff – borrowers, trolls and nasty fairies who live in the walls and sneak about while you sleep. There was something moving inside.

The door wasn't as small as a mouse hole, not as big as a coal-cellar door. Maybe slightly bigger than a cat flap? She wasn't sure if she could get through it if she needed to. Not that she'd ever want to. Unless something was coming from behind her, and this was the only way out.

She was lying on her stomach, feeling the sting of the grazes on her stomach, only now worrying about what the soft substance smearing into her wounds really was, when a light came up in the space beyond the door.

Before she could see any further she snapped out of the hallucination, gasping, almost tipping herself off the counter stool as she drew herself up and out. She swatted at her stomach, put her hand under her top – no grazes there. Only now did she notice the customer glancing over at her from the kitchenware shelves.

'We'll be closing up in a few minutes, sir,' she said. 'But if there's anything I can help you with?'

The middle-aged man bought an espresso pot shaped and painted like a cartoon circus rocket and Petra cashed up and shut the shop.

Spillage, Aisle Four!

Falling, Metamuse, Sakurashinmachi,
Setagaya City, Tokyo, 23–31 December

It's Christmas and I'm pushing a trolley in the Inageya
supermarket in Sakurashinmachi, an upmarket residential
suburb of Tokyo. Metamuse has offered me plane fare and five
nights' accommodation in Tokyo in exchange for 'an honest
review' of their new show, *Falling*. I had plans to spend the
festive season with my wife's family, but she's a good person;
she spared me and told me to take this opportunity instead.

Here goes: my attempt at an honest review, whatever that
might mean.

I've never been to Tokyo and I'm surprised by it. It's
massive, yes, but it's human-scaled – it seems to have been
built by lots and lots of people with a sense of society.
I don't feel like an alien in an alien world; I don't feel lost
in translation, and I find my way out to the supermarket on
the highly efficient public transport with an hour to spare.

If you read my <u>review of *Idiopathy*</u> that ran in Paris this
May, you'll know I had issues with sharing headphones. This
time you can use your own device. Some people might have
similar squeams about uploading apps and allowing them
full access to your data and location, but I don't give a shit.
I know Big Brother is watching, and I prefer to be entertained
while they do.

So I plug in my own earphones and activate the app as instructed on the confirmation email. There are no red carpets or dapper staffers to welcome me this time, but I know they're watching.

'Collect a trolley and make your way to the fresh produce aisle,' the voice says. It's not *her* this time and I'm disappointed. I've found myself thinking of the intimate instructive voice from *Idiopathy* a few times too often these last few months – she seems to have lodged somewhere in my psyche, rippling there sometimes, stretching languidly.

But my guide today is a bland male voice. 'Let's start by feeling,' he says. 'Choose two large fruits or vegetables and hold them in your hands. Consider the texture of the skin, feel the heft in your hands.'

I was trained not to play with food, and I especially remember my mother's warnings not to fondle the veggies in the supermarket when I went to the shops with her as a kid, but I follow instructions – of course I do. I've come all this way, haven't I?

I pick out a pineapple and a melon, thinking of my fellow earthlings as I do, knowing that they'll have to peel these before they eat them and won't digest too many of my microbes. Come to think of it, I should probably buy them after the show, have fruit salad for dinner.

I'm supposed to be feeling, considering texture and heft, but all I'm feeling is a bit of a fool. Maybe it's the jet lag, or maybe it's that tune that's softly playing behind the guy's voice – what is it? I know it from somewhere – maybe it's because I suddenly feel so bloody far away, but I don't really want to be here.

I know where this is leading, I think. I've seen this before. It's just like *Psychomart*, a show I reviewed in London seven or eight years ago. Back then it was cool – defamiliarising the familiar, making us 'really see' our urban surroundings and the other people in them; elevating our mundane existence – but we've all been there and done that and de-elevated again. Could Metamuse, the group who made me feel invisible hands touching me, who made me rip open my soul in a dark room, really have dragged me across the world for this?

Now I'm told to drive to the cheese and dairy aisle. I put the pineapple and melon in my trolley and concentrate on acting normal as I scan the signs along the aisles.

Fuck. The song that's playing from the supermarket's ceiling is the song I had my first-ever slow dance to. It was our primary-school farewell dance – five o'clock on a Friday afternoon. We were damp still from the games we'd played in the afternoon – apple-bobbing and water-balloon races – and I was self-conscious about whether anyone could see through my T-shirt and I'd gone to the girls' changing room to spray on even more of my cheap deodorant. I was too tall, even then – about a foot taller than Gabriel, but he was a kind boy, and I hugged him to my chest through that song and forgot.

It was my song they were playing – not yours, not anyone else's who happened to be playing this game. There was no way they could have known this detail of my life – I've never written it down, never even told my mother any detail about that dance. Gabriel died during high school.

'Pick up your favourite cheese and find a security camera in the ceiling,' the voice says. Tom, I've dubbed him – he sounds like a Tom. 'Smile at the camera and say cheese.'

They're taking the piss, aren't they? This is not a thin copy – it has moved through pastiche into parody.

Why here? I'm wondering. *Why did this have to happen in Tokyo?*

I didn't find the answer, but the question became irrelevant after what happened next.

Annoying aside klaxon: remember *Psychomart*? It's easy to forget just how *big* it was back in 2010 and 2011. Its popular appeal spilled way beyond traditional theatre-going audiences. The app sold over two million copies – decent numbers for any app back then and incredible for a pretty expensive experimental art app. For a couple of months in cities around the world, *Psychomart* was the thing for fashionable clever kids to do. It ushered in serious investment in AR technologies beyond mainstream gaming and entertainment, and inspired countless bad knockoffs that ultimately hastened the collapse of the oversaturated scene. *Psychomart* was the fidget spinner of immersive theatre. Remember fidget spinners?

But what's interesting about *Psychomart* is the quieter news that happened after the craze had passed. *Psychomart* had started off as an art show created by two independent producers, Rafe Charlston and Linda Verazzi, but as early as its third tour a controlling stake in the small shell company had been bought by Qubit, a marketing consultancy and seed funder headed by Martin Trengove. It was then that *Psychomart*'s familiar branding and smartphone-based VR experience was designed and delivered and the model quickly exploded into hundreds of iterations across the world.

In 2014, Trengove was convicted on fraud and charges relating to the then-UK's Data Protection Act. Probably instigated by Charlston and Verazzi themselves, an investigation showed that *Psychomart* under Qubit became a mass consumer-profiling experiment, charting shopping styles, gaits, attention spans and emotional feedback to thousands of planted products throughout the network. This user data from all the *Psychomart* shows was compiled and illegally sold on to advertising packagers.

So what? you might ask – Google and Amazon do that every day. True, and Trengove was small fry compared, without enough legal and financial heft (speaking of heft) to change the law to match Qubit practices. But he had just enough juice to have the jail sentence commuted in favour of a fine before relocating – you guessed it – to Tokyo in 2016, where he's on the board of several marketing research companies but has stayed deftly away from company operations.

All this passed my notice after I'd moved on from *Psychomart*, and it may have evaded yours too.

Okay, back to what happened next at the Inageya supermarket. It was here that the script diverged from *Psychomart* homage and became something altogether different.

Tom instructs me to choose a microwaveable meal and a drink from the convenience food section. The unfamiliar packaging makes this quite challenging, but I guess I can recognise a pizza when I see one in a photograph. I choose a small bottle of white wine and an orange juice to go with it. Next, he says, go to aisle four.

But there is no aisle four – the supermarket has superstitiously skipped from three to five; the word for four is related to the word for death – and it takes me several self-conscious minutes to notice the hand-printed sign on yellow paper stuck next to what looks like a delivery bay door. 'Aisle 4 inside,' it says, with a wonky arrow pointing towards the door. There's a more permanent no-entry symbol on the door along with some Japanese text that I'm guessing means 'Staff Only'.

What do I do? Obey the norms of global supermarket etiquette or Tom's instructions? That's my dilemma. The option of obeying neither instruction doesn't enter my head. I'm here to be directed.

I look at the pizza slice sweating in the trolley alongside the fruit and the wine, which is looking quite tempting at this stage, and figure the authorities at the shop must be in on the show and I probably wouldn't be arrested if I'm just playing a game. Besides, I want to see what's there – whatever lies beyond will either elevate this rather humdrum experience or confirm that Metamuse was a one-hit wonder and has slumped to join the rest of post-late-capitalism's moribund creative practitioners, both of which would be satisfying in their own way.

With one last glance over my shoulder, I push through the service doors, the rubber buffers of the double doors sucking at each other like lecherous toothless monsters with overactive salivary glands. (Remember, at this stage I'm still trying to make my own excitement.)

Through the doors is a wide corridor lined with movable shelving stacked with cling-wrapped cans and bottles and sacks, leading into a vast stockroom. The smell is of layered spices and flour and an undertone of astringent chemicals. Three women loading carts look up at me as I pass but turn back to their work without comment.

There's another yellow sign across the stockroom floor and I hurry across to follow it, through another pair of double doors that lead me outside onto a freezing cold ledge overlooking a delivery bay. Someone's unloading vegetables from a van onto a—

—woman falls out of the sky, right in front of me. She flips gracefully through the air two metres from my face. Time slows to an incremental crawl. I have time to replay the curve and cartwheel of her body, to trace the woman's trajectory from the upper floors of the building above me, before she ploughs into the conveniently placed skip full of plastic and paper padding.

Time and the world rush-suck back into place as I hurry over to the skip, where the woman is standing and brushing herself off like an action hero. She hoists herself over the rim and onto the ledge where I'm standing, and for an extended moment she's on hands and knees in front of me and I'm standing over her, thinking about power for a minute too long before squatting down to help her up.

'Thank you,' she says, her hand strong and warm in mine, not flinching from the touch. For God's sake, you *never* touch the actors. It's the unwritten rule of immersive theatre – otherwise where is the line between art and fantasy and wish-fulfilment and desire and consummation? It would not be safe to blur that line. 'Come with me, Rose. I have something to show you.' And I recognise the voice. It's her – the woman who's been living in my braincore for the last seven months.

She doesn't really look like I imagined her, and that's something of a disappointment, but at the same time I realise that this woman could look like anyone. She's wearing a jet-black wig, and her beautiful, bland face could be painted in any imaginable way. She's a canvas, this woman; a screen for my projections.

But her hand is warm, and I follow her back inside. I forgot about the cold when she fell, but it's a relief to be back in the building again. It's also disturbing, because the space is no longer the supermarket delivery bay I just walked through. The pallets of groceries and the staff and the concrete walls and floors are gone – writing this now, I still don't know how they did that – but I'm in a night-lit desert camp, sensuous dunes undulating me towards a cluster of tents richly lit with golden light from within.

I can see the stars rippling in the sky above, feel the warm, dry air wafting up from the sand, which shifts and slips and scrunches under my boots. There's the smell of sumac and garlic and saffron; also of the goats and camels that rest serene in a wood-fenced pen, a small bleat or a tinkle as a beast flicks its head to warn off flies.

I have been transported to the other side of the world in one step, and the plunge and plummet is bewildering and invigorating all at once. You know that feeling of the first cool morning in autumn, the animal instinctive sense that the seasons have turned, or that feeling you get if you've landed in a new country in a different hemisphere, how that change lodges in you, makes the tips of your body tingle? Like that, condensed and concentrated, whacked into a wall of change in one second.

Like in *Idiopathy*, it's the transition that strips me, makes me obedient. My sense of certainty and authority over my own life have been seductively and lovingly flayed away from me and I will follow wherever Metamuse leads me.

Today, Metamuse – in the guise of this black-wigged *her* – beckons me into a tent, where she proceeds to heal me. From the outside, it may look like a spa treatment, maybe – a copper bucket of amniotic water, a loofah with which she washes me, intimate questions that are only for me.

Maybe it is an overblown spa treatment, maybe it's a psychotherapy session, but I emerge stripped, dismantled, reconstructed, reset.

I need to be critical. I am a critic. *Falling* is two shows – a bitter, blunt takedown of the *Psychomart* trend that disorientingly swivels into the thing of intense beauty that is the desert hammam. The two sides are frustratingly unequal – but as I fly back home, once again feeling the ghostly hands on my skin, I know Metamuse played me perfectly. First, they softened me up, letting me slip into my critical complacency, before sucker-punching me with love. Again.

If you manage to attend a viewing of *Idiopathy*, I don't know who your guide will be or where Metamuse will lead you or how they'll treat you, but do yourself a favour and follow if you can.

11 *<7 Panther Road>*

Petra waited for more, but that was all.

She should just disregard it. He owed her more than that after ghosting her for the last three days. She should just make him wait, see if he could bring himself to write a little more, or, hell, even give her a call. At the very least, she should follow up tomorrow, not come running like a little dog.

But she couldn't. If he'd said something like, 'Sorry, I've been busy,' she would have gone home, but it was the very impersonality of the text that swayed her. Sure, he was a rubbish texter, but this was unlike him. Unlike the little she knew of him, at any rate. But still, she wouldn't be able to live with herself if she went home and sulkily ignored him and all the while he was in some sort of trouble.

She checked the address on her phone. It wasn't far. Right here in town – Helena would be pleased – and she headed that way.

Number 7 was a neat and narrow semi in a road of tightly packed similar houses. Probably built a hundred years ago for workers but no longer occupied by them, judging by the cars parked along the road. He'd told her he lived with his grandmother, but the small front yard, bounded by a uniform low gate and little wall made of the same red brick as the house, was tidy and anonymous and offered no secret hints to Vincent's character or history. If this was even his house, she reminded herself. Maybe it was just a neutral staging post for a break-up chat. If that was the case, he needn't have bothered. He owed her nothing.

Too much thinking, Petra. Just get on with it.

She took the few steps up to the front door and knocked. The knocker was a version of a lion's head, more friendly than the scary creature on the studio's red door. Unlike that one, the ring in this creature's mouth wasn't welded down and made a satisfying *clack* when she rapped the brass baseplate with it.

Still, no one came.

She stood for a minute, straining to hear any movement inside, tiptoeing to look through the textured glass in the door. There was a light on inside, but no shadows moved. Outside, it was dark now, and it had begun to rain again. She'd rather be doing something else than standing here getting cold and wet. She tried the knocker again, conscious now of the urgent sound reverberating along the street. It sounded needy, not the sort of feeling you wanted to broadcast on a strange street just gone dark.

She took out her phone and checked the address and then responded to the text.

<I'm here. Are you in?>

Curtness was catching. She still couldn't quite shake the feeling that her messages might be being read by other eyes. She'd keep herself to herself until she saw him. *If* she saw him.

She stepped over the flower bed, its neatly pruned rose stalks waiting for spring, and peered through the bay window. The curtains were drawn, a heavy red-lined material, but they weren't quite fully closed. Over at the far face of the bay window, a slant of light showed through. She edged across the window ledge, trying not to get her legs tangled in a viney bush, and found an eyeline into the front room.

A lamp, an abstract painting on the wall above a fireplace. Shifting across, she saw a couch, someone's legs in dark trousers.

A slam behind her.

'Hi. Petra? Come in.'

Petra wheeled round, stumbled in the plant. She battled her way through the undergrowth to where Vincent was standing.

'Did we have a...' he trailed, apologetically scanning his outfit of dressing gown and baggy track pants, his hair clumped and tousled. Even in the dim light, she could see how drawn he was, almost grey, as if all the warm hue had been sucked out of his skin. He looked a hundred years old.

'Did we have plans?' he said, ushering her between the plants and to the door. 'I'm sorry if I forgot. I've been...' He looked so withered that for an ungenerous instant the thought that this old man had wound his body around hers just a fortnight ago repulsed her. But then he turned, and the light from the doorway did its work and he looked a little more like himself. Still, what the hell had happened to him?

'You just asked me to come. I think.' She held up her phone like it was ID. 'You sent me your address.'

'Nah, wasn't me.' He frowned for a second before his face changed. 'God, you have to see this, Petra. Come in, come in.' He warded her into the house and hustled her along the passageway so quickly she could hardly get a sense of the place.

The hallway was unlit, so all she got was a glimpse of the darkened stairwell going up, a low shelf with shoes at the entrance, a picture or mirror sourly reflecting. As she passed, she tried to glance into the front room she'd seen through the bay window, but the door was ajar. She had only the sense of low rose light touching up a shelf full of large art books and feathering off a framed poster of an exhibition. A waft of cigarette smoke, the slumped dark-hued couch, possibly green but turned the colour of sludge in the lamp's saturating glow. A fragmentary glimpse of the person sitting there – dark jacket sleeve on the couch's armrest, a relaxed foot in a shiny shoe and a black-trousered leg slanted away.

She saw no more because Vincent didn't slow, herding her on towards the kitchen at the end of the passage. Along the way, she glanced at a series of beautiful framed photos, clearly Vincent's moody work. Night-time scenes of softly lit moonscapes and mistscapes, a point of humanity in a sweating winter window, the contours of a face rendered abstract by neon and darkness. They were unmistakably his pictures; she recognised a couple of the images from the selection he'd shown her on that first weekend. The prints in real life here on the wall, liberated from the tinted phone screen, expanded to incredible life. The darkness was like a warm blanket, the mist like a swaddling shroud. Thinking of her own wavering, uncertain creativity, she admired and envied his distinctive vision.

The kitchen was lit by a too-bright pendant lamp over a small oval table that served to cast the rest of the room into jarring shadow and smelled of cold grease, saturated fish batter. The mouth of the kitchen bin gaped, full beyond the brim with crumpled paper and plastic. Dirty dishes and a couple of half-crumpled beer cans were piled in the sink. There was a fluorescent strip light on the ceiling and Petra wanted to find the switch for it, bathe the room in a more kitchen-like light, as if it might chase the dirt off the plates and the stale smell out of the room along with the shadows. But she held back as Vincent sat in a straight-backed chair at the table.

'Come sit, please,' he said, gesturing at the chair next to him as he shoved the mugs and bottles away and more carefully moved his camera and notebook aside. He angled the laptop screen towards her. 'Look what I saw.'

Stop, she wanted to say. *First tell me where you went on Friday night. You shouldn't just get away with ignoring me and then showing me your cat memes or whatever the hell you want to show me without apologising first.* But his urgency was compelling, and under this harsh light his face was even more leached, there were beads of sweat on his brow – there was something wrong with him. So she held her tongue and looked to the screen, hoping she'd get the chance to have a normal conversation later.

The computer was a decent brand, but pretty old, and the screen was scuffed and spotted, from this angle reflecting the light back from a glass-fronted cabinet. 'Do you mind?' she asked before she touched his computer, something that struck her as an awkwardly intimate invasion. He nodded and she re-angled the computer, adjusted the screen, but still she didn't see what she was meant to be looking at. The photo on the screen was mainly dark with just some blurred patches in the lower right-hand side. A brighter shaft of white light cut across the top third.

'I'm not sure what I'm looking at,' she said.

Vincent leaned over and hit the cursor, cycling through a series of stills of the same blurred shapes. As a series, she could see that the photographer had approached the white slant and the indistinct shapes gradually – the smudges got bigger as he progressed and seemed to be moving just a little, leaning in towards the centre of the frame perhaps – but just as she was starting to discern some direction in the smudges' movement, Vincent flicked through the images, jittering forward and back until the shapes just looked like random smears again.

'You see her, yeah?'

'Who?'

'There, Petra. Please.' He pointed to the smudges.

'Christ, Vincent, stop flicking through the bloody pictures. I don't know what I'm supposed to be looking at.' This was ridiculous. She took a deep breath, tried to reset. 'I haven't seen you for days.' She reached out for his hand, touched it softly. 'Can we start at the beginning?'

She took another deep breath, offered him a tired, worried smile, and to her relief he mirrored her, breathing in and raking his hands through his hair. 'Yeah, sorry. You're right. I'm sorry. I guess I have a lot to apologise for.'

'Just tell me what's going on. Are you okay? That's all I wanted to know.'

Vincent stood up and turned on the strip light, looked around him as if noticing the mess in the kitchen for the first time. He muttered something under his breath and found a glass in the cupboard. 'Would you like something to drink?'

'No, I'm good.'

He filled the glass with water and downed it, still staring around the kitchen as if he'd just woken up on a strange planet.

Petra stood and went to the sink, running her hand down Vincent's back as she passed. She cleared space on the draining board and started removing the dishes from the sink, scraping their contents together.

'Stop that, please,' he said. 'I'll do it.'

'If you can just pull out that trash bag and find a new one, that'll help,' she said.

He looked at her for minute, then went to a drawer and found a roll of bin liners. He changed the bin bag and started tidying the mess on the table and countertops as Petra started on the dishes.

'Who's your friend, Vincent?' A tall woman with luxuriant grey braids had appeared in the kitchen doorway. She was wearing a bright skirt and a smart patterned blouse whose elegance was diluted by a loose knitted cardigan coat, which she drew around her when she noticed Petra standing there. She walked over with a deliberate stride that just failed to disguise the hitch of a limp, and extended her hand. Her smile was warm and generous, even in her drawn face. 'Hello there. I'm Gloria.' She could tell where Vincent had inherited that warm and open countenance.

Petra wiped her hands on a dishtowel and took the woman's hand. 'Petra. I'm really pleased to meet you.' She was going to add *Vincent's told me a lot about you*, but he hadn't, not really.

'Lord, I'm sorry,' Gloria said. 'He invites you to our home and makes you do the dishes.'

'Nan, please,' Vincent grizzled, and he instantly became

the boy this woman had raised. It was as if thirty years had vanished. 'You should go back to bed.'

Gloria rolled her eyes and Petra laughed. 'He didn't make me. I'm just glad to make myself useful.'

'That makes two of us,' Gloria said. 'Vinnie likes to coddle me, but I'm not dying.'

'Nobody said that,' he said, 'but you're not well. What do you need? I can bring it up to you.'

Petra looked between them, directing a questioning expression towards Gloria, knowing she was more likely to get an answer from her than from Vincent. 'I'm alright. Just a bit of asthma,' she explained in an aside to Petra, then turned to Vincent. 'I just came down for a cup of tea.' She filled the kettle and turned it on, then gazed around the half-tidied kitchen. 'I've let the domestic things slip, I know. I did my duty for a long time. Just now I'm... I've just lost a bit of interest in it.'

Losing your husband and your granddaughter, selling up the creative business you'd built, would do that to a person, Petra thought. But she didn't say anything, unsure whether she should admit she knew some of this woman's painful story.

'It's all good, Nan,' Vincent said.

'Besides,' Gloria added, 'Vincent's able-bodied, isn't he?'

Petra and Vincent stood on pause and spoke with their eyes as Gloria added water and squished the teabag around a bit before topping the mug up with milk. Finally, she made her way to the door. 'It's nice to have some living people here,' she smiled as she passed Petra.

Vincent shook his head. 'Just call down if you need anything else, alright, Nan?'

Petra went back to the sink and washed a couple more dishes in silence as Vincent took a broom to the floor. 'I'm glad you're still with us,' she said at length. This part of the conversation was easier with her back turned. She could imagine any reaction she wanted.

The sweeping stopped. 'What do you mean?'

'I didn't know where you went.' Petra tried not to sound defensive, kept her tone level, like someone coaxing a frightened child out of a dangerous situation. *Drop that knife, sweetie. I'm not angry.* 'It was no one's fault that we split up at the show. But I was hoping to meet up afterwards. I was hoping you'd text me at least.'

'I'm sorry, I... I lost my phone for a while and I didn't have your number.'

'You found it again? Your phone.' Scrubbing hard at a caked-on smear of egg and ketchup.

'Yeah. When you say it like that, it sounds like a lame excuse. I see that.'

'I honestly don't want to make an issue of this, but I was scared. I didn't know if you were in trouble or something. And that show – it freaked me out. It frightened me. I could have done with...' *Debriefing*. Last week, another life, she might have said it. 'You could have at least called. Once you found your phone again, I mean.'

'I didn't have your number, I swear. All my contacts were gone.'

She wanted to drop it, but couldn't let his lying slide. Mainly because he was doing such a fucking bad job of it. She turned, and enunciated, 'But how did you text me tonight, then?'

'I told you – I didn't text you,' he said. He stopped wiping down the countertop and came over to stand mawkishly in front of her. 'I'm really sorry that you were scared. But you'll understand that I was freaked out too, won't you? By seeing her.' He pointed at the computer on the table.

She dropped the sponge and wiped her hands on the dishcloth and went to sit back at the table. 'Show me, Vincent. I still don't know what you're talking about.'

He brought up a photo and turned the screen to her, and now she could recognise what she was seeing. The image brought an instant spurt of shock through her, the set still bringing a visceral reaction. When she'd wandered through that eerie chapel set, she'd thought about her father's funeral, the overstuffed emptiness of the gesture, and had started to cry.

Vincent framed a section of the photo, a segment with the window from the chapel set and the right side of the altar, and zoomed in. Now Petra recognised that this was what she'd been looking at before – the white slash was the edge of the altar lit by a bright spot from beyond the fake window. And there, under the altar, someone was crouching.

The more Vincent zoomed in, the more grainy the shape became, until she was seeing the same segment he'd shown her before.

'Can you see her now?'

'I did, I think, for a second. But I don't anymore.'

'Look again,' he said, highlighting the blur under the altar – and as it was selected, the image switched to a negative, and there, clearly, was a young woman's face. Like an optical illusion, she'd been looking at it all this time, and now that she recognised it, she couldn't unsee it.

'Okay, I see her now.' The idea that this actor could have been hiding there every time she'd gone through the set creeped Petra out. 'What about her? Did she jump out at you or something?'

'Oh,' Vincent said. 'Oh, yeah, there's no way you'd know… Petra, that's Beccie.'

She put out her hand towards Vincent for a moment, retracted it. 'No. It's not.' Looked into his face. Her heart was literally aching. 'You know it's not her. These shows, they mess with you deliberately. When I went in there, I thought of my father. There's all this imagery – they do it on purpose, draw on our emotions, our losses. It makes for good theatre, I suppose.'

But Vincent didn't seem to be hearing her as he scanned through another folder and clicked on a file. A picture of a lovely, pretty girl came up – her eyes looked tired but she was beaming a warm smile. She had her ringlets tied back in a red ribbon; she was wearing a sweat top with narrow horizontal blue and white stripes.

Vincent brought up the image from the fake chapel, adjusted the contrast, upped the colour saturation. The actor was wearing a narrow-striped top and a red ribbon in her curly hair. And, yes, she did look a hell of a lot like the smiling girl in the photo.

Had Vincent convinced himself he'd seen Beccie in the warehouse? That show was custom-designed to make your ghosts emerge. If you had any emotional baggage, it was no surprise if it took shape in that intense atmosphere. The poor man.

'I heard her calling to me,' he said. 'I followed her there.'

Petra didn't know how she should handle this. It didn't seem the right thing to let him suffer these delusions, but who was she to correct him? Maybe it was best to just help him in the direction of common sense. 'You couldn't have taken this picture. We weren't allowed cameras, remember?' Vincent would realise he was mistaken. He'd probably been as sleepless as her – after tripping out on 'seeing Beccie', he might have disappeared home, found some publicity shots of *Cabinet* and photoshopped her image into them. He certainly looked like he'd been doing something obsessive all weekend.

He frowned, thought. 'Yeah, I did have it with me. I always have it with me, you know that. I took these shots, Petra. You have to believe me.'

It was true: Vincent did carry his camera wherever he went, always ready for a rare image. Petra could imagine him firing off some illicit frames of the inside, even if it meant he'd be kicked out. Illicit shots, the pictures few others would take – they were what a photographer like him thrived on. Though she couldn't remember him having the camera with him, they'd been separated so soon, she honestly couldn't swear to it. 'And no one stopped you?'

'No.'

'Mysterious, isn't it?' The voice came from behind Petra, in the kitchen doorway, and there he stood. The man in the cheap cream suit, the shiny patent leather shoes. Petra recognised him immediately, and her heart punched her ribs. The man she'd seen at the basement pizza place, who'd been watching her at the pub. He wasn't wearing the white-banded fedora, and in the bright light of the kitchen she could see his face properly for the first time. He was wearing a layer of foundation but the stark light picked out the pits in his skin. His thinning brown hair was slicked back over a pasty scalp and his eyes were still, their focus unchanging. They made Petra think of a dead shark she'd seen at the oceanarium in Umhlanga. They ran educational shark autopsies, and the day she'd gone on a high-school trip, the thing stared right at her as its hide was sliced open and its liver and belly removed. It almost seemed to be smiling as the Coke bottles and plastic bags were stripped out of its guts.

The man sat down at the kitchen table opposite her, hands in plain sight, folded on the tabletop. 'I think they *wanted* him to take the photos. Olivia Jouval gets what Olivia Jouval wants.'

Vincent looked across at him with a strange expression – resignation? fear? – something passive and doomed. Like a schoolboy would look at a bully he knows he has no chance of outrunning. Taking a deep breath in before he gets his ass kicked again.

'Who is this?' Petra asked Vincent, and when he didn't reply, 'Who are you?'

'I'm Ellis,' he said, twirling his hand and offering her a stagey seated bow. 'Ellis Brown. Surname like the TV mentalist, but not named after him, you must understand. We do have our professional jealousies in the... *industry*. But my skills are for real, and I had the name *long* before him.' He snuffled a laugh to himself.

'Why is he here, Vincent?' She could read from the glances between them, Vincent's browbeaten slump, that they weren't friends or housemates. What lay between them was the opposite of familiarity – there was an obnoxious spikiness beaming from the man.

'He's helping me with Beccie.'

'How? What is he doing for you?'

'He says he can get in touch with her, that he can help me find her.'

Oh, Jesus. One of those. Conman spiritualist ambulance chasers; they come out like cockroaches at the slightest sniff of desperation. 'You know he can't do that, surely.'

He shrugged. 'I know it sounds crazy to you, but he talked to her yesterday – she told him things only we would know. I can't really explain it to you.' *I don't need to explain it to you*, is what Petra heard.

She shook her head, turned to Ellis Brown. 'And what are you charging him?'

Ellis shrugged and turned his empty hands over. 'I'm not charging anything. I'm delivering a message from Rebecca, that's all. It's between Vincent and me.'

She glanced at Vincent but he looked back at her and shrugged. She stood up, walked behind his chair, and put her hand on his shoulder, aware while she was doing it that she was staking her claim on him, hoping to show Ellis Brown that she had some influence over him too. 'If you need anything, just let me know. I'm around, okay.'

Vincent nodded, touched her hand for a second. 'Thanks. Really. I need to do this, but I want you to understand why. I'll speak to you soon.'

'It's fine. But I still don't really understand why you called me here.'

'I didn't. It was him, probably.'

'Guilty as charged,' Ellis smirked.

He let this guy into his phone? That was just stupid. But she didn't ask Vincent – while Ellis was in the room, at least, it was clear her opinion was not wanted. Instead she turned to face the conman, her arms tightly folded across her chest. 'So why did you want me here, then?'

'I wanted to meet you. You're a significant energy in Vincent's aura and I need to know how to mitigate it.'

'Mitigate? What exactly do you mean by *mitigate*? Are you planning to *mitigate* me?' Saying the words, she felt distinctly less brave than she wanted to sound.

He ignored that, but said, 'And Vincent doesn't let me into his phone, by the way. I have a skill – a trick, if you will. I can send text messages with my mind.'

'Whatever,' Petra said. She'd had enough, she was going home.

Her phone buzzed. She pulled it out of her pocket.

<Vincent: I can, honest>

Petra tried not to react, but Ellis's hands were on the table, folded calmly where they had been all along. At least, she thought they'd been there all along. It was a voice prompt or a button on the floor. Whatever. Idiot.

Her phone buzzed again.

<Suki: See?>

'Yeah, very clever. I'm going now.'

An easy enough trick. Probably used the Wi-Fi to hack into her contacts. Bastard.

<Helena: Soon, you will believe>

'Okay. Now it's time to stop it. Call me, okay,' she said to Vincent as she hurried down the passage.

12 *He had her mother's contact details.* She shouldn't have left her Bluetooth unsecured – that's obviously how he'd performed his parlour trick, hacked into her phone somehow. The moment she stepped out of Vincent's house, she immediately put the phone into offline flight mode and jammed it deep in her pocket, resolved to change her passwords as soon as she got home.

Petra strode along the street, trying not to seem too hurried to anyone watching – it wasn't a good idea to advertise panic or rush, anything that may be seen as weakness. Though it was just after seven, it was dark and the houses gave off a forlorn, shuttered feeling. The squally wind kicked leaves and litter around, making the ground feel alive with scuttling things. The road curled in on itself in a way she didn't recall coming here – the main road should have been straight ahead, but now she was being led into a lonely cul-de-sac. As she tried to backtrack, the abandoned cars littered in the drives and the houses' empty eyes made her think of a video game she'd seen at an art gallery, where the inhabitants of an English village all disappear into the Rapture.

It was a relief, then, when she stumbled out of the suburb's ingrown curlicues into the edge of the Midland Oak park. She'd come out a couple of blocks north of where she'd been heading, but at least she knew the direct route home from here.

The park was apparently the geographical centre of England, and it seemed appropriate, that far from the lofty ideals of Westminster, that this heart of England should be marked by a pleasant enough patch of grass and reeds, a playground whose high-quality but fading equipment accurately measured the temporal distance from the last socially minded government, an 'Elderly Crossing' street sign, a rusted metal bench, an ignored memorial plaque and an overflowing dustbin. The Midland Oak itself had been cut down years ago.

By day she'd see the cheering bloom of the crocuses and daffodils that were already starting to poke their heads out and promise the end of a bland and grey winter. But playgrounds were a different prospect after dark, and Petra stuck to the periphery, and was relieved when she made it across to the broader, busier avenue that led into town. There were living people and moving cars here, and she slotted in alongside them and made her way towards the top of the Parade, where the bus rank and the late-night supermarket were busy with workers going home and diners and drinkers arriving for the evening.

When she got to her building, he was lurking outside, leaning with one foot up against the wall; that irritating, entitled, suggestive slouch that was already becoming too familiar to her. He was wearing a pair of silvery white headphones and he nodded along to the music, nonchalant, twirling his hat in his fingers. That fact that Ellis Brown knew where she lived enraged her more than frightened her – he clearly had nothing better to do than sneak around after her. She couldn't bring herself to call it stalking – that seemed too dramatic, somehow; too threatening. This arsehole was a two-bit faker, and out of Vincent's home she'd stopped feeling threatened by him; now she was just put out, annoyed. Maybe she was dangerously underreacting to the risk. Countless women had made the same mistake, the threat seeming unreal until it was too late.

She could pretend she didn't see him, pretend this was not where she lived, walk by on the other side of the street, but already at this distance, half a block away, she knew it was pointless. He knew exactly where she lived. Still, she stopped three doors away from her entrance, hoping to draw him away from her building as if it would undo the damage.

When he realised Petra wasn't going to step any closer, he came over to her, flipping the headphones down around his neck.

'What do you want?' she said.

'There are things you should know about your friend. Let's go inside. It's cold.'

'No. I'm not inviting you into my flat. Say what you have to say.'

He shrugged. 'You don't trust me, do you?' he said.

'I have no reason to. Just tell me what you want to tell me.'

He smiled, his thin lips stretching over unnaturally veneered teeth, and his shark eyes narrowed. Petra realised, probably a bit too late, that she should dial down the hostility – not because he didn't deserve it, but to protect herself. But still, her gut told her that he wasn't a threat – physically at least. If anything, under the showy swagger and the stage make-up, he seemed fragile, a shell. It was his words and his games she'd need to be careful of. 'Alright – let's cut to it, then. Vincent's planning to do something stupid.'

'What?'

'You know about Beccie. He told you his daughter died. But he didn't tell you how.'

'It was you watching us in the pub the other night, wasn't it? You were listening to every word we said.'

He shrugged again.

'So you'll know he told me that Beccie was sick.'

'Correct. And that she needed a kidney transplant, but that it *didn't work out*. Do you want to know why?'

'Tell me.'

'He and Beccie were on the low-budget level of their medical insurance, and the procedure was not considered essential.'

'But it would have saved her life.'

'MyHealth disagreed. They calculated there was a sixty per cent chance she would die anyway. I've looked into it, and the actuary's risk assessments in similar cases become more favourable the higher your MyHealth membership tier.'

'In other words, the more you pay, the more essential your operation is seen to be.'

Ellis nodded.

'Jesus,' Petra sighed. 'But why are you telling me this? What's it got to do with you?'

'Wait,' he said, putting up his palms with a graceful, fluid flourish. 'There's more.'

Petra waited.

'He's currently doing odd jobs for the man who let his sister die. How tragic is that?'

'Who? What do you mean?'

'Curtis Worthing, the man who's buying his family's studio, is the outgoing CEO of MyHealth. The studio's changing hands from one family business to another – only there's a slight difference in, shall we say, capacity.'

'Oh.' A thousand questions jostled through her mind – but they were questions she had to ask Vincent himself. First of all, *Why the hell would you do that to yourself?* 'Why are you telling me this? What has it got to do with you?' she asked again.

'I know that you and Vincent are being targeted by Olivia... I can't pretend that warning you is a pure, selfless act of public service, but hey...'

'Olivia Jouval? Of Metamuse? What do you mean, "targeted"? We're just attending her shows.'

'Did you ever wonder how you and Vincent came by those tickets? Did you ever wonder why you met Vincent when you did?'

It was an absurd question, but he was looking into her face, apparently waiting for an answer. 'Luck? Coincidence.'

He snorted out a laugh. 'Anything you've experienced in the past few weeks as luck or coincidence is not luck or coincidence. When he fell at your feet that day—'

'How do you know that?'

Ellis Brown ignored her question and talked over her. '—he told you he'd been distracted by something, didn't he?'

'How—'

'That *something* was Beccie. He may or may not tell you if you asked him, but he thought he saw Beccie in the street for a second. And that's because he did. They scouted you two for this task at the same time as they scouted for locations.'

The world seemed to press in around Petra. She glanced around her, wondering which of the scattering of Tuesday-night clients heading to the bar down the block was watching her, whether someone was monitoring the feeds from the CCTV cameras slotted on the street corners.

'I'm here to tell you to beware of those women. Look into their shows. You may wonder why Metamuse is performing here in Leamington, of all the insignificant towns – it's not luck or coincidence. If you're feeling the shows ripple into your real life, know that it's not just you. Every show ripples into the real world.'

'Okay, whatever. I don't know what all that vague nonsense means, and I'm not really that interested.'

Ellis Brown rubbed his chin and then looked at his thumb, where a smear of his thick stage make-up had rubbed off. It was hard to be sure in the gloomy shadows of the street, but the skin beneath it looked grey. 'Yes, I see that. Maybe you don't need to understand. What you should know, though, concerns Vincent. I can tell you have a strong connection.'

He paused, infuriatingly, but still Petra was flattered – to have the strength of her bond with Vincent recognised by a stranger. 'What is it?' Ellis Brown was a conman, she reminded herself – he knew what she wanted to hear and he would say it at the optimal time to gain her trust.

'Before you get too involved with him, you should know that he doesn't plan to be around much longer.'

He delivered it as if it were a shocking denouement, and Petra took pleasure in deflating his grand climax. 'He already told me. He was planning to leave, but changed his mind. He might stay on a bit.'

'I don't think you're quite aware of where Vincent's intending to go, Petra.'

'Tell me then,' she challenged.

'He's leaving to join Beccie.'

13 'How can you plan something like this and just act normal?' Petra pleaded. She wanted to punch him. 'Why would you even agree to go out with me?'

'I'm sorry,' he said. 'When we met, Ellis Brown had spoken to me once. I didn't believe him then. Not until the second show. Not until I saw her with my own eyes. He showed me the proof.'

She drew her coat tighter around her and fiddled with her scarf. The sunken park trapped the depressed cold air and swirled it around, making it even colder.

She'd left Ellis Brown where he stood on the street and gone straight back to Vincent's house, hammering on the door until he answered. In the end, Gloria had poked her head out the upstairs window, and gathered him up and sent him out to speak to her. He'd suggested they go out for a walk – a bit of time away from his screen and the stifling miasma in the house would do him good – and they'd ended up in the dell. The children's playground at the far side, so bright and cheerful by day, now threw menacing shadows across the dewy grass and against the stone walls surrounding them; the jagged angles reminded her of the sundered legs of a giant, crushed metallic spider. Tendrils of mist were rising, framing the silhouettes of three teens slouched sullenly around the swing set. It was precisely the sort of scene Vincent would make into art. He'd find a way to lift the green tinge in the mist and flare the scars of the street lights. This night-time world was his element, not Petra's.

'Even if you *could* join her – whatever that means – what good would it do?'

She watched the leaves eddy for a long time. She didn't think Vincent's silence was evasion; more a respectful consideration of the question. 'I made a promise.'

She took his hand, not daring to look into his face. 'I know nothing, but I know this: she wouldn't want you to stop living. I know it because nobody would want the person they love to die. Can't you see that?'

'But Ellis says there's a way. I believe him. People don't get that chance. If they did, they'd take it. Can't *you* see *that*?' He withdrew his hand and clasped his forearm in a defensive girdle around his chest.

Petra closed her eyes and wished herself away. Yes, his pain was unbearable, and what she was feeling was unforgivable – she was feeling rejected for a ghost, jealous of this man's dead daughter. How could she compete? She should just stand up, apologise and leave.

But she continued to speak, as if she had the power to reach directly into his broken heart and soothe it with her prattle. 'Ellis told me about the studio too – about who bought it.' She looked at him, and when he didn't return her glance, she pressed on. 'You're working for the man in charge of MyHealth, the same people who let Beccie down. Why are you helping him, Vincent? Why are you doing this to yourself?'

'I need the money, don't I?' he said, shifting his body to disconnect Petra again.

The talk of money, the mundane matter of making a living, at least proved that he hadn't entirely committed to the insane notion of 'joining Beccie'. 'You can find other work. You're torturing yourself. Please—'

'I don't understand why you're so interested.' He spoke into the air in front of him.

'Because I... Because I care for you.'

'Why?' he said. 'Am I some charity case to you? Are you looking for a cause to make your life worthwhile?'

Petra felt like she'd been slapped. She gasped and drew back. 'Jesus.' She wrung her arms around herself, mirroring his position of a moment before. 'Okay.' Suddenly they were a metre apart on the bench.

'Sorry. I didn't...' He shifted over to her, reaching out his hand abortively before grinding the heel of his palm into his eyes. 'I didn't mean that. I'm just so tired.'

A smash of glass and a belt of forced laughter. Two of the kids across the park were jostling with each other, play-fighting in a loud, attention-seeking way. They were wearing maroon-and-navy tracksuits that looked lifted straight out of the eighties; retro two-stripe trainers. The third boy was hitting a rubbish bin with a stick. *Thunk thunk thunk*.

So many signs blaring at her that she should leave. Just go home. Right now. But she returned to the falling man who had located a sore spot, telling her a truth about herself that she'd spent a lifetime trying to evade, and sat. 'That Ellis Brown...'

'Yeah?'

'How did you meet him? Did you know him before or did he just turn up now?'

'I met him a few weeks ago. He—' Vincent paused, frowned. 'He just turned up at my front door.'

'Let me guess. Just before you won the Metamuse tickets?'

'Yeah, you're right.'

'What did he say?'

'He said he could show me how to contact Beccie.'

'Did he use her name? I mean, was there any proof that he knew about her before you told him?'

'I can't remember. But I'm not totally stupid. He knew things that nobody would know.' But he sounded less adamant in the cold night air than in the fraught, sleep-deprived atmosphere of his house.

'They're good, these people. Cold readers, conmen. They make a lot of money from what they do.'

'He hasn't asked for money.'

'Not yet.'

Vincent shook his head ruefully. 'Maybe you're right. Maybe he's just messing with me. But…' He stopped talking, probably playing back all the things Ellis Brown had told him. 'I'm just so tired.'

'Me too,' Petra said. 'I haven't slept properly since that show. God, I feel so… foolish. Betrayed.'

Thump thump thump sounded again from across the park, and now there was another laugh. No, not a laugh – a stifled cry. Security lights had flicked on in the houses overlooking the dell.

Petra stood up, took a few paces towards the boys, vague now through the tendrils of fog.

'What's up?' Vincent said.

Petra didn't say anything, put her hand out towards him:

wait there. She went closer to the boys and now she could see through the fog, all three boys alive. The tall one who'd been banging the bin had flung the stick aside and was smiling at her sheepishly.

Vincent had trailed her steps. 'Everything okay?'

'Yeah,' she said. 'I thought I saw something that wasn't there.'

14 'Mom, can I come over this morning?'

'Are you alright, love?'

Petra looked through her narrow window, down at Regent Street, the peeling map in the shuttered travel shop, the homeless man's bundle of orange sleeping bag in the doorway. 'I'm fine. I'm just feeling... not great. I'd just like to come visit before I go to work.'

'Sure, of course. Come along. Ida's here, but she won't mind.'

'Who's Ida?'

'Ha ha. Funny girl. See you now-now. Pick up some coffee and milk on your way, won't you?'

Petra heard the women laughing as she came out of the stairwell and turned along the third-floor corridor. Her mother's earthy bray, designed and developed in a distant country where there was more space, along with the thin chime of someone else. Through the small kitchen window that looked out onto the corridor, she heard their conspiratorial voices, then another volley of laughter. Petra hadn't heard her mother laugh like that for ages, wasn't sure if she'd ever made her mother laugh that genuinely, so deeply from the gut.

'Door's open, love,' Helena called through the kitchen window as she saw her pass.

Petra shouldered through the door and closed and latched it behind her – sure, this was Leamington, not Joburg, but her mother shouldn't be leaving her door unlocked anyway. Helena was carrying a tray with a jug of lemonade and the smart green-and-yellow art deco glasses she kept at the back of the cabinet. She pecked Petra on her cheek as she passed and left her to unpack the groceries as she continued the conversation with her friend.

'And then when I showed her the sketch, she pretended she didn't recognise herself,' Helena was saying. 'A bloody cheek, hey?'

'It was a perfect likeness.' The other woman's voice was softer, a demure hybrid of a Midlands accent, but with a clear tone that carried perfectly into the kitchen. 'You captured her essence, Hellie.'

Hellie? Who the hell called her mother 'Hellie'?

'I know. I was pretty pleased with that one. She was probably just bitter that I did a better job than her with her larney inks.'

'Oh, don't worry about her. She'll get over it.'

Petra had brought a couple of extra bags of coffee and a couple of cartons of long-life milk, along with some biscuits and fruit, and took her time packing the items away properly and rinsing and drying the fruit before arranging it in a bowl, all while she racked her brains to remember Ida. She was sure her mother had never spoken to her about this friend, but they were laughing and chatting so comfortably, they had to know each other well.

Weird. It just went to show, she supposed, that her mother had her own life, wasn't stuck on pause between Petra's visits. That was a good thing. She took a breath and walked through into the lounge.

She smiled at her mother and at Ida. The woman was fifty maybe, fifty-five, wearing thick, grey knitted socks and thin patterned cotton trousers that looked like pyjama bottoms, with a chunky striped sweater and scarf. Her fading dark-blond hair was kept back in a ponytail. She looked vaguely familiar but Petra couldn't place where she might have seen her.

Petra put out her hand. 'Hi, nice to meet you.'

Ida smiled and shot Helena a look. Helena rolled her eyes back in a way that eloquently said, *See what I mean?*

'We have met, Petra,' Ida said.

'Oh, yeah. Of course,' Petra said. 'Sorry. Um, would you both like some coffee?'

'Thanks. That'll be lovely. Of course, Ida won't touch hers. She's got an appetite like a bird. But we always offer, don't we?'

'That we do, Mom.'

Once Petra had made the coffee and settled on the couch watching the women's conversation for a few minutes, she started to relax. It was obvious from the details they were sharing about the art class rivalries and the way they chatted about their weekend plan to visit a National Trust property that they knew each other well. Petra was probably preoccupied when they'd met before, that's all. In fact, it was starting to come back – she might have met Ida that time they went to the Artbridge Gallery and Petra had bumped into Reena and Emma from college and had stayed by the bar with them while her mother browsed.

Petra only realised she was dozing when her mother spoke. 'Go have a lie-down on my bed if you want, love. You look tired.'

Petra started awake, the cooling coffee in her mug slopping dangerously. 'Oh, God, I'm sorry. I've just… I haven't been sleeping well lately. But I'm fine.'

Both women were training worried looks at her, and Petra squirmed under Ida's scrutiny. Evading their eyes, she checked the time on the clock on the mantel. 10:45. She only had to be at the shop at noon today.

'Are you sure you're alright?' Ida asked. 'I can tell that you're troubled.'

'Ida's clairvoyant,' Helena said.

Oh, God. Not Helena too now. Petra opened her mouth, about to say something but not sure what it should be.

But Helena started laughing. 'Look at her face!'

Ida cackled along. 'We got you, alright.'

'You really thought I was being serious!' Helena said. 'You think I've finally gone soft.'

Petra shook her head. 'Not funny, Mom. I've had a weird week. People have been trying to convince me of all sorts of rubbish.'

'What do you mean?'

'Just last night I crossed paths with a conman. He was pretty good at his job. He was taking advantage of a friend of mine, who's grieving.'

'Those guys irritate the hell out of me,' Helena said. 'The ones who pretend to talk to the dead. Offer fake comfort to poor grieving people as if they could ever talk to their dead loved ones.'

'Ja, that's exactly what this guy last night was doing.'

Ida tutted as Helena said, 'Bloody vultures. Remember that guy who tried to rip us off after Dad died? He was really good too, wasn't he?' She turned to Ida and explained. 'After Rod died, this shyster came to our door, said he was from the wills department of the bank and we just needed to sign some papers. He was perfect in the role – the cheap suit, the comb-over, just the right amount of sweat; he knew so many details about Rod's accounts, his work, everything. Turns out he was a crook, and I only found out in time because I phoned the bank to find out Rod's account number to fill in on his form. I still don't know how he knew all that stuff about Rod.'

'There was nothing magical about it,' Petra said, a little too vehemently. 'Dad wasn't great at internet security – anyone could have read his emails. Or the guy could have gone through his trash and collected his bank statements. This guy I met last night was a different level. Made himself out like a showman, a magician. Like those TV psychics.' Helena and Ida nodded, leaning forward towards her, something in Ida's face jarring – where did she know her from? 'It's all cold reading, of course.'

'Of course.' Ida pursed her lips and shook her head, and said, 'It's not right,' but because she was English, Petra wasn't entirely sure whether she was being ironic. She couldn't be certain, but she thought she detected a smirk around Ida's lips.

After a moment when the conversation had dried up, Petra got up and started to gather the glasses and mugs onto the tray. As Helena had predicted, Ida's mug was untouched, the coffee in it slick and cold.

'Can I refresh that for you?' she offered.

'Not for me.'

She picked up the tray and turned towards the kitchen, and a cloud shifted and sunlight from the window fell full onto Ida's face and reflected off the TV screen back to Petra. Petra stifled a gasp. She jerked to clutch at the tray and only just avoided tipping it and smashing it all over the hallway tiles.

The face that stared impassively at her from the black mirror was younger than Ida's but also far more ravaged. Her eyes were puffed with grief – the same swollen eyes that she'd seen the other night, downstairs in the lobby. This was the same woman looking back at her now. The smirk was plainly plastered across her mouth, as a black tear drained from one of those empty sockets.

Petra scurried into the kitchen to shove the tray onto the countertop and try to remember how to breathe, before she would rush back out again to confront the false apparition. For what? For posing as her mother's friend? For looking fine when she was really brutalised? What the hell was happening? But when she got back to the sitting room, the clouds had obscured the sun again and the reflection was gone, and Ida's voice sounded as it had all morning.

'You alright, love?'

'Yeah,' Petra started, rounding the back of Ida's chair to get to the couch.

Ida pushed back the loose tendrils of her hair from her face and gathered it back behind her ears, collecting it and repositioning her ponytail. 'This weather, it makes my hair insane.' Holding her hair with her left hand, she fished in the handbag at her feet for a barrette and clipped her hair back tidily. The barrette was covered in rose velvet.

Ida turned, looking over her shoulder to where Petra was immobilised. She smiled. One top incisor was missing and the other was shattered diagonally, and there was blood behind her lower lip.

The light shifted.

No, not blood – a smear of lipstick.

Not a broken tooth – a raisin stuck in her teeth.

Pull yourself together, Petra.

15 Petra stepped back from the shop window with a satisfied sigh. Her shoulders and forearms were aching, but in a good, distracting way. Cleaning a massive window was not something she would have chosen as therapy, but it had done the job on this unseasonably mild day – she hadn't thought ugly thoughts for almost an hour.

She watched the streaks of the window cleaner evaporate. Now the glass reflected the sunlit buildings across the road with mirror-like clarity. A chubby wood pigeon flumped down on the ledge above the window, fluffing out its butt feathers, and Petra turned her back and picked up the bucket, rags and the spray bottle and went inside. Nature would be nature, the cycles of maintenance would recur, and she would let it go. There was no point in trying to control what she couldn't control. She was feeling somewhat relaxed for the first time in a while.

In the back she washed her hands, poured the dregs of cold coffee and microwaved it. She flexed her feet in her boots; all morning they'd been feeling uncomfortable – sweaty and grainy in her socks, sticky almost, as if she hadn't dried them properly after showering. On the walk to the shop from Helena's flat, something in there had been chafing, her but she hadn't bothered to stop on the pavement and unlace her boots to shake out the grit that was caught in there. But now, if anything, it felt like there was even more grit than before.

The bell dinged at the counter. Petra showed the shelf of hand-shaped wabi sabi tableware to the dour woman in a slumping grey everyday coat before walking behind the counter and bringing up the daily banking sheet. Suki was perched on a display table like an emo-themed centrepiece, reading a comic – *My Solo Exchange Diary*, by the looks of it. Apart from the wabi sabi woman, there were no customers downstairs but the CCTV showed four upstairs – a man and a woman together, a woman alone, and a single man. Petra didn't remember the singletons coming in. The customer heat map she kept in her head was generally pretty accurate – not a particularly taxing skill at Needful Things.

The spreadsheet was more boring and less absorbing than the window cleaning, and the mental chatter she'd successfully shunted away for a couple of hours began to up its volume. The trapped thoughts started circulating again: what had happened last night at Vincent's house and at the dell, what Ellis Brown had told her, the weird hallucination she'd experienced at Helena's flat. Well, she had to call it a hallucination, because it would be even more disturbing if it was real. It was clear that Helena hadn't seen what she'd seen, and when she'd stumbled back and rounded the couch in a defensive lunge towards her mother and got a front-on view of Ida, of course she looked fine – the late-middle-aged woman she'd been introduced to, teeth intact, no bruises or blood. Not the young, battered woman she'd morphed into.

But she hadn't imagined it. What she'd seen was as real as this pen in her hand, the glass and plastic of the computer, the boxes on the countertop – she tapped them all ritually as she thought, concentrating on the feel of their solidity against her fingers, pressing her palm into the sharp edge of the Pokémon card display case. Yes, a line pressed into her palm, pain triggered. What was real if not that? If she'd reached out the same way and touched Ida's face, she would have come away with blood on her fingers, she was certain, evidence to prove what she'd seen.

But she didn't. She had no proof. Her mind was playing tricks on her, and that was far more unsettling than if the world had started to break its rules around her.

She could try to explain herself to Suki – Suki of all people understood mind games and she'd help her rationalise what she was feeling, explain it as the result of some sort of logical trickery, nothing supernatural or psychotic. But she'd keep it to herself for the moment. She minimised the cash control sheet on the computer, opened her browser, and searched for 'Curtis Worthing', perching her boots on the narrow rail under Suki's absurd chair.

A squelch. There was definitely an audible squelch there. Her feet were sodden. Jesus, she was probably having a rare somatic foot-sweat stress reaction. She was almost tempted to run a web search on 'somatic foot-sweat stress reaction', but kept focus.

Though Worthing appeared in a listing of the top twenty highest-earning CEOs in global healthcare, he didn't even have his own Wikipedia page. Clearly rich enough not to need a public profile. The real power lurks in the shadows, as any TV-watcher knows.

Petra slid off the chair and came around the counter, and went to join Suki across the shop floor.

Suki was unpacking new stock into the electronics display case. Nobody was going to buy this sundry assortment of satellite phones, luxury tablets, bespoke game consoles and audio equipment from Needful Things rather than a proper shop. More fanciful invoices for the Barlows' laundering scheme. They were beautifully designed, though – nice to look at.

'Uh, Suki...'

'Yes, darling?'

'I think you got the price wrong on that one,' she said, pointing at a pair of headphones on a marble stand that were tagged at £50,000.

'Nope, that's right. They're limited-edition Sennheiser Orpheus. Eight valves. Carrara marble chassis. Perfect gift for the man who will never be famous.'

'Who the hell would...' Petra shook her head, decided to let it go. 'You don't happen to know someone called Curtis Worthing, do you?' It was a long shot, but if anyone she knew had access to inside information about Curtis Worthing, it would be Suki.

'Who's he?'

'He's the CEO of MyHealth. He's retiring here in Leam, apparently.'

'Oh, yeah, it's ringing a bell. Why?'

'No real reason. Vincent's doing some work for him. His middleman's a bit of a dick.'

Suki raised her eyebrows. 'Really? As I remember, there was some unpleasantness with the Worthings – the name's always mentioned with a bit of a sneer, you know.'

'Why's that?'

Suki shook her head. 'I don't know. I don't really keep up with the corporate gossip. Couldn't be less interested. But let me ask Ben. He'll know if there's any dirt to be dug, and if there is, we can drive this mean CEO who's tormenting your boyfriend and his dickish supervisor right out of town. What do you say?'

Petra laughed. 'Go for it.'

While Suki was in the back office calling her brother, the wabi sabi woman sloped out and the couple came downstairs and bought a sizeable stack of vintage LPs, and another handful of customers came in, the door grinding and tinkling every time. It had turned into an ad hoc post-lunch mini-rush, a bit of daytime wine always helping with impulse buys of unnecessary items.

'Oops,' a man with a pinstriped hat giggled as he turned and swished Suki's Tattooed Dudes colouring book stand over, the books sliding impressively far across the polished-concrete floor. Another side-effect of wine o'clock shopping.

Petra squatted and started to collect up the books while the giggling man evacuated. She'd gathered up maybe three quarters into a pile and moved closer to the countertop to collect the ones closest to the toppled dump bin, shifting her weight, when she felt it. A distinct seepage, up her sock, a definite grind of gritty soil, as if there were boggy puddles in the bottoms of her shoes. Instinctively, without looking, she stuck her fingers into her sock, shoving them down her ankle, to wipe at whatever was causing that sensation. She moved to the next book, picked it up and slapped it onto a new low stack she'd made on the floor.

There was blood on the cover. Glistening, wet blood, streaked on by her fingers. She turned her hand and looked at her fingers.

She probably screamed or whimpered a little as she yanked at her bootlaces and flung her boots away from her, ripped off her socks. She should have thought more about where they landed, splatting as they did with their heavy load of fine blood-soaked sand, painting apocalyptic designs over the white-painted load-bearing columns, the white cabinets, the glass display cases, the books, the toys, the houseware.

Petra was standing barefoot and bewildered in the middle of the shop floor as Suki emerged from the back office.

'Well, that was weird,' she said, then swallowed her words as she looked around her, at Petra, down at her feet. 'Um, maybe a bit less of the casual, darling? Probably best to keep your shoes on, at least when we're open, alright? Aren't you cold, anyway?'

Petra rubbed her eyes and looked around her – at the polished surfaces, the clean white paint, her dry, sand-free socks and boots jettisoned against the front display cabinet. Down at her sock-printed and somewhat puffy feet, the nail polish she'd applied a week before her first date with Vincent growing out and cracking. But no blood, not especially damp. The panic had dispersed as quickly as it had arrived, leaving her feeling foolish and cold-toed.

'Sorry,' she said, flinging together an excuse for her dubious behaviour. 'I thought I felt a spider in my sock.' *Really? Both feet?* It was the best she could come up with. She put her shoes back on, finished repacking the dumpbin, and walked back behind the counter.

'So, Ben was really weird,' Suki said. 'We talked a little like normal, but when I asked him about Worthing, he clammed up, became rather cagey. There's something there, but he's not saying what it is. I know when he's lying to me.'

'What do you think it can be?'

'I have no idea, but now I'm determined to find out.'

Suki spent a while searching alumnus networks and private club registries for any information about Curtis Worthing. He was fifty-nine years and 358 days old, with an undergraduate degree in humanities from Beauchamp University, pivoting to higher degrees in management and biomedical sciences from Harvard and Cambridge. Divorced once, remarried then widowed, two adult children from the first marriage. He was indeed born in Leamington, and attended Barford School. But for all the routine biographical information, he didn't seem to have lived a life beyond going to school and becoming, by apparent social osmosis, a mega-wealthy tycoon. Some news articles from *Private Eye* and the *Morning Star* tried to hint at unsavoury relationships with Tory cabinet ministers that gave him a competitive advantage back when the NHS was dismantled. Then again, people with the right connections and money in the bank tended to have a competitive advantage in any crisis. It was the way the world was set up; you didn't officially need to be a criminal to make an obscene killing.

Around four, Helena phoned. Petra got the nod from Suki and took the call into the kitchen. 'I just wanted to check that you were alright,' she said. 'You seemed unwell this morning.

Are you sure you shouldn't be off work, at home?' It wasn't like Helena to fuss about Petra, and the fact that she was brought home to Petra just how weirdly she'd acted.

'I'm fine,' she said. 'Sorry about this morning. It's just… I haven't been sleeping well.'

'Hm.'

Her mother's dubious response needled Petra. She doubted herself enough already – first, the boy at the park last night, then seeing Ida's reflection this morning, and now this unsettling freak-out over her feet. And try as she might, she couldn't shrug off the experiences as products of her tired imagination. She remained convinced she'd seen what she'd seen, felt what she had felt – she checked her hands again and her stain-free fingers controverted her. Vincent, the Metamuse shows, Ellis Brown – they had all invaded her life at the same time. It was starting to make sense now, what Ellis Brown had said – that she'd been *targeted*. And it had all started that day she saw the young woman in Helena's lobby; the woman she was convinced was now masquerading as a friend of her mother.

Utter any of it aloud, though, and it would all sound crazy.

'Tell me, Mom – how long have you known Ida? You act like I should know her, but I can't remember meeting her. Where did you meet her?'

'This again. You'd better get some rest, love. You want me to get you some groceries?' Helena stopped speaking and drew in a sharp breath that Petra heard clearly.

'What's the matter, Mom? Are you alright?'

'Fine, love. Just a little twinge.' Before Petra could interject again, she ploughed on. 'I can drop something off. Chicken soup, you know. Act like a mom should act.'

Petra couldn't exactly explain the anger that was building up in her. She should feel lucky to be getting some TLC from her mother. Not everyone had that luxury. But Helena was currently annoying the shit out of her. Was this how *she* felt every time Petra fussed over her? 'I'm fine. I have to go,' she said, cutting the call before she said anything regrettable.

A few minutes later, a lean guy dressed in black jeans and polo neck like a young Steve Jobs pushed through the door. It took Petra a few moments to recognise him, and it was his dark curls that clued her in.

'Hi, Freddie,' she said. 'Where've you been?' Looked like he'd spent the week getting a makeover. 'Is there a new dress code at Gravity's End?'

He nodded at her without smiling, and scanned the lower level of the shop before walking wordlessly up the stairs. Petra followed him on the CCTV screen as he peered around every corner of the top floor, checking every section, as if looking for someone. There was nobody upstairs.

When he came down again, Petra said, 'Are you looking for something? Or someone?'

'Just you,' he said, and his voice was a husk, just a functional sound played on a dry instrument. He sauntered around the main floor displays, selected a glass paperweight from Prague with a cast-iron rose set into it. He held the heavy sphere, turning it around in his hand, stretched his arm out in front of him—

'Hey, what—'

—and dropped it onto the concrete floor. The smash shattered the air and time seemed to stop as the shards skimmed across the floor, shearing and reverberating like ice on a frozen lake.

'—are you doing?'

Petra pushed up from the chair and took a few steps out from behind the counter; the look on Freddie's face – blank, mean, emotionless; a shark's expression – stopped her in her tracks. The black-shirt mayor character in *Cabinet*, the one she'd stumbled across attacking the woman in his office, came to mind.

As she hesitated, Suki was rushing out of the back office, phone to ear, and also jarred to a halt as she took in the scene. 'What are you doing?'

'What's the matter with you, Freddie?' Petra asked.

Freddie said nothing, only turned to the door, locking it from the inside and flipping the closed sign outwards. He advanced towards them. Petra stood rooted behind the counter and Suki braced herself in front of it. 'Don't you dare come a step closer.'

Freddie finished his pace, and then stopped. 'I've got a message for you.'

He was looking at Petra, but it was Suki who spoke for her. 'Yeah? About what?'

'About Curtis Worthing. She says he's the root cause.'

'The cause of what?' Petra said. 'Who's telling us this?'

'That's all she told me.' He took three steps and shoved his boot through the glass display case of executive toys. 'She also said make it memorable.' He went to the door, flipped the sign, unlocked the door and left.

Petra hurried after him. 'Who's *she*? Who's telling us?' she called down the pavement, but Freddie had already disappeared around a corner.

Suki was glowering over the mess on the shop floor.

'Jesus. It was like he was in some sort of fugue state, wasn't it? Like hypnotised. I knew there was something off about him when I saw him out of his plaid shirt and stained chinos.'

'He's a troubled man,' Suki said. 'He needs help.'

'It could have been worse, I suppose. I was scared when he locked the door.'

'If he'd tried anything, I would have broken his arm. I know kung fu.' It was her usual brave bluster, but Suki was shaking.

Light out of Darkness

Elemental, Metamuse, Fjellstrand,
Norway, 14–28 June

The truth comes to me on a ghost-lit midnight shore in
Norway. The rest of the audience are out in the half-dusk,
singing joyfully at the water's edge as they float the corpse
they made into the water as an offering, but I'm cowering
in the dank back corner of the boathouse, covering my ears,
afraid to look.

That corpse is not a prop, I want to scream at them, but
the suck and slurp of the water, the rip of the wind, is too
loud. These things you're feeling, I'd tell them, the hook in
your soul, the fingers in your brainstem and your groin, those
are not effects. They're in you. You shouldn't be here.

It's been six months since I fell in love with a ghost in a
desert hammam out back of a Tokyo supermarket, and since
then I haven't been quite right. I've been distracted, obsessed.
I've put a hell of a lot of strain on my wife; she's getting tired
of my wandering attention. I've been unable to concentrate on
my work. And without a home and an income, I've needed to
move away from the city, away from the theatre that's been
my livelihood.

And who should turn up again, offering me an all-expenses

mystery tour to Oslo for the summer solstice? Olivia Jouval and Metamuse, of course. I don't know what she wants, and why she wants it from me. (And I say 'she' not 'them', because the invitation was signed by Olivia Jouval alone. All along I've felt more compelled by Jouval, as if she's the driving creative force behind the company; it's her protean face I see shifting in my dreams.) There are a hundred out-of-work reviewers available, some of whom write better than me. But I come along, on her assignment – I've got nothing else to do, have I? I feel like John the Baptist – a prophet, an apocalyptic messenger, preparing the ground for Olivia's arrival.

The fifty audience members of tonight's show were rounded up outside the Parliament Hotel and it takes an hour in the bus to Fjellstrand, a little suburban village across the water. Wordlessly, we're led into a forest. Though the map on my phone tells me the patch of trees is only a couple of hundred metres across, the woods are primal and dark and terrifying. Ten metres into the trees, the midsummer glare on this sunny night is completely snuffed and the jovial tour-bus chatter has fallen into a cautious murmur.

In the scented dark, we've left the scrap of civilisation that clings to the rocks far behind. We could be in a different century; there's the sense in all our primitive brains that our ancestors were hunted in forests like this, by monsters we like to believe no longer exist.

We come to a clearing and are greeted softly by a man and two women dressed in pagan robes, flower crowns in their hair. The moment we're issued with the plain white robes to wear (over our clothes, to my relief), I find myself looking for the wicker man. I can tell from the nervous grins around me that I'm not the only one who's watched too many films and is worried about being a human sacrifice.

They need virgins, don't they? How exactly do they define a virgin in Fjellstrand? Untouched by man? Or untouched by the Devil?

I'm a little reassured when we're led out into the sun on a hilltop laid with colourful blankets and cushions, and share a picnic of bread and cheese and fruit and wine. The hosts play drums and tambourines and encourage the audience to sing along. We're a terribly clean, terribly polite, terribly bourgeois bunch of hippies.

Next, we're taught how to weave straw dolls and make floral headbands. Not really what I came to Norway to do – I could do crafts like this in my new home village's community centre on Tuesday mornings. But this is Metamuse.

The screaming girl almost trips over me as she plunges out of the woods. Too quick, just an impression: a flash of black and white and red – the piss smell of her fear, pungent sweat, the salt of her tears as she shatters through our space.

Some people in the audience gasp, cry out; some laugh nervously, looking to the hosts for direction. When the wolf-men and the monstrous, stinking ram-figure crash through after the girl, the laughing stops.

'Quick! Quick! Put these on.' We're issued with crow masks and instructed to follow the chase.

It must be subtle lighting, clever marshalling by the actors, great sound and set design, because although they've set a busload of theatregoers into a panicked flurry through what I'd swear is an authentic Scandinavian forest, we all come out into the next sequence perfectly choreographed.

Imagine it: fifty plague-crows all emerging into a circular clearing from every angle, converging on the scene. I am one of the crows and unprompted, unrehearsed, I step forward in perfect synchrony with the fifty other witnesses. I hesitate; they hesitate. I lurch forward three steps; so do they.

How does Metamuse achieve this? How do they fire the same signals into fifty different brains at the same time? I was impressed by the way *Idiopathy* and *Falling* got into my head, and in those shows, they toy with participants individually – but this… This is mass mind control. It's a bewildering effect. I am utterly in control of my movements, but entirely connected to the rest of the group. We're a herd organism; Metamuse has turned us into the Borg.

I can see the wide and darting eyes through the masks, flickering at me in fear and astonishment just as I know they can see mine. We step forward and witness.

Two men in wolf costumes with bloody muzzles eating raw meat. A giant man in a rancid ram's costume laying a white sheet over the girl. The blood blooming like live art as it touches her torn body.

The light changes like firelight glaring off the trees and the animals become shadows and melt back into the forest.

The hosts bring us sheets and instruct us to swaddle the corpse. In teams of six or eight, compliant, the audience lays the sheets out and folds and rolls the girl's body into it.

But I hang back – I don't want to do this. It's horrible. Why are they all so obedient?

All I saw of the girl as they turned her was a hank of black hair. As she sprinted past, toenails painted green. But that's enough for me to know – it's *her*. They brought me here to kill my desire.

When the body is wrapped, they place her on a wooden litter and raise her. They start chanting and head out of the clearing and onto a broad path through the forest. Glancing around me, I realise that the safest way to get back to the village or the road is to follow them. Worst case, I'll have to tag along with these murderers until the end of the show, but the alternative is being lost in the forest and in time forever.

Murderers? Sounds ridiculous. This is a show. I knew what I signed up for. I'll just go along with it. The audience's mood is celebratory, as if they're enjoying a summer festival rather than carrying a corpse.

Soon, the procession comes out of the trees at the island road. My relief at seeing road signs and lights on houses tucked into the cove is indescribable. As if there's zero chance of any passing traffic, or even suspicious neighbours, the hosts lead us along the middle of the road and down a slipway towards the water. It is midnight, after all, I need to remind myself in the moonlit dusk.

Just for a moment, I believe it will all be okay.

I spot the boathouse to my left and, trying not to stand out from the other white-robed crows, I shift to the left of the group. As I do, I pass the funeral bier being borne on the shoulders of hosts and volunteers. I glance at the linen-wrapped shape on top, and – despite how tightly she's been swaddled – she shifts and her arm flops out.

The green nails on her fingers. They reach for me.

She sits up, the black hair stuck in the gaping wounds on her neck and chest, clotting with the blood.

She smiles at me, with broken, gore-smeared teeth.

Her eyes are dead. She is dead.

And that's what has sent me scurrying and hiding from ghosts in a boathouse on the Oslofjord.

When the panic passes, I reassess what I've seen. It must be the stress. Maybe they added special ingredients to the wine or the food.

There is singing and laughing a little way down the slip road. The audience are performing their ritual. Somehow, right now, the lure of company is more powerful than the fear of what I will see down there.

Still wearing my mask and robe, I make my way out of the boathouse and down to the water's edge, where they've set the sacrificial litter down. Piece by piece as they sing and laugh, the audience is removing what they made and placed there and offering it to the water – straw dolls, little wooden rafts with flower-wrapped candles, paper balloons that rise up like sprites over the water.

There is no corpse on a litter. It strikes me that there never was.

Nobody here but me has a corpse to dispose of.

I've failed as a critic. I've been so immersed in this experience that I've forgotten myself. For a moment there, I believed the girl was dead, that she'd been ravaged by animistic spirits, that she'd been killed for our entertainment.

But the truth is that Olivia Jouval can see into my soul and show me my desires and my fears projected into the real world. Like the best psychoanalyst, she has identified and shown me the parts of myself I needed to sacrifice. The experience of cutting that part of myself away and surrendering it has been profoundly cathartic.

In *Elemental*, Metamuse isn't showing me their ghosts; they help me to exorcise my own.

---

16   Standing outside the red door on Brook Street on that blustery Thursday night, Petra remembered the day she first met Vincent. First he was up there, between the upper-floor window of the studio and her face, and then he was down here, crumpled on the pavement. How fanciful she'd been that first night, imagining him bowing at her feet in a funny, kinky way, as if she was a pop star in a music video. It felt like another life – so many impressions crammed into her quiet routine: the thrill of first contact, knowing how much they had in common, how much they had to learn from each other; the intensity of the sex; then the intimacy of the shows – and the horror. That second show was when everything went south. She hadn't fought with a man for a long time, felt so bitter, so worried, so angry – she hadn't felt so scared or disoriented. It felt like ages ago, but it was just less than a month.

And it felt like a different place, too. That day had been cold and sunny, a blessing amid the grey, like a crisp Highveld winter's morning. Now the swirling squalls were driving dead leaves and litter around her feet, spattering icy drops into her face. Tree branches writhed around the stark LED street lights, making the walls and pavements undulate. Petra shuddered and tried to pull her fleece-lined hood tighter over her head, only to have it plucked away again by the fingers of the wind.

Again, she looked at the electronic door panel. She didn't know which unmarked button to press to ring a bell, and didn't want to wake any neighbours who may be connected to the system; so, feeling like a character in a Gothic novel, she battered at the door a second time, then fished her phone out of her pocket to check if he'd sent her any message.

Nothing.

She texted him. *<I'm here.>*

She heard footsteps behind her. Trying not to look scared, she turned. Two young guys across the road, the scuff of their boots too loud, highlighting the sudden death of the wind. They were just students or something, minding their own business, cutting purposefully towards the pub or back home. Since when had she started becoming paranoid about her neighbours? In the lull, she strained to hear noises behind the door. She'd give it another minute. She heard the breeze approaching through the dark stand of spruces behind Milverton House and then it funnelled its way along Brook, kicking up all the detritus in a flurry. Her hood flipped off her head and her ear was filled with wind and wet dust and her hair pulled out of her collar, and she pictured herself as she'd look to those boys; then she remembered the boys in the dell, and for the first time since Vincent had called she considered that he might be messing with her. Or that it might be Ellis Brown, setting her another trap.

But Vincent had sounded so genuine this time – a call instead of those terse, ambiguous texts. His voice, sounding like himself; it felt like they had passed over this last rubbish week and it was a chance to start over. She hadn't hesitated to join him here. She turned away.

The red door opened. 'Petra. Hey, sorry. I was in the back. Come in. Jesus, it's foul out there.'

Petra closed the door behind herself – just latched, not locked with a key – and followed Vincent down the corridor. Homely lights were shining over the staircase and there was a warm glow spilling out of the rooms at the end of the corridor. It was stripped bare now, no frames against the wall, no building supplies spilling out of closets. Everything vacated and swept; it looked like an empty show house.

'This is my last night in the house,' Vincent said. 'I hand over the keys tomorrow. I wanted to mark it somehow...'

Petra nodded.

'I thought it would be nice to say goodbye with you.'

Petra stopped, probably even took a couple of involuntary steps backward. 'Say goodbye? Vincent, you're not...' *God – he's not planning to take me with him, is he?* 'I thought we'd discussed this. I thought you were okay.'

He smiled, tiredly, but a genuine smile. 'Oh, ha. That came out wrong. I meant say goodbye to the studio. Nothing else.' He gestured down the corridor. 'Come, please. I just... you'll see what I mean.'

He led her into the first, larger room at the end of the corridor, the one she'd hidden in while listening to Picton insulting Vincent that first day. 'This was the main performance room,' he told her. 'Tiny compared to most pro studios; with the mics and the amps, you could fit six in at a squeeze if they had small instruments. On some of the tracks, they had to come in on shifts, half the band playing at a time. You know, those big, sociable reggae and ska numbers, all recorded in parts in here. And look...' He turned and gestured through the soundproof window to the control room next door. The console was alight, ranks of switches and slides lit up like a modern painting.

'You're leaving it behind.'

'Yeah. It belongs here. It lives here.'

'But Worthing's coming tomorrow. He'll just rip it out, throw it away.'

'Tomorrow's problems are for tomorrow,' Vincent said. 'This is my wrap party.'

Petra still didn't like the way he said that, and didn't like the way he included her in his end-times plans. But now he was spreading out a red blanket in the middle of the empty floor, and unloading a cooler from the corner, a bottle of the wine she'd enjoyed at the pizza place, a pack of beers, crisps and a salad from the grocery, a packet of bread sticks and a thing of veggie hummus – the luxury sort with the seeds on top. A big bar of chocolate. It felt too much like a uni date to feel afraid; that comforting familiarity – the ease – was just what she needed right now, and Vincent knew it.

'This is nice,' she said. 'You should have told me to bring something.'

'I've got everything I need right here.' He sat down on the blanket. 'Except maybe a cushion. The floor's bloody hard.'

Petra sat down across from him. The sounds reverberated in the room, swallowed in padded corners and spat out strangely between floor and ceiling. Their voices were focused, amplified, the crinkle of the bags sharp and defined. Petra was conscious of the wetness in her mouth as she chewed on a slice of green pepper.

'I wanted to say sorry,' Vincent said. 'I shouldn't have just disappeared. It's been a weird week.'

'It has, right?' Petra laughed. 'It wasn't just what we thought we saw in the dell. It's the whole week. Have you been seeing weird things?'

'Uh, kind of, I suppose.'

It was the same polite, dubious tone he had taken when she'd asked him to confirm that he'd seen the hanging boy in the dell. If he hadn't shared her experience this week, there was no way she was going to say anything more. She'd just end up feeling crazy. *I could have sworn I knew a man who I'd apparently never seen. I totally forgot a woman I should have known. I've been waking up with nightmares that feel way more real than nightmares. They feel like things that have really happened. They feel like things that are going to happen.*

But if anyone had been acting mad, it was Vincent – sitting at his computer, obsessing over those photos of nothing. He'd almost convinced her that there was the figure of a girl in there.

'That show affected me a lot,' was all she said. *Affected us*, she wanted to say. *They're still messing with our minds.*

'I didn't think you'd worry about me.'

Petra was relieved he'd pulled the conversation back from her hallucinations and delusions. 'It's alright. I knew nothing about you. I know not everything's about me. I'm just so sorry about Beccie. It was none of my business.'

'It's not that. It was just hard to tell you about her. That weekend was the first time I felt happy in a while.'

'I get it. I really do.'

'I didn't want to spoil the mood. But at the same time, I couldn't pretend Beccie didn't exist. I think when I imagined her in the second show, it was just my mind telling me not to try to sweep her under the rug. That she's always with me.'

Petra shifted closer to Vincent, the blanket rumpling as she moved, and grabbed his hand. Nobody watching now, no external judgement about how she should act. He squeezed hers back. 'I understand.' Also, she was so relieved to hear him say he'd imagined Beccie in the warehouse. 'So, Ellis… you realised he was just trying to use you?'

'Yeah. What he says can't be true. Anyway,' he said, standing abruptly and leaving the room. He appeared in the window of the control room and pressed a button. His voice came over a speaker in the corner of the room. 'Tonight's for celebration.' He hit a couple of keys and a mellow dub beat came rumbling out of the walls around her. 'Brook Street's Greatest Hits.'

As Vincent came back around to the performance room, Petra scanned the walls and noticed all the speakers embedded there. 'You can't leave all this equipment for Worthing,' she told him. 'He doesn't deserve it.'

'I'll take what I can in the morning.'

'I'll help you.' She could borrow Suki's car. Maybe they could even get the console out, in pieces. She could store it in the shop. Why hadn't she thought of it before? She jumped up. 'We should start now. If you take it all apart now, we can get it out of here by the morning.'

But Vincent was shaking his head. 'No, no, no. Let's relax. Tomorrow's problems for tomorrow. I just want one good last night, alright?' He held her and slid his warm hand under her clothes, up her back, and kissed her, moving to the soul-resonant beat. She tasted the beer and spice on his tongue and agreed that some things were for tonight and some things for tomorrow.

When they had danced a while, they sat again, Petra leaning her back into his chest, sipping her wine and feeling satisfied and unhurried. The tracks kept coming, changing from dub to trio jazz to folk to rock and around again, advertising jingles and electronic computer game themes peppered the mix. Every chord of it taped right in this room. Petra could feel ghosts again, but this time the remnants of harmony, the sort of residual expressive joy that in enough quantity could surely defeat the ghosts of fear and despair. She leaned back and looked over her shoulder, turning Vincent's cheek with her hand and kissing him again. Their bodies vibrated at the same driving frequency.

'Will you play something for me?' she asked.

'I can't play.'

'I bet you can.'

'Nothing like my granddad.'

'Yeah, but nobody could play like Max, could they?'

He smiled. 'True. But all the instruments are gone.'

'You could play with your voice, with your body,' Petra sang. She didn't know what had come over her. She felt like she was channelling some muse or a siren from ancient mythology. She only ever sung in the shower. Okay, maybe some karaoke when she'd let her hair down. And in her kitchen, all alone. 'Sing with me, Falling Man.'

It was just the wine, just the mood, but she felt she was actually holding the notes and the sound that was coming out of her throat was seductive, rich, someone else's voice, like Adele or Joss Stone or someone, their singing so different from their day voices, a different being when she vibrated her larynx just so. God, she felt powerful just then. She wound words around the trancy beat that was playing and Vincent started to respond, beating out a complex complementary rhythm on the floor, on his thighs, on her thighs. They became a living instrument, and she could feel the heat of his groin at the small of her back, every surface of her body sensitive to the air's vibration. They moved together until the track changed, then fell back, laughing.

'Jesus, you've got a voice,' he said.

'If only I knew someone who owned a studio. I could make a demo, become famous. I used to know someone who did, but the idiot sold it.'

'Hey, hey. Not nice.'

He grabbed her arm and started twirling her in a flatfooted jive. She was dizzy from the wine, her feet utterly uncoordinated, but she didn't care. She danced as if no one was watching, the bottle of wine dangling in her hand like she was a liberated spirit from the sixties.

After a while she was lying back, her head in his lap as he ran his fingers through strands of her hair, looking up past his face to the ceiling, the overpainted bevelling and the cracks, a water stain the size and shape of a human heart. His gentle fingers always moving, teasing out, extending, placing, as if he were drawing her. Part of her wanted to ask him to still his hands, but she was so comfortable on the warm blanket, the soothing bass hum working through the floor and massaging her muscles, aligning her bones, her body melting into the floor...

And she must have fallen asleep because now she was lying on her stomach, and Vincent was gone. So was the blanket, now that she woke to it, and she felt the jagged wood of the floorboards in the skin of her stomach and she was being dragged across the floor by someone, something that wasn't there, felt its tug at the base of her skull. She scrabbled her hands against the floor to try to gain purchase. The floor of the performance room was much rougher than she'd first thought; thick, septic splinters driving into her palms. And she couldn't stop herself from being dragged towards the wall, papered in peeling, piss-yellowed vertical-striped paper. *There's no wallpaper in Vincent's studio*, she managed to remind herself as her naked body grazed across the floor, scraping up clods of greasy, organic dander, her whole body grazing and merging with the stuff on the floor, being pulled to the low door in the skirting.

Her face jammed to the skirting now, her head being manhandled through the too-small gap, but slowly enough that she had time to take in the troll-creatures' half-size boudoir within, stagnant sickly yellow pools of light illuminating the contents, like the front window of an antique shop up a side street in a failed plague-stricken town.

And inside, beyond, the scene she didn't want to see. Couldn't unsee.

Now, somehow, her shoulders dislocating and crackling as they squeezed into the hole, which had become a tunnel; the force dragging her deeper, right to the site of the red-haired woman's humiliation, and beyond into an even more unnerving intimacy. It was warm and moist, this tunnel, slick with an organic patina, and she felt pushed by the walls now, rather than dragged, peristaltically processed, shunted along this building's intestine into some inner sanctum, too deep to be witnessed, too raw to be touched. Down the end of the undulating tunnel, a bright light silhouetting two figures, both women with their heads hanging. A regular flicker of red strobing onto their shapes, revealing them. One of the women, the slick hair and bruised eyes and bleeding lips of Ida. Next to her, Helena, slumping forward at an unnatural angle. She couldn't hold herself up like that; she'd fall flat on her face if she didn't move her arms.

But she was limp, as if emptied. And when the red strobe scanned across her face, her skin was sallow, her eyes staring lifeless.

'Mom! Mom!' Petra called.

She was still shouting when she woke.

The zipper of her bundled coat cutting into her cheek. Vincent hurrying somewhere across the floor. Her eyes taking time to focus in the low light. The music going off. Silence flowing in, smothering. Then voices.

She turned her head and saw two men in the doorway.

Petra stood up, ridiculously aware of the creases in her cheeks, and glanced across at Vincent, who had taken a tense position between her and the men. Shielding her, maybe.

The smaller man was Francis Picton; she recognised Curtis Worthing from the photographs she'd found online. He had sandy-grey hair waxed around a balding pate and healthy, tanned skin, clear eyes and his well-tailored suit lining a trim body. He was surprisingly tall and strong, as if he'd been expanded by fifteen per cent; he looked like a man who had made the most of a good life.

'What are you doing here?' Vincent asked.

The men took in the picnic on the floor, their gaze sullying their private pleasure, trailing over Petra, her mismatched socks.

'Door was open,' Picton said.

'You'll get the keys tomorrow,' Vincent said.

Worthing tapped his wrist. 'It is tomorrow.'

'Five minutes after,' Picton added. Vincent sighed and let go of Petra. 'So it's time to go. Either that or you can stay and help. The party's in six days. Lots to do.'

Worthing stepped into the performance room and strolled around it with his arms behind his back, scanning the beading at the ceiling and the skirting, knocking with his knuckles at the soundproofed window frames and the plaster of the wall. 'It is a lovely space,' he said. 'Glad it will get some appropriate use. You know you never should have been running a recording studio in here, don't you?' he said to Vincent. 'This house was never zoned for business.'

Vincent shrugged.

'Quiet neighbours increase resale values, don't they, boss?'

'Is that it?' Petra said. 'You're just going to flip the house, aren't you? Destroying a family's legacy for a quick profit. Nice work. You're used to that, aren't you? Destroying people's lives for money.'

Worthing stopped walking and turned to face her. 'How so?'

Even from metres away, she could feel his eyes hook into her. This man had faced down and defeated stronger people than her on his way up the corporate ladder. 'Forget it.' Petra turned her back and squatted down, gathering the bottles and wrappers into the shopping bag and starting to fold the red blanket.

'Since you're here already,' Picton said to Vincent, 'you could always stay on once your girlfriend's gone and get started. There's lots to do.'

'In the morning,' Vincent said.

Petra waited until they'd got out onto the pavement and closed the red door behind them. They walked a few aimless metres towards town, not really knowing where they were headed next – they lived in opposite directions. Then Petra turned around to face him. 'Why? Why are you selling the house to him?'

'I told you. We need the money. Gloria and me.'

'But why sell to Worthing of all people? You know who he is. Anyone else would snap up the house.'

Vincent shrugged. 'His was the first offer. It met the asking price.'

'I don't believe you.'

'Yeah?'

'I think you're trying to punish yourself. It's the same reason you're working for him as opposed to practically anyone else in the world.'

'What do you mean? What do you think I've got to punish myself for?'

Decision point, Petra. You say what you mean now, or you never get the chance again. You drift through the rest of this relationship, however long it lasts, and you never get the chance to say this again. Is it so important to say it? Can he really not see it for himself? Who the hell are you to come into this man's life, glean a minute of his pain and assume you know the magic breakthrough that's going to heal him? It was blindingly obvious to her, and if he couldn't see it, then someone had to tell him. 'For losing Beccie, Vincent.' She was prepared to sacrifice this happiness to be the messenger.

He frowned, opened his mouth. Everything in his face shut away. He exhaled and turned his shoulder towards her.

'You blame yourself, but it's *not your fault.*'

'Nobody said it was my fault,' he snapped back. '*I* never said it was.'

'But then why are you torturing yourself? How can you bear to be so close to that man? Do I have to be the one to remind you: his profiteering killed your daughter.'

He shook his head, a scathing pity in his eyes. 'You really think you've got the power make a difference in the world, don't you?'

'Yeah, I—'

Snuffing out a bitter laugh, Vincent shook his head; he hefted his bag and stalked off without looking back.

17

'Hello. Am I speaking to Petra Orff?'

'Uh.' For a moment, she honestly wasn't sure – she'd been dreaming, lost in the shadowed forest from *Cabinet* again, the crucified angels hanging backlit like terrible Christmas ornaments, undulating mechanically, pretending to show her the way out, but only leading her deeper, deeper into the centre of the wood, where the feast table was set up. 'Yeah. Yeah, it is.' What time was it even? She felt like she'd had negative sleep.

The details of the last night filled themselves in. The sweet time with Vincent that had turned bad. She took the phone away from her ear and glanced at the time. 5:17. No good news could come at 5:17 in the morning.

'You're on the next-of-kin register. I have some news about your mother.'

Petra shifted up to sitting. 'What? What is it?'

'I'm calling from the MyHealth Clarendon Hospital. Your mother's been admitted for emergency surgery.'

'What? Why?'

'She complained of pain and weakness. The site of her recent cholelithotomy was bleeding.'

'When was this? When did she come in? Is she alright?' Why hadn't Helena called her? How had she got to the hospital? Who had taken her? She didn't have ambulance services included on her plan.

'She's out of surgery. It went well but she's staying in intensive care for the next few hours.'

'Why?'

'Just routine observation. Her system was fairly stressed and we need to ensure she has the fluids she needs.'

'I'll come there now.'

'I can't say when she'll be able to see you. When she's moved onto the ward, visiting hours will be two to seven p.m.'

Regardless, Petra was in the waiting room by ten past six in the morning. The receptionist told her she'd have to wait for the doctor to authorise her to see Helena for a minute, and no, she didn't know when she'd be in, so she'd taken up a seat in the corner, by the window, moving the magazines to the other side of the low coffee table. The morning light had been rising softly for a while now and Petra remembered this corner from the last time she'd been here with Helena, for the procedure that was meant to be routine. That old man had been sitting in this corner, the one she'd expected to be nasty to them but was surprisingly warm to Helena, along with the orange-haired woman. The way the light had slanted, making her look like she had half a face. She'd thought it was just a trick of the light back then, but now, after all she'd imagined, it seemed that hallucination had clearly been the start of some mental dissolution. If she could afford one, she'd ask to get put on a psychologist's waiting list while she was here.

Before long, a small doctor, her ponytail shot through with greying strands that gave her an authoritative cast, approached. 'I'm Amina Saidi. You're Helena's daughter?'

'Yes. How is she?'

'She's fine. Sedated now, so I'd prefer if you don't disturb her. If you want, you can see her through the window now and you'll be able to speak to her a little later.'

'What happened?'

The doctor studied her for a moment, assessing what register to use in her explanation. 'We're not quite sure how, but the site of the extraction ruptured. It's very unusual because it's such non-invasive surgery. You can imagine it like an ear piercing turning into a large tear. Unusual. We're investigating how it happened.'

Petra didn't want to sound accusing, but the doctor was almost admitting it. 'Did someone make a mistake?'

'No. I was on the surgical team. It went without a hitch. Whatever happened seemed to have happened from some subsequent trauma.'

'What do you mean? What sort of trauma?' Petra had visions of someone hitting or kicking her mother. But that was impossible. If she'd been attacked, Petra would have known.

'There could be many causes. Trauma doesn't necessarily describe deliberate or personal violence – it might be an accident. A bump or a fall.' The way she scanned Petra when she said *doesn't necessarily* meant that she hadn't ruled it out. 'You might not even know it happened. Anyhow, there was some internal bleeding and a rupture into the intestine that might have led to sepsis if we hadn't caught it in time.'

'Oh, God. Is she going to be fine?'

'Yes. She's on antibiotics and the ruptures have been sealed. There's no indication of contamination. But that's why we're keeping a close eye on her. Just for careful observation.'

'Thank you.'

The doctor led her through the labyrinthine viscera of the hospital, which somehow seemed much larger and deeper than the building could contain, to the high-care ward. As promised, she was allowed to peek in at her mother, who was looking peaceful in the bed, and totally out of it. She had a drip line in her forearm and oxygen into her nose, but no deep intubation or scary-looking appliances were connected to her.

'So, we'll let you know when she's awake, and you can come and speak to her briefly. I'm sure she'll like to see you.' That small acknowledgement, the word of human recognition, almost made Petra cry.

Back in the waiting room, she texted Suki then opened the drawing app on her tablet and started to sketch, in deliberate evasion of the reality overload. For the first time all week, she left the noisy, superficial space in her mind, and felt focused and quiet. It was almost nine when her phone vibrated her out of her bubble. Her coffee was cool and half a worked-up portrait was staring at her from the screen – a woman with orange hair and her face in half-light. Pale, freckled skin in the light, and in the shadowed part the etchings of the bones and rictus teeth of blown-away flesh.

Coming to as if out of a dream, she refocused her eyes and looked around her. The waiting room was busier now, the day patients checking in, outpatients waiting for their appointments. Leaving her coat and coffee flask on her seat to reserve it, she went to the reception desk.

'Is there any update on my mother? Is she awake?' The receptionist, Geeta by her name tag, was not the same woman she'd spoken to earlier. 'Helena Orff. Dr Saidi said I could see her when she was awake.'

Geeta checked a list on her computer. 'Not yet. We'll let you know.'

Back at her corner seat, Petra scrutinised the woman on the tablet for a long moment – who was she? where had she come from? – before turning the screen off and picking up her phone.

The text came from Helena's number. An instant of relief. But: <*I'm sorry she's involved your mother now. She shouldn't have done that.*>

Her heart plummeted. Ellis Brown was playing his stupid tricks on her again.

<*Who is SHE?*> But Petra knew – Ellis Brown had told her Olivia Jouval had *targeted* Vincent and her.

The next message was from the Warwickshire County Council's billing enquires number that she'd phoned a couple of weeks before. <*You know who. Now you need to know why. You need to connect the dots.*>

Petra recalled the vague conversation she'd had with him. Something about the shows rippling into the real world. <*Why don't you just tell me?*> Replying to the council's number would be pointless, but she pressed send anyway.

<*Message failed*> was followed by a text from Sandy Ratcliff, the organiser of the book club she never got round to attending. <*I can't explain like this. The walls have eyes. Rose Devriendt, a journalist – look her up. She got closest to the truth.*>

Petra didn't send a text to Sandy, but typed the name into her browser. There were plenty of hits. Rose Devriendt was an established arts critic who'd written reviews for several papers and magazines. She wrote regular columns in *The Guardian* and *LA Weekly*, a page in *Art Times* and slots in the *New Yorker*. Used to, anyhow. Her print work died around five years ago with the rest of the industry, and since then she'd been running what looked like a pretty well–respected blog.

Connect the dots, Ellis Brown had told her, so Petra tried, scanning down the index. Devriendt had written a new review almost weekly for a few years, but then they'd dried up. Her first review of Metamuse, from May three years ago, was listed as number 138. A show in Tokyo that December was number 152, but her output had dropped dramatically after that – the Metamuse review from Norway the following June was number 155, and also the last post published on the blog. Comparing Devriendt's reviews with the Metamuse page on Wikipedia showed her that she'd reviewed one show from each Metamuse season, except for the latest one, in Boston six months ago.

Devriendt's first Metamuse review had a knowing, superior tone that belonged in a social column in *Tatler* rather than an informative arts review. But as Petra read on she became immersed in the impression of a professional woman unravelling in real time. As Devriendt travelled from one Metamuse show to the next, the reviews became increasingly personal, and by the time she wrote the article from Norway, the voice became downright haunted and paranoid as Rose Devriendt was drawn in, seduced, touched. Rose had begun to feel that Olivia Jouval was speaking directly to her, that Metamuse was for her. She began to feel… *chosen*.

Metamuse had been playing with Rose then, just as they were playing with Petra now. Where had Rose disappeared to after the Oslo show? What had happened to her?

18 The contact page on Rose Devriendt's blog brought up only a form. Petra wanted to get hold of her urgently, but she'd searched for phone numbers or other contact details and this was the best she could do. It was the one time in her life she regretted not showing an interest in the dark-web exploits of her more paranoid friends at college.

Dear Rose, she wrote. *I have also been caught up with Metamuse and I urgently need to know what OJ & RB are doing and what they plan to do next. I believe what you've written because I've been experiencing it myself. If you read this, please get in touch with me urgently.* She left her contact details in the form.

It was close to noon when Suki came into the waiting room, accompanied by a man who couldn't have been styled any differently from her. Next to the dark, jagged lines of her hair and clothes, the painful sharpness of her necklaces and cuffs and bangles, he was a premonition of a summer's day. He looked like he'd stepped off a yacht in the Mediterranean, with a healthy tan and an expensively informal cotton shirt and pale-blue linen jacket, not like someone who'd been cowering in the unrelenting gloom for the extent of an English Midlands winter. He was tall and lean and his light-brown hair curled forgetfully on top of his head. But despite their differences, his lucid green eyes and the prepossessing way he held himself identified him as unmistakably a Barlow.

'Petra, darling,' Suki said, sweeping across the waiting room to her corner. 'I'm so sorry. What news of your mum?'

While the man stood a respectful few paces back, Petra gave Suki a rundown of what the doctor had told her earlier. There had been no further change in the course of the morning.

'Ben's here,' Suki said after she'd finished, casually indicating her brother, who stepped forward and took her hand in a practised double-handed, magnet-eyed Carnegie shake.

'Susan tells me you've been wanting to learn more about Curtis Worthing.' *Susan?* Petra bit back a laugh and glanced at Suki, who was clenching her jaw. 'I have some background info that may prove illuminating.'

'And guess whose name comes up in the story?' Suki added.

'Whose?'

'Olivia Jouval and Rashida Barnes. Small world, right?'

Suki was pushing a limp tomato around her untouched salad with a five-star scowl on her face, but Ben Barlow had tucked into his hospital-cafeteria burger with surprising relish. If Suki was to be believed, her family commonly feasted on swan cheeks and gold-plated caviar, but uncomplaining consumption of what lay before him was likely a survival instinct ingrained from Ben's boarding-school days.

He dabbed a dry oven chip into a neat swirl of ketchup. 'So there's nothing much to Curtis Worthing. His father was a money man at Jaguar Land Rover, back when it mattered. Curtis attended Barford School and Beauchamp.'

'What's Beechum?'

'The university, darling,' Suki said. 'It's spelled *Beauchamp*, but we pronounce it *Beechum*.'

'Oh, God, I've always called it *Bo-shump*. How embarrassing. Next you're going to tell me *Oxford*'s pronounced *Coventry*.'

'Don't worry, darling. What's the fun of class traps if nobody falls into them?' She patted Petra's hand. 'Anyway, Worthing wasn't at the most venerable college there. Greville.'

'Venerable enough,' Ben countered. 'Despite all the authors sullying its pedigree.'

He was one of those Englishmen, Petra had quickly realised, who don't laugh when they're joking. She'd never quite cracked the English code of humour. Where she came from, when you were making a funny, you overcompensated with confirmatory laughter, exclamation marks or smileys, just so everyone knew it was a joke. When they'd first met, Suki had told Petra something: *England can feel like a party you haven't been invited to*. She'd never forgotten that. It had seemed like a shallow quip, but sometimes it perfectly described her experience.

Petra smiled thinly, then hid it behind her glass of iced tea. 'Barford School? So Curtis was born and bred here?'

'Yes, the Worthings own a nice little pile at Haseley Knob, just up the bridle path.'

'That makes sense,' Petra said. 'It helps explain why he's buying property here. But he really could afford to buy any property anywhere, couldn't he?'

'Yes, I think it's some sort of homecoming. This I'm

hearing from scuttlebutt – one of his solicitors, Busby Catte, is a member of the Society and we're good friends. Of course, Catty shares nothing that's beyond the public record, but it saves one from looking it up, doesn't it? At any rate, Worthing's retiring and consolidating his personal investments here. It could be worse. I often think I should leave the clogged gutters of Mayfair and come visit my darling sis in her bucolic countryside.' Ben shrugged and cast a look around him, as if the blue-tinged cafeteria metonymised this shire town in the middle of England. Maybe it did, with its busy staff hurrying through with their pastel scrubs of different hues and a full spectrum of the town's local inhabitants, from down-and-out people patiently nursing long-term injuries, through unfit families squabbling in packs, to stressed middle-aged white collars, to the well-heeled elective surgery candidates counselling each other before their procedures. But where the MyHealth Clarendon differed from Leamington at large was that all of them had to eat here, in this bog-standard canteen, a tease when outside there was a range of much better fare to suit all budgets. 'Do you know what a treat it is to stroll ten minutes from your doorstep and see actual arable fields where groweth sustenance for the glorious nation? I so seldom get the chance to escape.'

'Thank God for that,' Suki said, but Petra felt strangely proud. She and Helena had wound up in a town that one of the richest men in England envied.

'But the choice of Brook Street Studios isn't just happenstance. When he was a student, Curtis fancied himself an artist, a musician, a thespian. He realised he couldn't play a note, but the talent seems to have bypassed him to his son, who's currently living in Tokyo. Something of a digital busker, from what I can tell. Styles himself "Kun Jameso"' – the quote marks dripped stickily from his mouth. 'So, in order to entice young James home from time to time, he wants to keep rooms for him here in Leamington, which might appeal to him more lifestyle-wise than the manor in Haseley Knob. And what better pad than a house in the hippest town in Warwickshire with a culturally significant recording studio attached?'

'I don't understand. I thought they were ripping out the studio equipment and turning the whole house into flatlets. If Curtis and James are such keen musicians, why don't they just leave the equipment intact? Worthing's manager is almost forcing Vincent to throw the kit away.'

'I couldn't say. But I can guess. If you're a very wealthy person, buying a recording studio for your son as a present, you'll want to have the latest, top-of-the-range equipment, not some second-hand fare.'

'Nuh-uh,' Petra shook her head. 'That doesn't add up. If he wants the studio for its historic value, he'll want to keep that beautiful control desk at least. It's a classic, from the little I know. Important music has been recorded with it.'

'It may be a strategy of some sort,' Ben said. 'You don't get where Worthing has got without being shrewd.'

'What a waste,' she said. But as she was shaking her head, the penny finally dropped. 'What a bastard!'

'What?' Suki asked.

'They intended to keep the studio intact all along. They've been threatening Vincent that they're going to throw the equipment out, but they've wanted to keep it all along. They're tricking him into giving it away for nothing. They're charging him to store it there! What utter bastards!'

Suki pursed her lips. 'Aka good business.'

'But wait,' Ben said, bringing attention back to his story. Worthing's profiteering treachery clearly left him cold. 'It's this connection with the dramatic arts where we come across your Mizzes Jouval and Barnes.' He paused to eat another chip.

'Yes?' Petra stole a glance at Suki's watch. There was still no word about her mother, and reception would call her as soon as there was. She had time to indulge Ben's storytelling style.

'Back before he'd been disillusioned as to the accurate limit of his creative skills – i.e. when he was in college – young Curtis was deathly serious about acting. By 1981, in his last year at Beauchamp, he was a leading proponent of the Beauchamp Drama Society. It is there that he met Olivia Jouval and her *friend*, Rashida Barnes.' Petra noted the emphasis on the word *friend*, but let him continue. 'Rashida was a first-year scholarship student at Highfield College and she joined the club with Olivia. Radical performance art was their thing.'

'That sounds right, doesn't it?' Suki said.

'1981 you say?' Petra said. 'So they'd be… nearing sixty now.'

'Yes,' Ben said. 'They were the same age as Curtis, who's also sixty this year.'

'This month, in fact,' Petra said. 'It's in *Who's Who*,' she added.

'Early retirement, then,' Suki said. 'Lucky for some.'

Petra shot a skew look at her.

'What? I'll be indentured to my doting family until I'm seventy at least.'

Usually, Suki's tone-deaf, glib remarks washed over her, but today they rankled. Maybe it was having met Vincent, learning about how the system had failed Beccie, and of course the worry of what exactly the insurance was going to cover of Helena's treatment and how they were going to pay for the rest. Again, she bit her tongue; at this rate, it was going to start bleeding soon. 'It's funny what assumptions you jump to, based on interviews and media coverage. I guessed she was younger than that.'

'They scrupulously stay out of the limelight,' Suki said. 'Metamuse is always in the media, but we hardly see them beyond Olivia's fake portraits. We know nothing about the women behind the company. It's a brilliant campaign in these oversaturated times.'

Petra's phone rang. It was an unknown number.

'Sorry. I'd better take this,' she said.

'Of course,' Suki said. 'It might be reception.'

But it was a woman on the other end, with a European accent and a rich tone cracked at the edges. 'Hallo, Petra. This is Heike Maslow. I'm – I *was* Rose Devriendt's wife. I called you as soon as I received your message.'

Petra excused herself from the table and hurried out into the small courtyard beyond the eating area. A couple of weathered wooden benches spaced around a silver birch struggling bravely in the low light, already emitting tentative buds.

'Thanks for calling. You say you *were* Rose's wife. Is she...?'

'She died last year.'

'I'm so sorry. In that case, I didn't mean to intrude, and you needn't have called me. It's not that important.'

'I think it is. I know what Rose was going through.' Heike took a deep breath. 'Her fear, what she was believing towards the end. I still think a lot of it was in her mind, but not all. I looked into it. I did some research. I think some of it was real. If you say you are experiencing the same thing, I think you must be careful. You should have all the information.'

'Okay. Thank you. I don't know how much you know about Olivia Jouval or Rashida Barnes, whether you've heard of Curtis Worthing. But I think something strange, and possibly dangerous, is about to happen. If you have any information – if you're in the position to share it – I'd be really grateful.'

'I'm going to send you something Rose didn't post to her website and some news articles she'd collected. She died in Boston last September – during the Metamuse show. She was writing a blog post that weekend. The things she's written there, I can't believe them all. Rose had become mentally ill – she was paranoid, she was afraid. And I blame this Olivia Jouval for doing this to her. She never had any problems before Metamuse.' She paused, taking another deep breath, controlling her voice. 'But she was starting to uncover things that were true. As you say, dangerous things – and that wasn't in her mind. I looked into it,' she repeated. 'The people who died – they're all connected. They all knew each other.'

'I'm not sure what this all means,' Petra said. 'Can you help me understand?'

'I would warn you to just leave it behind, but I don't know you. I don't know how deep you are. Maybe the only way I can help you is to send you what I have. Maybe you'll be able to make some sense of it.'

Unpublished blog post retrieved by Heike Maslow

[Heike, I'm not coming home this time, and I want to tell you why. I've emailed you the link to this page.

Maybe that's what Olivia and I have in common. I've always expressed myself better in writing than talking, and I'm sorry about that. I love you.]

Casting Couch, **Metamuse, Boston**
Friday, 13 September
19:15

It immediately feels like a game, another elaborate Metamuse hallucination. Following the instructions, I check in and am assigned a room key. The Back Bay Hotel is an old-fashioned residential hotel with thick, dark and musty carpets and overpainted doors. When I get up to my room, number 401, green neon is pouring through the window against an overcast evening sky. Metatextual vibes shimmer knowingly.

There's an outfit laid out on the bed for me, along with my character notes. So far, so unsurprising. The invitation led me to expect a two-night immersive murder-mystery weekend. I am Rose Dee, an aspiring actor. I'm nineteen years old, I've done some community theatre in my hometown of Kansas City, and I've come to Boston on the invitation of someone called Harry Warren, apparently a famous movie producer.

The jeans are high-waisted and too tight, the camisole too strappy and revealing, the white blouse too big, ballooning in the shoulders. But they are exactly what I wore in the nineties, when I was nineteen. I feel stupid dressed like this, critically aware of every misstep that girl took in the last twenty-five years; bitterly aware of every way she's been screwed over by mean-spirited people, by sheer bad luck, and by history monster-trucking over all her hopes and dreams.

23:25

Nonetheless, I tease and gel my hair in the bathroom and go downstairs to the dining room in character, just as instructed. I'll play along; there's never a question that I will. Who the hell am I to resist?

The dinner's actually fun. Meeting the other guests and the hotel staff, trying to figure out which of them are actors and which are participants. I scan the faces, but *she* is not here. That much I'm sure of. I think I recognise some of the players from Fjellstrand, but I can't be sure. Everyone was in masks there and I was freaking out most of the time. It's been less than three months but it already feels like a dissipated dream.

Everyone's in awkward nineties gear, so I start to feel more comfortable – shoulder pads and big hair for the yuppie roles; skinny jeans and plaid for the alternative types. The story is we're casting acting and technical jobs for a new big-budget movie, and over the next couple of days will be living the process. I learn that most of the guests are amateur film fanatics. The show was only advertised on a few selected, very niche internet film groups, and potential guests had to apply with a motivating letter. None of them have worked professionally in film before, but all of them harbour dreams of being on set.

I can't help asking – yet again – why they've chosen me.

I'm upstairs watching TV when I hear the scream. It's a short, dismayed 'Ow' but it pierces through the wall and straight into me – it's the sound of a woman in pain.

I rush out of my room, ready to fight off an attacker or call for help or something. Before I've thought about it, I've shoved through the open door of Room 402 and am seeing a woman in a red dress sitting on the couch, mascara or bruise-smeared eyes, blood trickling from a cut in her lip. Harry Warren is sprawled across the floor at the foot of the bed between us, taking up a lot of space for such a short man. His hair is mussed and there's a purple gash over his left eye.

'I hit him,' she says, pointing at the marble-based lamp flung in the middle of the white bedspread. 'I think he's dead. Will you help me?' The scene is elegant, meticulously staged; so artful and hyperreal, it's clear that this is a private scene.

'Sure,' I say, flattered to have been called into an intimate one-on-one.

She wipes the lamp down with the corner of the cover and places it back on the nightstand, then rips the sheet off the bed and lays it on the floor next to the body.

Which is when he lurches up and grabs at me, trying to pull his mass up against my legs. As he grabs and pulls, he pinches at the flesh on my inner thigh, his long fingernails scraping the thin skin. It's fucking sore, and just instinctively really I raise my knee into his face. The timing is perfect. There's a sickly shattering crunch as the rest of his nose crumbles back into his skull and something else pops, and he crashes back to the floor.

'That's fucking disgusting,' I say with a giggle, also secretly pleased that I've been graced with this key scene and these visceral horror effects – they're gross and they're great. Metamuse have really upped their game, even after *Elemental*, which, as we know, really had me going.

I squat down and help her roll Harry onto the sheet. He's fucking heavy and he's not cooperating, and it takes some time to shimmy him properly into the middle of the material. When we're done, the woman goes into the bathroom and washes her face and hands, and when she comes out she's crying and shaking, and it's hard not to get caught up. It's easier and more entertaining to park your cynical doubts and just go with it, as I've discovered. I tell her not to worry, that it'll be over soon.

'We can take him down to the pool,' she says. 'Pretend he tripped and fell.'

'There's a pool?' I say.

She nods, chewing her lip like a starlet. 'In the basement.'

'Okay,' I shrug. I don't say why don't we just dump him in the bathtub, put some soap on the floor? It would be a hell of a lot easier. Nobody appreciates script notes in the middle of a performance.

So we drag him out the door, down the corridor and into the elevator. Luckily, nobody sees us. When we ping out into the basement, it's only a short drag along a smooth stone floor to the poolside.

I must say, by this time the realism's getting a bit too much and my muscles are straining. The guy playing Harry Warren hasn't moved at all; he's clearly a very dedicated actor with a high pain threshold. Then again, I don't really care about his comfort. He really hurt me when he grabbed at me – this Stanislavski shit's going to leave bruises.

'Damn,' the woman says. 'If he came down here to swim, he'd be in his trunks, wouldn't he? I'll go check his room. Can you strip him in the meantime?'

'No,' I say, backing away. 'It's been fun, but I'm heading out now.'

The woman comes over and grabs my arm, presses her face towards mine so all I can see are her big, smeared eyes. 'Please, for God's sake. I don't know what else to do. Why are you acting so… calm about this?'

'Very funny,' I say as I leave the scene and go back to my room.

Saturday, 14 September
2:21

At two in the morning there's a knock on the door. I'm not asleep – wired from the evening and jetlagged, I've been churning the information I've gleaned from the players, determined to solve mysteries that don't even exist. The green neon throbs outside my window as I stare into the dark corners.

I open my door to a man in a cheap black suit slouching in the doorway, his white-banded fedora askew on his head.

190

I remember seeing him earlier in the night, thinking he was cast as a musician, but now that I think of it, there was no live music.

'Can I come in?' he says.

'No,' I say.

'I have something important to tell you,' he says. But his face and his voice are bored, like he's running lines for a grudging favour.

'You can tell me from there,' I say.

He shrugs and then goes on to tell me that I'm in danger, that I was chosen to do something I shouldn't have done. That Olivia wanted me to kill Harry Warren, that it's not a game.

'Sure, okay,' I say, closing the door on him. I'm tired. They can advance my character arc in the morning.

He shoves his shiny black shoe in the door and pushes a manila envelope at me. 'Read these,' he says. 'Please,' he adds after what seems to be a battle with his will. 'Don't doubt yourself. It's all real.'

SUICIDE OF TOP LAWYER STILL BAFFLES

The Parisian, 15 May

THE DEATH OF high-profile lawyer Audrey Godard three nights ago still leaves police and Godard's family and colleagues baffled. The fifty-seven-year-old senior partner of Godard, Duclos and Debuchy threw herself out of the window of her rue de Navarin apartment on Friday night in front of seven friends and colleagues at a dinner party.

Friends who spoke confidentially to *The Parisian* cannot understand why she would commit suicide. She was successful and appeared happy and gave no indication of depression or undue stress. After gathering witness accounts, police certified the death self-inflicted and closed the investigation.

But Ms Godard's three adult children suggest that there was undue pressure to close the case from Etienne Duclos and Elisa Debuchy, the law firm's other senior partners. They think the circumstances surrounding their mother's suicide should be examined.

'It is outrageous that our mother's death should be hushed up simply to avoid negative publicity for the firm,' said Marcel Godard (27) speaking on behalf of his bereaved siblings, Robert (25) and Amelie (23). 'Of course we want the firm to avoid negative impact as much as they do, but we need to understand what caused this tragedy. A few days' extra investigation would not harm the business, and would provide us with closure.' They have appealed to the magistrate's office to reopen the case.

Audrey Godard was born in Birmingham, England, in 1960, as Audrey Cartwright. She was educated at Henley School and Edgbaston Arts Academy and studied dance and drama at Beauchamp University before undertaking an MPhil in law. She started her legal career as an entertainment contracts specialist and became one of France's highest-profile entertainment litigators by taking on diverse cases for celebrity clients, most notably the defamation suit of Harold Karnac and the fascism row of President Pasteur vs Penguin Random House.

In 1988, Ms Godard married automotive designer Philippe Godard; he died of colonic cancer in 2007. Audrey Godard is survived by her three children and her mother, Elizabeth Cartwright.

ENGLISH BUSINESSMAN DIES IN ACCIDENTAL FALL

Tokyo Daily News, 2 January

TOKYO – AN English businessman has died in an accidental fall from his apartment in Sakurashinmachi.

Mr Martin Trengove (58) was celebrating New Year's Eve when, according to his partner Ms Jennifer Russell, who was with him at the time, he slipped on ice on the balcony and fell the four storeys onto the road, dying instantly.

Mr Trengove, a self-employed marketing executive, was embroiled in a fraud scandal in the UK in 2014, but the Japan Chamber of Business lists him as an active member in Japan since 2015.

Metropolitan police have interviewed witnesses to the accident and confirm that no foul play is suspected.

OSLO CITY COUNCILLOR
FOUND DEAD IN NESODDEN

Norway Post, 3 July

OSLO – THE body of Oslo City Councillor Annette Hansen has been found in the woods south of Ellingstadåsen on the Nesodden Peninsula. Municipal and county search teams made the shocking discovery yesterday evening at 9:30.

Dr Hansen had been missing from her home in Oslo since 21 June, when it was believed she attended a solstice celebration. When she did not return, the alarm was raised and an immediate and urgent search operation was launched. The recovery efforts were initially hampered when Dr Hansen's husband, Frank Barber, reported the location of the solstice party as the Nordmarka Forest rather than in Nesodden.

According to a source at the coroner's office, preliminary examination of the body revealed a broken leg and wounds 'consistent with the bites of a large-toothed carnivore such as a wolf'. As there are no wolves still living in Nesodden, initial speculation is that Dr Hansen was attacked by feral dogs, possibly after being immobilised by a fall that caused the broken limb.

The daughter of a diplomatic family, Dr Hansen attended schools in Norway, Sweden, the United Kingdom, Japan and the United States. She studied arts and theatre at Beauchamp University in England before moving to the United States as a political campaign director. She returned to Norway in 2008, where she married Barber, an American trade attaché to the Business and Industry Committee in the Storting. Dr Hansen became a member of the Oslo City Council for the Conservative Party in 2012.

She is perhaps best known for piloting the 'Feed Ismail' campaign in 2016, and was a well-liked figure from all sides of the political spectrum for her cross-party and collaborative initiatives.

She is survived by Mr Barber, along with her first husband Kris Landvik and three daughters.

At first I think they're just story props, made to immerse me further or to toy with me. But I check the newspapers' websites, run through their archives – and the articles exist.

This is real.

My first instinct is to bargain, to rationalise it all away: So what? People dying in big cities at the same time as the shows isn't a major coincidence. People die all the time.

But Beauchamp University is mentioned in two of the articles, and it doesn't take long to find out that Martin Trengove went there too, at the same time as the others. I don't want to enter the next web search, but I know I have to. It spits out the answer I've been dreading:

Harry Warren (59), producer, Beauchamp University, 1979–1981.

This is no coincidence; the deaths are all deliberate.

I was wrong about it all.

I was desperate to believe Metamuse was some sort of beneficent therapy service, but I was so wrong.

I should have trusted my gut. I should have turned away the moment I felt their fingers probing into my mind, but I didn't. I had to follow. I was seduced.

That's why they chose me. Despite my pretensions at being a clever critic, I'm just so fucking gullible. From the moment she felt me in Paris, she knew I'd follow. She knew I'd do what she wanted me to do.

Tonight, Harry Warren died. It might be made to look like an accident or a suicide, but I know it will be murder. Olivia Jouval chose me to kill him.

I don't know why. I don't have time to find out. The police have arrived downstairs. Real police, not a nineties or fifties or thirties pastiche, but real cops with tasers and lethal force. From my fourth-floor window, I see how they've cordoned off the hotel, and the gaggle of bystanders ogling from across the road.

I hear them in the corridor.

Soon, they will come for me.

My room is painted in throbbing green.

---

19 'That was a long call,' Suki said when Petra got back to the table. An uneaten hospital panna cotta forlornly reflected her bleak gaze back at her from the tabletop, while Ben poured creamer into his canteen coffee from a tiny plastic catering pack.

'Sorry,' Petra said as she slumped back into her chair. 'Can I have that?'

Suki pushed the dessert over to her. 'Who was it?'

'Someone with information.' It seemed the simplest way of explaining what she'd heard from Heike Maslow and what she'd just spent the last twenty minutes reading. 'I got in touch with a reviewer who knew a lot about Metamuse. I hoped she'd be able to cast some light on Olivia Jouval and Rashida Barnes, and if there's really anything sinister behind Metamuse.'

'But?' Suki asked, reading Petra's disappointed pause.

'But Rose died.'

'Oh.'

'That was her wife on the phone, and she sent me some links. But I'm not sure what to believe – Rose was imagining things, seriously deluded. But she included news articles, too. I need to double check her facts, but if they're right, I know it sounds bizarre, but Jouval and Barnes could be using Metamuse to target specific people.'

'Target them?' Suki asked. 'How so?'

'In the same week as every Metamuse season, there's been an apparently accidental death.'

Suki pursed her lips as Petra offered more details. 'That doesn't necessarily mean anything,' she said at length. 'People die all the time. It would be unusual for someone not to die in an accident in one of those cities in any given week.'

'Yeah. That's what I thought, but Rose seemed to be uncovering a connection between each of the victims. I've got a list of names here.' She slid her phone over to Ben. Audrey Godard, Martin Trengove, Annette Hansen, Harry Warren. 'Do you recognise any of them?'

Ben glanced at her grimy and cracked old phone. 'Harry Warren, yes – there was some question of misdemeanours, wasn't there? But the others...' He shook his head. 'I can have a look.'

Petra's phone rang: it was the reception desk. Helena was awake and the doctor had cleared her to look in on her. She thanked Suki and Ben for coming, and when she got to the high-care section, Helena was propped up on her gurney much as Petra had seen her before, only the drip line and oxygen tube connected to her. Petra pushed into the room quietly, but Helena turned her head and managed a weak smile.

'Hi, love,' she croaked.

Petra hurried over to her bedside and grabbed her hand. A little too hard, she realised when she felt just how light Helena's return grip was. She let go and smoothed her mother's hand on the starched sheet. 'Mom. What happened?'

'I had this pain. I thought it would go away, but it didn't.'

'Why didn't you call me?'

'I did try, love. There was no answer, so I didn't leave a message. I didn't want to trouble you.'

'God, Mom,' Petra keep her voice low, her relief that her mother was talking outweighed her frustration just at the moment, 'it would have been no trouble.' But the truth was, if Helena had left a message last night, while Petra was dancing and getting drunk with Vincent, she may not have noticed it for hours. Guilt crashed in. After all her self-righteous preening, complaining that she was always there for her mother but that Helena never seemed to trust her enough to call on her, she'd failed her just when she was needed most. 'How did you get here?'

'Ida brought me.'

'In the middle of the night? That's—'

Helena gestured weakly with the back of her hand. 'She lives in my building. She was happy to help. She's a friend, love,' was what she said, but Petra heard, *Let it go; it's none of your business.*

Petra looked away for a few seconds, then turned back to her mother. She took her fingers, lightly this time. 'Well, it doesn't matter how you got here. I'm glad you did.'

'Ja. It could have been bad, they say. But they caught it in time.'

Helena had never seemed old before, but now the skin of her hand felt like parchment, the thinnest of barriers between all that was her and utter dissolution. A slight tweak of luck or timing, and she might have been dead. Why did this have to happen last night, when she'd been on call for her mother night after night, year after year?

'You mustn't feel bad, love,' Helena said, reading her thoughts in her face as only she could do. 'You don't have to look after me. You have your own life to live.'

Petra shook her head. 'But we're supposed to look after each other, be there for each other. I failed you.'

'Oh, nonsense, love. It all turned out okay.'

Yeah, Petra thought, *only because I was usurped by that dodgy stranger who's insinuated herself into your life.*

'I was scared, Mom. What if Ida hadn't been around, and my phone was broken or something. What then?'

'I would have called a taxi, an ambulance, anything. We're not alone, love. And you don't need to control everything. Trust life, trust society. We're stronger than you think.'

Helena's pragmatism brought a little comfort, but still Petra couldn't forgive herself as she left the ward. The nurse at the desk said Helena was stable, and if the night went well, it was likely she'd be discharged into the general ward in the morning.

Petra wouldn't be able to see Helena until the morning, so she decided to go home to wait. She should be ten minutes away if there was an emergency, but having seen Helena and heard the doctor's report, she was feeling positive. Suki had closed the shop for the afternoon – she had some Line Logistics work to do and wanted Petra to take the day off. 'You don't believe it matters to anyone if the shop is open or closed, do you, darling?'

As Petra walked out of the hospital, she saw Ida – the real one, the middle-aged unbruised woman, not Petra's mirror-world hallucination – stepping out of a little blue Fiat 500 in the parking lot. Without thinking, Petra dodged behind the brick pillar at the portico and waited for Ida to pass, trying to find an angle to catch her reflection in the sun-proof laminate on the window.

Though Ida was facing forward, unselfconsciously walking into the reception area, for just a second the young face in the window seemed to look directly at Petra with battered eyes, and smiled at her with bloodied lips. Then the low sun disappeared behind clouds and Petra saw the real woman glance behind her through the glass, like a woman feeling eyes in her back.

20   By four-whatever in the morning, Petra had given up trying to sleep and was listening to the early-morning road sounds as she textured her drawing of a drowning girl she'd imagined, drifting serene under the surface of a city river among plastic waste and weed-bearded shopping trolleys, battle-scarred fish surviving and crabs scuttling.

She'd already thought of phoning the police and sharing her suspicions about Metamuse, but what would she say? Corporate CEO to be targeted by an accident vaguely related to an immersive theatre show that was run by someone who may have gone to college with him? She'd end up sounding like a lunatic blogger, or *The Sun*. If anything, she should get in touch with Picton and warn him to be careful, but in the insipid light of dawn, speaking to him didn't seem such an enticing prospect. Let Picton and Worthing look after themselves. She couldn't help thinking that if anything bad happened to them, they deserved it.

She couldn't concentrate on the drawing so took to staring at her phone. No signal that her mother was awake yet, nothing missed from the hospital this time. When she noticed Vincent was online, she called him.

'Petra?'

A sterile background hum buffered his voice and she wondered where he was. She tried to picture him lying in bed just like her, to make herself feel less vulnerable, but she'd never seen his bedroom.

'Hey,' she said. 'How are you?'

'I'm okay, thanks. And you?' His voice was grainy.

Petra checked the time display on the alarm clock. 6:07. Shit – his voice would be grainy, wouldn't it? 'Yeah. I just wanted to say thanks for the other night.'

'Uh, sure.'

'Anyway, I didn't realise how early it was. I'm really sorry. I'll call back later.'

'No, no. It's alright. I'm awake. I'm on a job, actually.'

'Where? It sounds like you're inside a fridge.'

'Something like that.'

'How's the studio? Have you finished moving your things out? Is Picton treating you alright?'

'Can't complain.'

'Listen, Vincent. I found out something about Worthing and Picton that I think you should know.'

'Yeah?'

'I found out that Worthing's planned to keep the studio intact all along. As a gift for his son. So basically, they've been scamming you. Making you pay to store your equipment there. All along, they've planned to grind you down until you signed the equipment over for nothing.'

A long silence. Then, 'Where did you hear this?'

'Suki. My boss – her brother knows Worthing's lawyer. Knows all about the family, and that Curtis has been wanting to lure his son back from Japan.'

'You've been researching Worthing on my behalf?'

Petra couldn't make out his tone in the flat static of the

phone – was he angry? Grateful? It was hard to tell. The pause was filled by a slam and clatter on the road outside as someone dropped a handcart out of a delivery van.

'I wasn't prying, if that's what you think. It came up in relation to something else. I was looking into Metamuse.' She wanted to tell him about Rose Devriendt, but she didn't know how he'd react. What if he didn't believe her? What if he didn't care? Petra felt oddly protective of Rose and her tragedy.

'Oh yeah, it's the final show tonight,' Vincent said.

'You're not planning to go, are you?'

'I don't know. Probably not.'

'Good. I don't think you should. Did Ellis Brown tell you how they've been manipulating us?'

'I haven't heard from him since that night you saw him.'

That was a surprise. Why would he suddenly switch his attention from Vincent to her? Maybe because he recognised that she was more receptive to the story he was selling. 'Well, he told me to look into the show. That's why I asked Suki in the first place. It's scary—'

'Yeah, of course. That's why it's cool, right?'

'They used Beccie to draw you in. That's not "cool". That's evil and devious. Just like putting drugs in the drinks and the aircon.'

'Free hallucinogens for all? I don't think so.'

What more could she say to convince him? *The shows are a front for serial murders, Vincent. They target members of the audience and brainwash them to kill deliberately selected people in apparently random accidents. It's happened in Paris and Tokyo and Oslo and Boston – and now it's happening here. And this time* we're *the perpetrators they've chosen.*

She didn't say it because, after all the corroboration and proof she'd seen, she still couldn't bring herself to believe it.

'Okay,' Petra said, 'believe what you want. But please trust me on this: I've learned some things lately and it's clear that Metamuse is a front for dangerous stuff, real-world stuff, even criminal stuff. You need to keep away.'

'That sounds a bit paranoid, right? It's a theatre group.'

'It's true, Vincent. I should show you what I've read. It involves you as much as me, after all. But I can't do it today. My mother's in the hospital.'

'Oh, sorry. Is she alright?'

'She'll be fine. Thanks. But listen – promise me, please, that you won't go tonight.'

He hesitated.

'You think you're going to find Beccie there, don't you?' she said. Another affirmative silence. 'But you won't find her. That's what they want you to believe to get you there. But it's not true.'

He sighed. 'Okay. I won't go.' The concession was too easy, but Petra needed to believe him. If they stayed away, if they didn't help them, the show would run its course and Metamuse would leave and everyone in Leamington would be okay. Petra believed she had enough control to prevent the inevitable.

He hadn't said it categorically – *I promise I won't go to the show tonight, Petra* – and she should have let it bother her more. Instead of making a flask of coffee and heading back to wait pointlessly at the hospital, like a character in an American TV show with nothing better to do, she should have gone straight to Vincent's house and explained everything to him.

Despite the fact that he didn't seem to be interested in seeing her again.

As it happened, Helena had been moved to the general ward first thing in the morning and was subject to normal visiting hours. Petra had showed her face at the shop and Suki shooed her out, so she sat and doodled in the waiting room until two.

Helena was fine, already uncomfortable in bed, no oxygen required, the drip line out and taking mild painkillers by mouth. Dr Saidi had explained that the repair on the rupture had worked perfectly and there had been no adverse effects, and it was likely she'd be discharged in the morning. By four, Petra could tell that Helena was getting bored by her – probably wanted her peace to read her book, or stare at the football replays on the ward's TV with Olafur Arnalds in her ears. Anything better than Petra's guilty and cloying attempts at making up for her initial failure.

She texted Vincent. *<Are you home? Can I come visit?>* *<message failed>*

When she got to Vincent's house, she had to double check the number to make sure it was the right place. It was a clear, bright evening, the sinking orange sun warming the street – so different from the squally storm of the night less than a week before, when she'd first been here. But something felt different about Vincent's house, and at first Petra couldn't figure out what had caused the change.

Then she noticed that the bulbs that had been springing up in the beds along the short path to the front door were drooping and depleted, brown husks of the fresh growth she'd seen before. The bush she'd pushed through towards the bay window that night was dropping its leaves too, as if it was late autumn rather than early spring. The brown decay made the garden look burned and poisoned.

Tentatively, Petra rapped on the glass set into the front door, and then after a moment, feeling nothing stir inside, she knocked louder. There was a light on somewhere inside, a low and sickly sulphurous glow, like a candle in a hermit's cave. She rapped on the glass again, about to call Vincent's name, but somehow hyperaware of the ripples her presence was already causing on the quiet street. She didn't want to make a scene.

A shadow passed across the deep-set glow. Petra waited, but he didn't come to the door. She raised the lion-head knocker, and as she did, the door nudged open.

She stepped inside, pushing the door closed behind her. Now she could call out.

'Vincent?' To her right, the front room where Ellis Brown had been lounging last time she'd been here was vacant and lightless. Hurriedly, she advanced along the corridor towards the amber light, which was coming from the kitchen.

'Vincent?' she called up the stairs that led to darkness. 'Are you here?'

In the kitchen, a single low bulb was burning in the stove-top hob, yellowed by years of singe and grease. A pot was simmering on the stove, saturating the air with a rich, soupy aroma. A notepad lay on the table with something written on it.

'He's not here.'

Petra wheeled around to see Gloria in the doorway, buttoning a thick coat as if she was on her way out.

'Oh, hello ma'am. Sorry for letting myself in. There was no answer. Do you know where he went?'

'He left a note,' Gloria said, gesturing at the table.

Petra picked up the notepad.

I have to go. Beccie needs me.

'I'm worried for him,' Gloria said. 'I want to find him but I don't know where he's gone.'

If Petra had been any less of an emotional busybody, maybe she would have left Vincent to it. She'd warned him; he was a grown-up and could make his own decisions. But she couldn't expect Gloria to go hobbling off unprepared into the countryside to face down Olivia Jouval and her band of mercenaries.

'I know where he is,' she said. 'I'll go and fetch him.'

Gloria stepped closer and took her hand. Her skin was warm and dry, textured from years of work; it reminded her of her own grandmother's palms. Sometimes Granny Jo would visit, and if Dad and Helena started fighting, Granny would take Petra by the hand and lead her into the garden. That lavender-dusted parchment skin meant safety, peace.

She gripped Petra's fingers and looked her in the eyes. 'Thank you. You have a kind heart.' There was intense worry in her expression, such naked vulnerability that it cloyed with the sweet fat in the air and ashamed Petra.

She looked away, checked the time on the oven clock. 5:08. The show started at eight and it wasn't that far to the venue. She'd borrow Suki's car, pull Vincent out of the queue, bring him home and be back in time to say goodnight to Helena.

21   It was six-thirty on a darkening evening by the time
Petra got to the tiny village of Sling Sutton, on the northern
edge of the Cotswolds. She'd never been down here herself,
but she'd seen photos of the iconic brewery building, and seen
their beer listed on menus in some independent restaurants in
Leamington until the beermaker had ceased trading a year
and a half before. The village consisted of nothing more than
a small church, a village hall, the Sling Puppy pub, and some
disparate houses hidden shyly behind overgrown hedgerows.
Petra had to slow to a crawl to find the pitch-dark entrance
to the country lane the Abarth's GPS was indicating, but
as she rounded a narrow bend and cleared a gloomy copse
it was hard to miss the brewery. The massive Victorian
soot-stained brick monument to chthonic industries loomed
from the top of the little hill like a demonic cathedral from
William Blake's nightmares. Spotlights the colour of blood
and flame underlit the building's jagged face, exacerbating
the effect.

Marshals dressed in tuxedos and ball gowns were directing
traffic away from the brewery's car park to an overflow lot
in the churchyard. In small-town England, unlike in Joburg,
it wasn't so unusual to park next to graves, but still, on this
moonless night in the middle of what felt like wild and ancient
nothingness, the thought sent a ripple of fear through her gut.

She focused on the animated voices of the other guests, who were slamming their car doors and laughing in defiance of the heavy night, and followed them down the rutted lane back to the brewery building. The people ahead of her were dressed in elegant, formal outfits, and Petra felt like she was following them underdressed and uninvited towards an opulent country wedding or an upmarket premiere.

She followed a couple who had emerged from a car parked a few bays away from her, the woman holding up the hem of her deep-yellow dress in her right hand, her ankles buckling on the stilettoes as she navigated the rutted country path. Her partner, trim in a white-jacketed tux, was tugging at his collar.

'This is meant to be a recreation of a university ball, isn't it?' the woman said.

'Yeah, I think so,' said the man, adjusting the waist of his trousers.

'I couldn't afford a dress like this when I was a student, that's all I'm saying.'

In response, he put his hand on her ass. She leaned into him, and they turned left, then right, following the tiki lights towards the brewery building.

There were no more than twenty cars in the overflow parking lot; when she rounded through the gates of the brewery, she guessed there were maybe sixty cars parked there. A metal traffic sign was stashed behind the pillar of the gate: *Sling Sutton Brewery Temporarily Closed*. The buildings still looked in decent condition – simply shut rather than abandoned. A couple of brewery trailers were still parked around the back and there were still pallets and vats stacked up behind locked fences. When did a temporary downturn

turn into permanent collapse, Petra wondered. Had the owners given up hope of reopening?

Beyond the car park was a short queue at a security and baggage check outside a small gatehouse that served as the brewery's gift shop, and beyond it a couple of hundred people gathered outside the building's huge main doors in loose groups, waiting to be let in. *Intimacy* and *Cabinet* had run for six days each, but from what she knew, the finale of each season was a one-off event. If all the ticket holders were here tonight, she would have expected a bigger crowd. Maybe not everyone had received the invitation to this final show. She tried to scan for Vincent, but the figures were silhouetted by the glare of the uplit monolith – she'd have to get closer.

When she got to the security checkpoint, she joined the short queue waiting at the bag check table. She should have counted on delays parking and queues and checkpoints. It had been a simple plan – arrive, find Vincent, bring him back to Gloria – but she hadn't given it enough thought, even on the drive here, when her mind was entirely occupied with finding her way and not being crushed by a Land Rover speeding towards her on the pitch-dark country roads. At a linen-decked table, two cast members – one in a tux and slick side parting, and the other in a showy scarlet ballgown and luxuriant red Jessica Rabbit waves – were collecting bags and phones and placing them in lockers arrayed in a temporary rank behind them. Although she'd become used to the plague masks at *Cabinet*, Petra was glad the staffers weren't wearing them here – the dark night and the looming location were eerie enough, and Petra wasn't in the mood for more disquiet tonight. Simple plan: quickly in and out.

She watched as the usher in the red gown clicked a bracelet onto the wrist of the blond-haired woman in front of her, who was shivering in a gold designer dress, high heels and trench coat.

Jessica Rabbit checked her tablet. 'You're Lucinda James tonight. The gold Chanel. Mm, one of my favourites. Did you have any trouble at the outlet?'

'No, none at all. The process was incredibly smooth. They had the dress waiting for me and they did the nips and tucks within a couple of days. I'm really impressed.'

'I'm so glad to hear that.'

'I hope my hair's alright? The salon did it to order but I'm not sure how many classic chignons they've styled.'

'It looks great. You look lovely.'

'It's all just for fun, anyhow,' Lucinda responded.

'Will this thing also help locate us if we're lost?' her companion asked as the usher in the tux clipped his bracelet on.

'Yes, actually it does,' Jessica Rabbit smiled. 'Something like that.' She pointed along the driveway. 'Please, go through. My colleagues will let you know where to go next.'

When they'd cleared the table, Petra approached.

'Welcome to the Fallout Ball,' Jessica said.

'Thanks, I... I actually don't have a ticket. I'm just looking for someone.'

'Oh, I'm sorry,' the tux started. 'You need a ticket.'

'Don't worry, Ernesto – she's on the list,' said Jessica. 'Petra Orff, playing Camilla Martinez, right?'

'Uh, I don't think so. I didn't register. My friend had the invitation and I told him I wasn't coming.'

'But here you are,' Jessica Rabbit smiled. 'He must have registered on your behalf.'

Petra looked at the woman's face. Had she seen this person before? In the gloom, coloured only by this odd, jagged glare, it was hard to tell. Besides, she was wearing thick stage make-up, a wig, false eyelashes. There was no way to tell. 'I just need to go and find him. That's all. I didn't get dressed up or anything.'

And there was nothing weird, Petra told herself, about the fact they knew who she was. In the last few troubled years, facial recognition and SIM proximity tech had become widespread at concerts and sports events. There should be nothing ominous about the fact that they'd recognise her from the previous shows.

'Let me take your phone and your bag, anything you don't want to carry – you know the drill, don't you? – and you can go through and look for your friend.'

If she argued, she wouldn't be let in, but she needed to keep her phone in case Helena or the hospital called. The night she'd so willingly ceded her phone before *Cabinet* seemed like a different life. The man in the tux was helping the next guests in line, and it was only Jessica she had to pass. With a docile smile, she handed her sling bag over.

'Your phone?' Jessica said.

'It's in there,' Petra said, as naturally as she could.

'Right, then.' Jessica Rabbit locked the bag away and turned back to clip a bracelet onto her wrist. She indicated the number stamped onto the wristband. 'You're number 138. You'll need that when you get in.' Jessica smiled a glittering smile. There was a dark stain on one of her incisors; lipstick, maybe.

• • •

As she circulated through the cluster of guests outside the brewery's main entrance, she realised spotting Vincent would be harder than she'd thought. The crowd seemed to be thickening, arriving from God knows where, and milling and shifting in the stark-lit cold. There was no way Petra could scan the faces from a distance, nor could she go up to every guest in the cluster and stare at them without looking truly weird.

She was just a moment short of standing in the middle of the group and shouting Vincent's name. Not very likely to coax him out, but it was going to be her last resort.

Just then, a woman in a teal-coloured satin ball gown, more folies-baroque than Jessica's Hollywood Golden Age, appeared on a low platform outside the doors.

'Welcome, everyone, to the Fallout Ball. If one thing is certain, it is that you will have an unforgettable night. The more you give of yourself, the more you will derive, so please, join wholeheartedly in our celebration. My name is Rashida Barnes and I'm one of your hosts.'

So that was Rashida Barnes herself. Petra found herself battling a wash of star-strike as she craned over the shoulders ahead of her to get a proper look at the woman's face, but it was too dark and she was too far away to make out much detail. It was clear from the shift and murmur that rippled through the audience that there were many other fans here, excited by the knowledge that they were seeing one of the Metamuse founders in person.

'Tonight is our graduation,' Rashida went on. 'The Drama

Society alumni have come of age. It may be the last time many of us will meet, so let us share a final celebration of everything we have created together.' She raised her glass and most of the audience made an effort to respond. Some clapped and some whooped, but it was cold and the teal dancer was the only one with a drink.

'Sharing is caring!' someone heckled.

'Yeah, give us some of that!'

'It's cold!'

'It's only twenty past seven,' someone near Petra reasoned. 'You'd wait outside a theatre until they let you in, right?'

Rashida smiled, unruffled. 'Before we start with our programme, a bit of housekeeping. You, dear retiring members, know them already, but for legal reasons we must remind you. No phones, no cameras, no recordings. Be aware of the emergency exits. Follow any instructions from our ushers; they are there for your safety. I think that's about it.'

'You've forgotten the masks,' someone chipped in. 'We have to keep them on at all times.'

'There is no need for masks tonight,' Rashida said. 'We've been through a lot together. You know us by now, and we know you.'

'Does that mean we can touch the exhibits this time?' a man called.

The dancer smiled aloofly. 'We are all friends tonight. There will be stipulations communicated to you across the evening, only for your own enjoyment and safety.' Behind her, the vast doors began to open. A scattering of cheers came up from the keenest audience members.

Petra could understand their enthusiasm – this was an opportunity to take part in some opulent dress-up fantasy. It was like being a kid again, but instead of a box of old hand-me-downs, they had apparently been outfitted and styled by one of the most expensive costume departments in the theatre world. Instead of a hand-cut cardboard box, they got to play in this Gothic cathedral to intoxicating industry for a night. In other circumstances, she might be whooping along with the fans, but the shadows of Helena's illness and the void Beccie had left in Vincent's soul, the manipulative games Ellis Brown and Olivia Jouval and this elegant Rashida seemed to be playing, hung heavy. Petra didn't even have to half believe Rose Devriendt's paranoid theories to be wary of this place tonight. But what most focused her on her purpose was the way Gloria had gripped her fingers – the warmth, the appeal, the mortifying fragility: find Vincent and bring him home.

'As you've been briefed,' Rashida was saying, 'tonight is a recreation of the glorious year-end Fallout Ball of Beauchamp University's Drama Society in 1981, a significant year to us. Each of you has been assigned a role, and through the night you'll be prompted to undertake certain actions to ensure that our celebration reaches its culmination.'

'Sounds like a locked-room challenge mixed with a murder-mystery party,' a man standing to the left of Petra said.

'Fun, right?' his companion said, taking his hand.

Petra turned to look at the people standing around her, but lit only by the brewery looming over them and sharp white LEDs slanting in from the parking lot, it was hard to make out their faces very well. If she didn't find Vincent in this group it would be even harder once they got inside and started wandering through the massive building. She'd already wasted too much time. It was getting late, and at this rate she was going to miss the end of visiting time at the hospital. Helena wouldn't mind – that much was obvious – but still… Petra should have been there tonight instead of here. But she was here now, and for one reason – not to save Vincent from himself, but to help Gloria, and if the evening wasn't going to be a complete waste, she had to at least do what she had come here to do.

That is, if Vincent was even here. The weird thing was, she couldn't feel his presence. Yes, it was stupid, but she believed that if he was standing in this group of a few hundred people, she'd know it. All she could feel at the moment was a cold absence, an artificial wall being built around her, hemming her in.

She pushed out from the middle of the crowd and made for the brewery's doors, trying to find a way up to the platform Rashida had stood on. That might be her last chance to scan the crowd.

As she approached the stack of wooden pallets and glanced around her, checking if any of the Metamuse ushers would stop her, she felt a touch on her shoulder. She turned to see Ellis Brown; his two-tone suit and fedora would have made sense in the context of this show, he would have looked like one of the cast. But today he was wearing regular casual clothes – jeans, boots and an everyday waterproof coat over a sweater. He pulled the hood further over his head.

'Quick,' he said. 'Follow me.' He took Petra by the forearm and hurried her around the side of the building and into an alcove filled with neatly piled towers of aluminium beer kegs. Ellis drew Petra behind one of the towers and checked to see they were out of sight.

'Why are you here?' he said to her. 'I told you it was dangerous. Didn't you believe me?'

'I honestly don't know what to believe. I'm not sure if I buy the whole murder conspiracy thing, but I'm willing to accept they're using us in some way. I'm not interested in being played with.'

'So why are you here?' Ellis repeated.

'I need to find Vincent and take him home. I tried to stop him but he's come anyway.'

Ellis sighed angrily. 'That was really stupid. We can't save him, Petra.'

'What do you mean?'

'I know he's here. I know he was always going to come. Rashida and Olivia have him where they want him.'

It hurt Petra to have her fears so plainly expressed by this presumptuous stranger – Vincent didn't give a shit about Petra's advice. Once he was tempted by the prospect of seeing Beccie again, there was nothing she could do about it, no matter how she'd deluded herself about their 'fated' connection.

Okay, sure. Of course her pleas would mean nothing to Vincent compared to Beccie – she wasn't vain enough to expect anything else. But what about Gloria's? If she found him and explained to him that Gloria was worried, that she wanted him home, then he'd come with her, surely.

'I have to speak to him. Where is he?'

'Are you sure you want to do this?'

'*Where is he?*' she repeated.

Ellis shrugged. 'He's inside. I can get you to him; I've worked this setup before. But you'll have to get dressed into your costume. You won't get anywhere without it.'

'Why?'

'Each costume is tagged. Doors open, lighting changes, sound, atmospherics – it all works on precise location data. You need it to make your way through the set.'

'But then they'll know where I am. They'll try to stop me getting to Vincent, won't they?'

He laughed. 'I suppose someone *might* be interested in micromanaging your movements, but in case you haven't noticed, there's a show going on. A highly complex and technical performance. They probably won't be interested in stopping you from seeing him. And I repeat – nothing you say is going to stop him. Come with me. It'll be quicker through the back.'

Queueing with the rest of the audience might be the safer way, but she didn't want to waste any time. She didn't know if she could trust Ellis, but still, going with him was her best shot at getting in and out as quickly as possible. She nodded: *lead the way*.

Ellis led her out of the storage pen and hurried her to a back entrance. Petra could hear the rising thrum of the waiting audience around the front of the building, but didn't dare look back as she scurried around behind him in case she caught someone's eye. Here, away from the gaudy light of the public face of the venue, the brewery building loomed heavily, its callused, stained outgrowths reaching up to pull at the sky. A chill wind channelled through cold-brick alleys to the delivery bay at the rear, where headless trailers lined up, waiting.

After pushing open a low door in a vast metal shutter, Ellis gestured Petra in. For a split second she hesitated before stepping over the steel threshold, but she was relieved when Ellis stepped in after her and quietly closed the door instead of slamming it and locking her in.

'We can go through here, I think,' he said. 'We'll link up with the dressing rooms and reception lobby.' Petra hoped he was right – it was ominously quiet in the delivery bay, the silence only broken by their own footfall and breathing, jagged back at them from the bare concrete floor and the stacked pallets of something wrapped tight in cling-wrapped blocks and kegs that dully reflected the standby strip lights spaced around the walls. When they made it across the floor and found the right door, Petra heard the comforting hum of voices punctuated by squeals and laughter – the sound of a party gradually starting up a few rooms away. 'Good,' Ellis said to himself, and this flash of doubt and vulnerability set Petra at ease. It looked like he was telling the truth. If he didn't know his way around this building, he probably wasn't trying to lead her into a trap. But the question still remained.

'Why are you here?' she asked as he paused in front of a riveted metal door. 'Are you still working with Metamuse?' She'd never asked, but after what he'd told her about Olivia Jouval, she'd got the feeling that he had left the group. In all his dealings, he exuded a disgruntled ex-employee vibe.

He turned to look at her. She couldn't make out his expression clearly in the low light, but it seemed open enough. 'I'm here to help you and Vincent. I don't think it's right, what she does. It needs to stop.'

For the first time, Petra wondered if there was some personal history between Ellis and Olivia; a failed romance or a spurning. He seemed to focus his bitterness on her alone, rather than what Olivia and Rashida were creating together. But she had more pressing questions: 'But why now? Why us? Why didn't you help prevent the deaths after the other seasons?'

'I tried. Olivia's persuasive. People do what she wants them to do.'

'What about Rashida? If what you say is true, isn't she just as guilty of orchestrating it?'

Ellis looked down and rubbed his brow. 'She's different. She has... more cause. And she's never been quite as... malicious as Olivia.'

It wasn't a convincing answer, but Petra had no choice but to let it go. He pushed open the metal door into a narrow corridor riven with bundles of high-voltage wiring and PVC plumbing conduits lit by brighter strip lights than the powered-down delivery bay. Glancing left and right to find his bearings, he chose a direction and led Petra further down the corridor, rounding a corner and a subtle jink. Petra tried to remember the route they'd come in case she had to double back this way, but she was starting to lose her bearings. The sound of conversation was louder here, but it wasn't clear where it was coming from.

Finally, though, Ellis drew up at a plywood partition wall at the end of the corridor. 'Yup,' Ellis said. 'This should be it. Listen.'

Yes, individual voices had emerged from the low thrum, and in the silence of the pause Petra could clearly hear a discreet conversation not far from the other side of the plywood, spoken in a language she didn't recognise. There was a metallic clang and a muffled thump.

'Alright.' Ellis's voice was jarringly close to her ear. 'Through there is the staff changing room. If I'm right, you'll find your costume in your locker. You've skipped the queue by coming through the back, so just open the locker matching your bracelet number and collect the costume, then you'll be able to circulate through the electronic doors. If you're quick, maybe you'll find Vincent in the lobby before the arc segments. Good luck.'

'You're not coming in?'

'I can't.'

'You're afraid of her, aren't you?'

Ellis looked away, sniffed.

'Is she really that bad? Do you really believe she made those people die? It doesn't make sense to me.'

'There's a lot you don't know. Just find Vincent and go home.'

Carefully, Ellis pushed the wooden door open and peered into the dark space beyond. Backing out, he gave Petra the all-clear and gestured her through.

22   The staff room lockers were each labelled with a stencilled number on a galvanised door. It was a small room with a couple of benches and bags, coats and belongings slung on hooks between the rows of lockers. Whoever she'd heard talking was no longer in the room.

When she located locker 138, she waved the bracelet at it, releasing the magnetic lock and unclipping the costume bag from the rail. Instead of a luxurious ballgown, there was a waiter's outfit in the bag – flat shoes, black slacks and a white button-down shirt. She swallowed down an irrational swirl of disappointment – she wasn't here to play make-believe, she reminded herself. Besides, throwing this outfit on in order to progress through the set would be quicker than making herself out like a Disney princess or a Home Counties heiress.

The clothes felt and smelled clean, so Petra hung up her coat and switched outfits. The costume fitted her well, and she didn't want to think too much on the invasive scanning that must have happened over the previous two shows to get this right. All this high-corporate technology, these incredible sets, the amazing costumes and styling most of the audience got, supplied for a short-run theatre show – it didn't make sense. How did they afford it? And why go to all this effort and expense for a single night of make-believe?

'Camilla,' someone called as Petra came out of the changing area to a pair of glass doors leading towards the vast lobby. A friendly voice, but insistent. Beyond the doors, the wide floor was chequerboard-tiled, its far end draped over by a broad, sinuous staircase swooping down from the mezzanine level. When the brewery was operating, those administrative offices would have looked down over the busy operations floor, but now the space appeared lifted straight out of a Busby Berkeley set in a Golden Age Hollywood musical. Several gowned and tuxedoed guests clustered around pedestals, nervously trying to get into the mood with coupes of champagne. Jazz piped from somewhere in the wings. Petra almost expected to see a line of chorus girls high-kicking down the stairs.

If she went up to the mezzanine, she could get a decent view of the audience. The lobby was warmly lit and it should be easier to spot Vincent if he was here. She pushed at the door.

'Camilla. Camilla!' It was only when Rashida hurried along the corridor from a darkened alcove, heels skitting skilfully across the hazardous polished tile and stopping right there, that Petra realised she was talking to her. For the couple of seconds she was allowed, Petra scoured her face. If this was one of the incendiary creatives behind Metamuse, surely there should be something supranormal about her, but there was nothing too unusual about her bland prettiness that was lifted by her make-up and styling. For a moment, Petra glimpsed something familiar about the woman when she stopped in front of her, but the recognition dissolved. 'Thanks so much for coming at such late notice, dear. Charlie dropped out at the last minute. He's so bloody unreliable. We're short-handed as it is, and we can't fuck this up. It's an important night. Lots of VIPs – as always at these university dos. So you know what to do, right?'

Rashida was putting on a stagey, public voice, and Petra guessed this was a scripted scene, one of those calls to action intended to get the audience moving in the right direction. She tried to avoid the conversation. 'No, sorry,' she said. 'I think you've got the wrong person. I'm not Camilla.'

Rashida pasted a toothy snarl-smile on her face, threw her head back and laughed. 'Yes you are, darling,' she said, pointing at Petra's chest, where a small name tag was pinned to the shirt pocket. 'You were briefed at check-in.'

Of course she was: outside, Jessica Rabbit had told her what role she was playing. 'Oh, God, I'm sorry.' Petra blushed genuinely. Stuffing up the game in front of its creator. 'I remember now. What do you need me to do?'

Rashida smiled thinly. 'Don't worry. Just go through to the kitchen. Salvador will see to you.' She pointed further down the side corridor. 'Remember, Camilla. This is a great opportunity for you and great things might happen to you. You should try your best.'

Petra didn't know how to answer, so she didn't say anything as she watched Rashida push through the glass doors into the lobby. Once she had disappeared into the crowd there, Petra tried to follow, intending to make for the stairs. She pushed at the door but it didn't budge. A magnetic lock held the top and the bottom fast, a discreet red LED shining on a pad on the door handle.

Shit. This wasn't her route. She'd have to go and see Salvador – the show would only let her advance from there.

Down the corridor, a large glass-fronted room with three massive stainless steel vats on one side and steel worktops along the other was doubling as the kitchen set. Back in real life, this room would have housed some technical stage of the brewing process – the vats were interspersed with blocky industrial machines with coloured buttons and dials on their fronts, and tubes running from them over stations on the worktops. Everything had been wiped down and polished, and the smell of food cooking from somewhere deeper in this area mingled with the persistent memory of yeast and fermenting barley. The room was staffed by a cluster of waiters dressed in the same black-and-white uniform as hers, and five or six white-jacketed kitchen staff. Two waiters were filling trays full of flat champagne coupes and sending others out to serve them, while along another long bench, the cooks were finalising trays of canapes. They were getting on with their job quietly and efficiently, clearly not playacting the part.

'Ah, Camilla. New girl, there you are. Come here.'

The man's voice was loud and dramatically projected – the voice, she was noticing, set the actors apart more than anything. She wondered what the staff thought of her, playing at being a worker while the rest of them did their jobs. Despite this awkwardness, despite her disciplined intention to focus solely on extracting Vincent, she felt a thrill of the immersion kicking in. No matter how disturbing *Cabinet* had been, it was tempting to follow another storyline, play along with this exclusive brand of opulent make-believe. To be utterly someone else for a few hours.

She located the fake chef standing between the two furthest vats.

Don't get sucked in, Petra.

I won't, she told herself. But playing along for now is the only way out into the lobby.

'You're Salvador, right?'

'Correct. Listen, Camilla. We have a special job for you.' He picked up a high-edged teak serving tray from a shelf and handed it to her. On the plush navy-blue velvet lining sat three cut-glass tumblers, an unlabelled squat and square decanter of alcohol, and an ornate silver ice bucket. 'Please deliver this to the VIP in the Club Room.'

23   Petra hurried out of the kitchen, the low, heavy objects on the tray securely balanced. Maybe Metamuse had read her CV, assigned her this role because of her three years' honourable service at Bread and Brewski. She was gratified to see the LED on the door flicking to green as she approached, and the door swung open smoothly as she pushed this time.

She cast around for a discreet place to leave the tray before heading up the stairs to get a good look at the audience, but she couldn't see a table near her. The crowd had thickened. Herded together now and plied with drinks, the guests' quiet nervousness had been replaced by a vibrant buzz. The volume of laughter and lively conversation had been rising subtly, along with the volume of jazzy swing. At last, she spotted an arched recess in the wall with a ledge. She made her way to it, scanning the faces of the people she passed. She set the tray on the ledge and turned – ramming straight into Rashida.

'Careful, now. Don't want to create a scene, do we?' Rashida's unwavering plastic smile was unnerving. She nodded to the tray. 'Our VIP is waiting. Don't you want to meet her? It's a wonderful opportunity for you. You won't get very far otherwise.'

Unable to muster a response, Petra nodded deferentially,

picked up the tray again, and scurried on. There was something scary about that woman. As Petra dodged through the crowd, she thought she felt eyes drilling into her from all around; she imagined her course being monitored from above, her own private arc being charted as she moved. She doubted Ellis was right that they wouldn't be interested in micromanaging her movements – he'd said it himself, hadn't he, that she'd been targeted. She felt singled out for special attention, and anyone here could be Metamuse plants, watching to see if she completed her task, waiting to divert or block her. Finding Vincent was all she was here for, she reminded herself – but sticking to the script for now was probably the best way to do it unchallenged.

Grasping the tray in front of her, she pushed her way through the gathered guests. A guy in a white jacket and puffing at a cigar tried to grab the decanter from the tray as she passed.

'Uh-uh, not for you,' Petra said, swinging away.

'Cheeky cow,' the man said to her back.

'Dave, for God's sake,' his partner hissed.

'Only trying to get in character. I'm meant to be an entitled toff, right? That's what the card says.'

'Yeah, it says nothing about being an arsehole.'

Petra made it to the stairs and ascended the curve to the mezzanine that wrapped around the cavernous lobby, feeling people below watching her, and the unnerving creak and sway of the steps under her feet. Despite how real the staircase had looked, once she stepped onto it she soon understood it was a stage set, a temporary scaffolding of steel tubing and wooden slats covered by lush carpet rather than a sweep of stone and marble. Though it seemed safe enough to hold several people's weight, as she ascended from the level of the brewery's main hall, Petra couldn't help feeling the suck of gravity from the deep empty space below her. She felt like she was climbing the frame of a rickety roller coaster, hastily assembled and veneered for a short-term show. That's what Metamuse was, wasn't it? An elaborate travelling carnival.

At the top of the stair-frame, she gratefully stepped onto the solid concrete floor of the mezzanine level. The corridor that overlooked the lobby below was blocked to her left and right by magnet-locked glass doors like the ones downstairs. In front of her were three half-glazed office doors done up in brass and green baize like saloon doors in a plush, old-fashioned hotel. The patterned and bevelled glass in the door closest to her was frosted, so she could only see the buttery light and indistinct shadows inside. CLUB ROOM was stencilled on a brass plate beside the door.

Petra turned and looked down towards the people below, leaning the tray on the railing and scanning for Vincent. But the crowd shifted and milled, and with their hats and costumes disguising them it was still no easier to recognise him from up here than down below. But there, off to the side – a man not in costume, but in a honey-brown sheepskin-collared jacket, squatting down and fiddling with something under a white-draped box. Petra craned over the railing as if it would make any difference, and felt the bottle shift dangerously on the tray. She grabbed at it to stop it from sliding and turned and squatted down to set the tray on the floor.

'What are you doing here?' someone said behind her.

Petra startled up and spun around. 'Vincent! Thank God.'

She'd been expecting something else. The snapshot she'd been carrying in her mind was of the last time she'd seen him, that night at his house. He'd looked addled then, dishevelled – deep rings around his yellowed eyes and his beard tufty. Half the reason she'd come looking for him tonight was that image of him, helpless and lost. But tonight he looked sharp and clear. He was dressed in an elegant dark-blue suit and his beard was trim and combed, his skin clean and his eyes clear. His lips were dry, though, chapped and red in fine slivers – too much smoking or not enough water – and she perversely took comfort in this small evidence of his deterioration; otherwise, why was she here?

She grabbed his fingers with her left hand and touched her right palm to his face. 'We have to go.'

He frowned at her for a moment, as if he didn't recognise her. 'You're Camilla?'

Petra pulled her hands back as if electrocuted. 'Nuh-uh. No. Don't give me that rubbish. Stop messing around.' Had they brainwashed him, rewritten him, made him forget who he was?

He sighed and rolled his eyes – as if *she* was the crazy one – and pointed to her chest. The name tag.

'Ah, yeah. Who're you meant to be?'

He ignored the question. 'Why did you come here? I thought you weren't interested.'

'Didn't you hear a word I said? It's not that I'm not interested. It's dangerous here. It's a trap.'

'Yet here you are.'

'Your grandmother was worried. She asked me for help.'

'In other words, you came here to rescue me.' He was trying to keep a level tone, but his sneer was nasty. 'God. She stresses for nothing.'

'*For nothing?* That vague note you left. No wonder she was worried.'

'I guess I should have spoken to her before I came.'

'You don't say? You're not very good at written communication, Vincent. Has anyone told you that?'

'Yeah, a couple of people.'

'When I got there, Gloria was actually on her way out to try to find you.'

'Oh. Shit. How would she have got here? How would she even have known where *here* was?'

'Exactly,' Petra said. 'You're bloody lucky I got there when I did, otherwise we'd have another missing person to look for.'

'*We.* Yeah.' Vincent sighed.

'So we need to go.' Petra took his hand and stepped towards the stairwell, expecting him to follow, but he stayed put, his sheer immobility jerking her fingers free. 'Come on, please.'

'Seriously, Petra. You can go home. I'm fine. You can tell Nan that.'

'You still believe you'll find Beccie here, don't you?'

He looked back at her with clear eyes. 'She's inside,' he said, nodding towards the glass door to his left. 'I'm just waiting for my cue and then I can go in.'

'But I thought you understood. That they're just using you. They're trying to draw you in.'

'For what, Petra?'

'I don't know exactly.' It was exasperating, not knowing what to believe. If she could just allow herself to channel Rose Devriendt's paranoid fervour, she could convince him, but it was all a mountain of bullshit, lie on top of lie. If she didn't know how deep the danger lay, how could she keep Vincent safe? 'But what I do know is that Beccie is not here. That's not possible. They're only using your grief to control you.'

'I know they are. I'm not stupid. I wanted to trust in rational sense. I'm not religious, I'm not superstitious. I don't believe in ghosts. But I believe my eyes. When I saw her at *Cabinet*, I doubted myself, but I can prove to you that Beccie's here. Right now.'

'How?'

'She's standing over there.'

She turned towards the glass door where the girl from the picture stood, her ringlets tied back in a red ribbon. The narrow horizontal blue and white stripes looked blood-washed, red and black, in the unearthly glow beaming from behind the door. Her vague smile looked slightly out of focus. She tried to squint her eyes but the photo would not resolve.

'See?' he said.

That's a facsimile of the girl in the picture. She hasn't changed at all. It's a clever projection. Why can't Vincent see that this isn't his living daughter?

Fuck this. 'Gloria's asked me to bring you home, and that's what I'm doing. Come.'

She grabbed his hand again and pulled, and this time she caught him off balance and he stumbled after her. She tugged him towards the main stairwell, not looking down as she felt the attention shift her way, as if she was putting on a scene for the assembled audience.

Vincent was too light, like a hollow model of himself, and she tugged him too hard, tripping on the first step and almost plunging face-first down the swirling staircase. She only just gained her footing, skip-tripping down the first four steps. Gasps below, someone laughing.

'You can't do this,' Vincent said. 'This is not your role.'

'Shut up,' she pressed though gritted teeth. 'Come with me.' There was only one objective, there had only ever been one: find Vincent and bring him home.

But Vincent was right: superhero was not her role.

They were waiting for her at the bottom of the stairs and would not let her pass. She judged Jessica the weakest and tried to push her aside, distantly hearing a cheer coming from the audience, but she felt Vincent lose his grip, and then a twist and a pressure in her arm, and—

24   'I'm still waiting for my drink.'

From where Petra was lying, she could see the stubby dark-wood legs of a squat armchair and a foot squeezed into a gold slingback. Although the toenails had been pared and freshly painted, the foot was callused and worked, squeezed uncomfortably into the ill-fitting high sandal.

Petra's cheek was pressed into the thick emerald-green carpet – an acrylic prickle over the skin of her face and, yes, over the rucked white shirt that exposed her belly. A chemical tang up her nose. White dust like concrete or talcum at the roots of the pile, circulating into her lungs as she breathed. She tried to move, but for too long she found it hard to coordinate her limbs.

As she tried to move her head to look around her, the woman leaned over, stretching her hands into the frame of Petra's vision. Armfuls of bangles – beaded, native silver, Tibetan string ties, hand-painted fabric; nothing suited to an evening ball – cascaded down her arms, gathering at the strong wrists, but oddly, where there should have been a loud jangle peppering the silence, the accessories whispered down like cotton against cotton. Again, Petra tried to move her head to look up to the woman's face but she could barely grunt out a twitch of her neck.

But her right arm was stretched out ahead of her body, and if she just tried, she could touch the woman's reaching hands. The woman bent further down and her fingers came to Petra's. They should have touched there, Petra should have been able to grip on and be pulled, but somehow they missed, maybe because Petra's right eye was squashed into the carpet and she was getting her depth perception wrong.

Once more, the woman reached for Petra's hand and grasped fresh air. She sighed, a heavy sigh weighted with immense sadness. Petra could feel the icy breath plunge onto her face. She straightened in her chair and drew her hands back.

'Help her up,' the woman said.

Someone squatted over Petra as she lay, squatted down and hauled her up under her armpits. 'Don't worry,' he said as he drag-lifted her onto an overstuffed leather couch, 'you'll feel better soon.'

Ellis Brown. She was not surprised he was here. The only surprise was that she had trusted him for one moment. She said nothing – both because she had nothing to say to him, and because she couldn't currently find her voice. But he cracked open a glass bottle of water and poured her a tumblerful, and she was extremely thirsty. Her control was flowing back into her mind and her muscles and she took a deep draught of the water. Along with the sense in her legs, she felt the comforting press of the phone still in her pocket. If they held her here for any longer, she could call the police or Suki to come and get her. But for now, she took in the room, assessing what was happening to her.

The room was furnished like a private parlour in a gentleman's club. Or at least it matched Petra's third-hand image of the parlours she'd seen on Agatha Christie mysteries on TV. Dark wood and green baize, heavy velvet drapes tied back with thick gilded ropes, venetian blinds lowered over the windows. A portrait of a horse and hunter over a mantelpiece, along with a clock that was showing ten minutes past ten. Petra couldn't tell if that was the real time or whether the clock was permanently set to advert time. Again, she resisted the urge to pull the phone from her pocket.

But the veneer of age and establishment wasn't supported by the smell of the room. Instead of dust and must and mildew and ancient smoke and animal fats, the brewery's yeasty funk asserted itself, overlaid by the astringency of carpet glue and printing ink. The cheap plush she'd been lying on, the paper on the wall, had all been recently pasted in for tonight only. The only organic odour came from Ellis Brown's cigarette as he leaned against the wall near the closed door.

The woman. The thought of whom Petra was avoiding, because she was still trying to make sense of her. This was the woman with the shock of red curls she'd seen in the hospital waiting room, the woman with half a face ripped away by a slant of sunlight. She was the woman with the hat and the ponytail she'd seen at the Ragged Boar with Ellis Brown and the group of fake office workers. Petra had only had a fleeting, scalding glance of her on those occasions. She looked at Olivia Jouval in her chair a body's length away, and Olivia Jouval looked back, expressionless. And even though Petra could scrutinise her face for as long as she liked – and she stared for longer than seemed safe – there was nothing identifiable in that blank canvas, nothing Petra could hitch onto if she were to draw her. The features blandly spaced with perfection. The eyes a watery grey, the lips a moderate thickness, the nose symmetrical and unremarkable. Her face was a model vacancy, waiting to be animated – a chameleonic canvas made for illusion. With wigs and dye and cosmetics, she could make herself look like anyone. Tonight, her orange hair was done in a 1981 Melanie Griffiths style, shaved back and sides, bouffed and sprayed on top. The hair elegantly partnered her emerald dress and gold shoes and nails and earrings; the mismatched bangles the only off note.

One thing didn't make sense most of all, though: as protean as this artist was, there was no way she was sixty years old. The smooth run of calf above the strap of her pumps, the taut skin at her elbows and upper arms, the forward push of her breasts against the silk and the smooth, pulsing skin of her neck – no amount of make-up or surgery could drop forty years off a person's body. Because Olivia Jouval looked like the twenty-year-old debutante who must have attended the original Fallout Ball all those years ago.

It finally made sense. 'You're her daughter, aren't you?'

Olivia puffed out a breath of derision. The hairs stood up on Petra's arm. 'You will only believe what you want to believe, won't you? This—' she turned to address Ellis, '— has always been the problem with "art".' Hawking out the word. 'All we do is service prejudices. We're just toadying jesters, entertaining our patrons by confirming their fallacious beliefs, that's all. Do you think we've changed one single mind in all this time?'

Ellis shrugged and took a draw on his cigarette before moving to the sideboard, unstoppering the decanter Petra had carried and pouring whisky. 'I don't think that was ever your aim, was it, Olivia? You've been as intractable as any of them. You do what you want to do, that much is clear.' He raised the glass towards Petra. 'Ice?'

Petra couldn't find her voice.

Ellis clinked two blocks into the glass and stepped across to hand it to Petra without offering anything to Olivia. Her body was cooperating by now, and she took the glass and had a deep swallow. She didn't usually like whisky but this was real – it smelled heady and it burned as it went down, and along with the cold condensation on the side of the glass beading and wetting her fingers, it proved to Petra that this was still real life. Gradually, she remembered what had happened outside this room, before she'd passed out.

As soon as she could trust her limbs to work to the same end, she straightened and stood. 'Where is Vincent?' she asked

'Vincent is with Rebecca,' Olivia said. Now, behind that facade of a body, Petra could discern the lifetimes exposed by this woman's nuanced voice and the weight between her words and the dark aura that radiated from her.

'Beccie is dead,' Petra said.

Olivia's smile dripped with cynicism. 'Yes. And what of it?'

'If you look through there, you'll see,' Ellis said, nonchalantly pointing his own glass at the venetian blind behind Petra, as he lit another cigarette with a cheap plastic lighter whose uric green clashed with the carefully curated stage set.

Petra put her drink down on the carpet by the leg of the couch and went around to the window. She pulled the string and raised the blind, revealing an expanse of plain brickwork that looked like an unadorned part of the brewery wall.

'What am I supposed to see?' She turned around to Ellis, but he was gone, Olivia was gone; the room was gone. Instead, Petra was standing in a low, narrow service tunnel that smelled of wet concrete and gently burning electrical wire. Behind her, bundles of cabling emitted a low buzz like a smothering hornet's nest, and to each side the dimly lit passage receded into darkness. In front of her, though, a window set into the tunnel's wall looked into a gold-lit cave whose walls were hung with racks with gilded lyres and medieval cornets, drums, cymbals and sticks festooned with small bells.

In the centre of the packed-earth floor stood Vincent and Beccie, talking. Vincent's voice was muffled by the window but it was clear that he was having a one-sided conversation. While Vincent pleaded and coaxed, Beccie stood impassively, turning her face occasionally, nodding, touching her cheek. When Vincent stepped forward, she stepped back and wouldn't allow him to touch her. It was a clever effect, yes, maybe performed live from another room, or perhaps with smart AI to react realistically to Vincent's motion, but it was obviously a hologram or a projection. Just as in the pictures Vincent had taken at *Cabinet*, Beccie was blurred around the edges as if they'd developed this hologram from a low-resolution original.

As Petra watched, it became clear that Beccie was on a short, regular loop. Nod, turn to the left, rub right thigh, nod, wipe right cheek... Nod, turn to the left, rub right thigh, nod, wipe right cheek... and repeat.

Why wasn't he seeing it? If she could just snap him out of it, make him see what she was seeing.

Petra knocked on the glass and it reverberated with a heavy, dull thud rather than the hollow sound she'd expect from a window. 'Vincent,' she hissed, aware of her voice carrying in the concrete tube. 'Vincent!' Now louder, hammering at the window.

He turned to her.

'That's not Beccie. Can't you see?' She beckoned in case he couldn't hear – *Come out of there. Come home.*

But his eyes didn't find her. He scanned the window for a moment before turning back to Beccie. A one-way mirror, perhaps. Blended into the fake rocks of the fake cave, Petra made out a doorway behind Beccie. A little way down the corridor, she found a turning that led to the entrance, on this side painted gunmetal grey. In the orange dust thickly layered on the cold, hard floor at its threshold, scuffs of several footprints tracked in and out.

Petra pushed at the door and it resisted heavily, but when she pushed the handle down and shoved with her shoulder, it grated open, an obstinate arc forming in the grit at her feet. From behind, the projection of Beccie was even more rudimentary, clearly made to be viewed face to face. The blue stripes in her sweatshirt seemed to run out of pigment halfway around her back, fading into an obscure silhouette against the bright objects and hidden sconces in the bright Aladdin's cave. Her hair, tied back in a ponytail, was roughly imagined, and her jeans and red sneakers were unpatterned and unlabelled.

Vincent didn't seem to notice her as she walked in and he carried on talking to Beccie. Petra strained to listen.

'I knew it was you, Bec. I would never leave you alone.' He put his hands out towards her, pleading for her to take hold of them, to come into his arms.

She spoke back. While some of her words had the tone and rhythm of English, with some clearly recognisable words included, Petra couldn't make out the meaning. 'There is no kotoba ni shoto for shyurta hodo.'

Vincent paused, mid-stride, wanting to believe that he was seeing what he so desperately wanted to. 'What did you say, honey? What does that mean?'

He waited for an answer that didn't come, but all Beccie did was cycle through her ritual: nod, turn to the left, rub right thigh, nod, wipe right cheek. Vincent tried again: 'Beccie?' Now he spoke to the walls, the low ceiling of the cavern. 'Is there something you want to say to me?'

Petra expected the hologram to stutter through its brief cycle, so when she moved in an organic way, cold fingers shot through her spine. Beccie took a step forward, lowered her head, and spoke back to her father: 'Floribunda selected to manage the script. This number less than two hours.'

'I can't understand you,' Vincent said, taking another tentative step forward.

'Everything was destroyed. The more I try to focus on words, it has become more confusing. We have just retreated from Ukraine. That train.'

Vincent began to cry.

'No, salmon are my favourite molluscs. It was frozen grass, my legs were sick.' The flash of the hologram's autonomy expired then as Beccie went silent and nodded, turned to the left... rubbed her right thigh, nodded, wiped her right cheek.

Vincent advanced, reaching out for her, but the image of his daughter floated back from him, her outline brightening as she blended into the wall, almost as if she was one more of the instruments displayed there. The flickering yellow light reflected warmly off her skin.

As he watched her disappear, Vincent's shoulders slumped. Petra hurried across to him to hold him together, to show him what was real, but as she reached for him her forearm and jaw juddered painfully against a hard surface, invisible in the space between them. The shock jarred through her bones, shooting a rippling pain up her arm and into her skull. Vincent – or really the image of him cast off this surface – wobbled. Wheeling around, Petra saw herself reflected back – several bewildered Petras in a shimmering cave of mirrors, Vincent and Beccie both become invisible in the shimmer. She twisted around, trying to find the originals. Turned once, twice, and stumbled.

Back into the Club Room, Olivia and Ellis Brown watching on, vaguely interested.

'You see? He's alright. He's with his daughter,' Olivia said.

'Alright? Do you call that *alright*? You're playing with his mind.' Her arm and jaw throbbed where she'd rammed them into the glass.

'Ah well,' Ellis said. 'He'll keep, at any rate.'

'Why are you doing this to him?'

'I'm not doing anything *to* him,' Olivia said. 'We were offering him a rare opportunity to act.'

Before she could say anything more, Ellis said. 'We need to go. It's time.'

'Oh. Good,' Olivia said, standing and straightening her dress, pulling the straps of her sandals over her heels. Petra watched her feet, trying to convince herself that she was walking in those elegant pumps across the pile carpet, but there was no clear evidence either way. 'It's almost time for the climactic scene at the Fallout Ball; I'm due on set soon. Then you'll understand why we do what we do. Ellis will take you to your position.'

Ellis came around the couch and pulled back one of the heavy drapes to reveal a small door cut into the panel, the entrance to a secret passage. 'We'll go through here.'

Petra got up and went to him. Any instinct she may have had to run out of the room, down the swirling staircase and out of the gigantic doors and into the night, find her car, go home, maybe find Vincent along the way, was distantly smothered. She knew she wouldn't locate Vincent or convince him to go with her until he was finished; she knew they wouldn't let her just leave the building – she'd tried already, and that was not how this scene worked. Besides, she felt safe to go with Ellis – not once had she felt physically threatened by him, and the consistency of his aloof pretension had mellowed into reliability, something even approaching charm. She believed that any risk was fictitious and designed for her entertainment. And she felt intrigued – sucked deep into the dream-logic of the show by now, she wanted to discover the narrative closure that were being offered to her.

If she just turned and went home, there wouldn't be a story.

That's what she was encouraged to tell herself.

Ellis opened the half door and squatted down, shuffling his way through into the shadows beyond. 'Follow me.'

Petra squatted down and peered into the doorway. From

what she could see beyond Ellis's folded form, into the space that was lit only in a low, gloomy red, the passage was organically carved like a narrow tunnel in a cave. The tepid air inside smelled of deep-dug earth and stale meat. 'Isn't there any other way?' she asked.

'Of course there is, but it's boring.' Ellis shuffled along and rounded a curve.

After looking back at the Club Room – Olivia's chair vacant, Petra's whisky glass sweating into the carpet, the stub of Ellis's cigarette giving up the ghost in the ashtray on the mantel – Petra shimmied into the tunnel, scraping her right shoulder and knocking the top of her head as she squat-hopped to chase Ellis. If there was more than one direction in this passage, she didn't want to lose him.

She managed to come up to a metre behind him, bumping her elbow and hip in the process, but just then he jinked right into a low archway from which most of the red light was spilling. Petra hurried after him, rounded the corner, and ran out of floor.

In her low squat, she wasn't able to balance herself as she fell off an edge of crumbling soil and onto a slick incline. Trying to twist as she landed, she ended up flat on her belly and sliding the three metres to where Ellis was sitting on a simple padded bench at a tinted viewing window, looking into a dining room with several round tables laid for a formal dinner. About a third of the seats were occupied, and couples and groups from the audience were being shown to their places by waiters.

'Oh, sorry,' Ellis said, utterly unrepentant. 'I should have given you a heads-up. Are you okay?'

Petra was lying flat on her face, her cheek scalding and her stomach painfully scraped, and pumped with a blend of mortification and déjà vu. But was there an element of endorphin rush there too? She'd had this sensation before – recently, and long ago as a child swimming in the ocean. It was that first embarrassed, stoked gasp after being dumped and rolled by a huge wave.

'I'm fine,' she said, straightening herself and sitting next to Ellis as he watched the dining room. The brick-walled siding where they sat would have been part of the brewery's original Victorian crenelations, an alcove with some arcane industrial function, but tonight it served as a small viewing deck for two. The thick glass pane was sealed and the close, earthy, yeasty, meaty smell in the small space made Petra think of a peepshow in a dingy strip club. She scanned the walls around the dining room and noticed several mirrored windows framed with antiqued gilt. How many other members of the audience were gathered in these dark alcoves, voyeuristically observing the chosen guests milling around the room and sitting down to their meal?

Ellis took a phone out of his pocket and scrolled. With an autonomic pat, Petra confirmed that her own phone was still there. 'They're a little behind,' he said. 'It's eight and a half minutes until our cue.'

Two couples who had been standing a little way away, their silent conversation and laughter playing out in front of them like a muted film, shifted closer to the mirror. The man in an emerald bow tie flicked around and stared directly at Petra. She flinched backward as he adjusted his fringe.

'Don't worry,' Ellis said softly. 'He can't see us. Shouldn't be able to hear us either if we don't scream. It's loud in there.'

Petra tried to keep her eyes on the man's face as he wiped a crumb off his upper lip and contorted his nostrils to check for residue, but she couldn't help glancing away. It was only when he'd turned back to his party and they'd all moved away from the glass that she would speak. 'All that stuff about exposing Olivia's secrets, the danger you'd get into – that was rubbish, wasn't it? You've been working for Metamuse all along, haven't you?'

Ellis spoke to the glass, his eyes trained forward. 'I really did want to warn you. I hoped you would stay away.' Now he regarded her with a look of tired resignation. 'But I should have known you'd come anyway, that the pull would be too strong. As I told you, Olivia gets what Olivia wants.'

'Why do you work for her? You don't seem to like her.'

'In this industry? If we had to like everyone we worked with, we'd never get a job.'

Petra shook her head, unimpressed with his cynicism.

'Besides,' he continued, 'look at this set, the production technology. It's streets ahead of any other company. It's amazing to be involved with this. She and Rashida pay for the best.'

'That's something I've been wondering. How do they afford all this? How can they even break even on shows like this?'

'Olivia had a good amount left over. She came from a monied family, unlike Rashida. She wanted it all to go into the company. I manage the money for her.' Ellis Brown shrugged. 'I suppose there's not really all that much to do with loads of money when you're dead. Why not fund the arts while you're fulfilling your immortal grudges?'

Petra turned to look Ellis in the face, but he wasn't smiling. 'You all keep saying that. The effects may be great, but she's not dead really.'

Ellis puffed a breath out and ground his jaw. 'You are so bloody stubborn. You're going to miss a lot in your life with those blinkers. I feel sorry for you.' Petra said nothing, so Ellis continued. 'There's that old cliché, but death really does become us. After the Fallout Ball, Rashida muddled along in functional mediocrity all her life, until she died. And look at her now – inciting quite the little flare-up of cross-media interest. You may not like them, you may not like their methods, but you have to admire them.'

Petra sighed. It was her fate to be locked in small rooms with sadly deluded people. She was starting to think she was some sort of weirdness magnet. 'You're all truly expecting me to believe that lithe Rashida Barnes out there is around sixty years old and... or... what? That she's been dead for four years? And that the young woman I saw in the Club Room is the same age as Rashida, but she's supposed to be dead too?'

Ellis opened his mouth as if to launch into an explanation of how things work, but closed it again. He checked his phone. 'We're up.'

25   Two minutes later, Petra was standing on an X marked in matte black tape on a black marble tile beside a vast cold stone hearth. Salvador the head chef had become staff leader here in the dining room, and equipped her with a heavy starched linen cloth to drape on her arm and a magnum of champagne to insert into the ice bucket standing by the fireplace.

'What should I do?' Petra asked.

'Stand by. Listen,' he told her. 'Pour the drinks when asked, Camilla. Do what seems appropriate in your position, that's all.'

Petra was situated at the bottom end of the hall, far from the high table where key characters seemed to be playing a scene in front of a dozen guests who were standing gathered around it. She was much too far away and the lively, lubricated chatter in the room was too loud for her to make any of it out, but she knew it wasn't her scene. They wanted her here, not there, for a reason. Trusting, knowing that she had no option, that her course would be corrected if she strayed, was comforting – it erased the pressure to make a choice. Meanwhile, the lighting had changed at this end of the hall. Any pretence at a real-world dining room had been dropped; bright spots of stage lighting now creating dark eddies and swirling curtains in cigarette smoke and dust, obscuring most of the diners' faces at the round tables in front of her. There were seven guests at each table and it seemed she was responsible for topping up the drinks at the two tables in front of her. Waiters stood by, spaced along the side walls to serve the other tables between her and the top of the room.

Now, almost subliminally, individual voices started to resolve out of the thrum from the table before her, as if they had been amplified. (*They have, Petra.*) A man raised his hand and clicked his fingers. Her cue, she guessed. She stiffened, then turned to grab the bottle of champagne from the ice bucket, and as she did, she felt a pull and pinch on her stomach, the fabric of her cotton shirt tugging painfully at her skin. Looking down, she saw three thin stripes of bright blood scoring the blouse, the grazes from her fall and slide sucking to the cotton. She adjusted the costume's apron to cover the wounds, took the bottle and approached the end of the table now highlighted by a murky blue spotlight.

'Don't know what she's doing here,' the man was saying in an actor's projected tones. He was young, playing a student, but with the tone of someone who had never doubted himself. 'Doesn't seem to be her thing.'

The young woman next to him turned and glared as the blue light came up to full, cold white – it was Olivia, her orange curls and green dress perfectly matching the prawn and avocado cocktail in front of her, her green-painted fingernails like garnishing. 'She's right here, Curtis.' She reached her hand towards the woman sitting next to her. The woman barely responded, looking down disengaged at her plate. And when she finally raised her head into the light, Petra recognised the dancer, Rashida, in her teal satin gown, the most elegant person at this table but crumpling into a void of self-consciousness.

'He's right. I shouldn't have come,' Rashida said to Olivia, looking younger, her voice shy and inflected with a regional accent that Petra could only assume marked her out in some obscure way, opened her up to ridicule by these privileged men.

'Oh, nonsense. You have as much right as anyone to be here.' Under the table, seen only by Petra, Olivia took Rashida's hand. 'Don't listen to them, Ida.'

Ida? Is that where she'd seen the woman? How could this gowned debutante be the same middle-aged woman who'd inserted herself into her mother's life? Could she possibly be the same hollow-eyed woman she'd seen in her mother's lobby? She made an effort to strip away the hair and the make-up, trying to recall the contours, any memorable feature, but like Olivia's, her face was an infinitely mutable canvas.

'Make the scholarship girl talk again!' the actor playing young Curtis Worthing chuckled, looking around the table for support. The resemblance was striking; Petra could recognise the older man in his features. The other night in the studio was still fresh in her memory. Instantly the lights over the whole table came up, freezing the faces around it in an accusatory strobe before plunging them away into the darkness again. Apart from Olivia, Rashida and Curtis Worthing, she'd glimpsed two men and two women. She thought there was something familiar about the blond in the peach off-the-shoulder dress opposite Worthing, but she didn't have enough time before the lights softened and centred on Worthing's end again.

'God, grow up,' Olivia said.

'Watch your tone, Liv.' The mirth fell off Curtis's face and shattered against the stone floor. All that was left was a substrate of cold, hard malice in his eyes, a bitter grey pallor to his skin. 'And you,' he scowled up at Petra, 'refill our bloody glasses.'

Petra fulfilled her part, clamping down her offence. *This is a scene*, she reminded herself.

'Leave the bottle on the table,' young Curtis ordered Petra, 'and go away.'

Petra backed off a few steps and watched as Rashida took a sip of her champagne. 'This is nice,' she announced to the table in a fragile tone. In a studious effort to pretend to give a shit, she drew the bottle towards herself and studied the label. 'Never heard of it. Must be the good stuff, right?' She smiled at the judging panel, getting only blank, appalled stares in response. Petra was mortified, watching the scene; how well the authoritative woman from outside channelled this insecure, fragile girl, who turned back to the label and read it aloud: 'Georges Perpignan Prestige. Hmm.'

Curtis let out a bark like a shot seal and some of the men opposite snorted. 'Purr-pig-nahn. Vehry nars,' the man clutching the hand of the peach blond snuffled. Had Petra seen this actor before? One of the estate agents at the pub, what seemed like years ago.

'That's not how you say it,' the fourth woman explained with a sigh, not meeting Rashida's eyes.

Rashida shook her head, dropped her napkin, which probably hadn't been lying in the right place to begin with, onto the table, and stood, scraping her chair back on the flagstones. 'I'm going to go. I'll see you later,' she said to Olivia. 'Thanks anyway.'

Curtis grabbed her elbow and yanked Rashida back. 'You will sit down,' he commanded. 'This is not a pot luck dinner round your parents' *gaff*.'

Petra could see her jaw grinding, her throat working, and suddenly felt herself fighting back the mortifying tears with Rashida, felt the burn of her eyes and the rip of the skin as she pulled away from him, sending the chair clattering back as she stood. She teetered on unfamiliar heels around the table and past Curtis – who stuck out a nonchalant brogue and sent Rashida flailing, face and stomach grazing across the stone, her ankle twisting wickedly as she fell, turning too far to ever return, twisting and shearing like a bundle of wet sticks, the crackle reverberating across the hall.

The snap was echoed by Olivia's hand striking Curtis's face with a resonant, meaty slap, then the grind and clatter of a chair, a scuffle, before silence.

Every face in darkness now, turned towards the single spotlight in the middle of the floor, where Rashida lay sprawled like a crime scene, her foot pointing in completely the wrong direction.

Lights out.

'So, what do you think?' Ellis Brown emerged from the wings and spoke to Petra as if they weren't surrounded by an audience of hundreds watching on.

'It's awful,' she said, deliberately trying to keep her voice low, between her and him, but the sound of it resonated off the tensely silent flagstones. She'd have to go with it, play her role. 'It's sad. If that's what happened, those guys are idiots, bullies. But from what I can tell, this story hardly justifies mass murder.'

'He shattered Rashida's ankle.'

'Yeah, I'm sorry. If that happened, he's a bastard. They all are. But still... you can't seriously justify killing people for that?'

'That's not all that happened.'

A spot came up in one of the glassed-off alcoves set above the dining hall's floor, illuminating Rashida performing a silent, broken dance that held the audience rapt until the main floor lights revealed an eighties 3-series BMW cabriolet in the middle of the floor, the top down despite the night-time chill suggested by the wavering slants of green and blue lighting. The two couples in the car wore thick coats and scarves. In the back seat, Olivia was tightly folded around herself, pointed away from the young Curtis Worthing.

Still, Curtis had his hand clasped on her thigh. 'I'm sure she'll understand in time, baby. She'll get over it.'

Olivia tried to shift away from him, but there was nowhere else to go. The car's engine was growling, the lights flicking past.

'Slow down, Martin!' the peach-blond woman was saying in the front seat. Nobody was listening. The wind whipped.

'She's in the hospital, Curtis,' Olivia said finally.

'I didn't mean it, baby. But she should show some respect.'

The blond turned in the shotgun seat to face Curtis. She laughed briefly and her mouth stayed pressed into a sour smile. 'You are so blind, Curtis. You do know you'll never have Liv, don't you?'

'Shut up, Audrey,' Olivia said.

'But he's right, you know,' Audrey said to Olivia.

'What the hell are you talking about? Respect? For *him*? Why on earth should she?'

'Watch yourself,' Curtis murmured. 'You need to relax.'

'If not for him, for the club, for the university,' Audrey said. 'She doesn't know what a privilege it is to even be here.'

'Fuck that.'

'Hey. Calm yourself, Liv.' He fished in his inner pocket and drew out a packet of pills. 'Here, take one of these.'

'No. You know I won't take that stuff.'

'Yeah, better not, right,' the driver, Martin, said. 'Remember what happened last time? She went all puffy.'

'It's called an allergy, dimwit,' Audrey told him, training her gaze back onto the road ahead.

Curtis rolled his eyes and picked up a bottle of champagne from the car's cup holder. He opened the bottle in the space between his hip and where the car door would be if it wasn't an open-sided stage prop, and tipped a handful of pills into it without anyone else in the car noticing. 'Have some of this, at least,' he said, offering the bottle to Olivia. 'It will make us all feel better.'

Olivia glared at him but took the bottle, swigging several gulps.

Curtis grabbed the bottle. 'Steady on. Leave some for me there.' Staring tiredly out of the car window, he absently swirled the bottle, dangling the neck between two fingers, dropping it, catching it with his other hand. Finally, he put it to his lips and tipped the bottle, before jerking towards her with a look of alarm. 'Christ, you nearly finished it, Liv. It was for us all.'

But Olivia wasn't listening. Her eyes had rolled back and a stream of vomit was trickling from the corner of her mouth.

'Oh, for God's sake,' Curtis said.

Audrey turned from the passenger seat. 'Stop the car, Martin!'

The lights and wind slowed, a frieze of cold black trees slowed to a halt behind them as the sound of tyres on wet gravel filled the air.

From the wing behind them, the sound of another car slowing and stopping, car doors opening and closing. Footsteps.

'What's going on now?' An American man's accent as the third couple from the table approached Martin's BMW.

'Oh, my God,' the woman said, the one who'd corrected Rashida's pronunciation.

'You'd better help us,' Curtis said.

And as the members of the Drama Society hauled Olivia's body out of the car, Rashida danced.

'I loved her,' Rashida said into Petra's mind, lines for her alone. 'Do you know what that means?'

'More than you can imagine,' Olivia said into the air.

'Take her shoes, her bag, Anette,' the American was saying. 'Wrap them up in this.'

Anette did, gathering Olivia's belongings and wrapping them in her satin shawl. Martin, Curtis and the American dragged Olivia into the woods. Audrey sat in the passenger seat, looking at her nails, muttering, 'God, can you hurry up. It's cold.'

Anette glanced between the receding men and the woman in the car, caught in two minds, the bundle in her arms like a dead baby.

'Are you just going to stand there and watch?'

Blackness. Only the spotlight over Rashida, frozen in an unnatural contortion in her window. Gradually, the light over Rashida faded, leaving the room in darkness for a few seconds, before a spattering of tentative clapping became a torrent of applause punctuated by excited, relieved whoops. The audience rediscovered their voices, nervous chatter at first and then becoming more relaxed as the dining hall's regular lighting came up again.

Rashida was gone and the tables cleared – dinner was over. The guests picked up their glasses and started to wander off to find their next scene.

Petra turned to find Ellis, but he had disappeared too. Shaken, she made her way back up to the Club Room, and found Olivia in her chair, her legs curled under her, waiting.

'It's a horrible story.' She recited the lines she'd prepared on the way up. 'If you felt that way when you were young, if those men were arseholes to you and Rashida, I'm truly sorry.' It was obvious the death and the burial scene was a metaphor of some sort. Olivia wasn't dead of an overdose and buried in the woods; she was sitting right here. Olivia didn't expect her to believe it really played out like that. What she'd seen was just a show, an allegory. 'There's something I need to know, Olivia.' Petra sat so that she could look Olivia straight in the eyes. 'Will you tell me the truth?'

Olivia offered a half-shrug, a half-nod. 'Go ahead.' Petra knew it was the most she was going to get.

'Have you and Rashida… caused the death of someone with every Metamuse season? Someone who was at the original Fallout Ball? Was Rose Devriendt right?'

'In many respects,' Olivia said. 'She was an astute journalist. She had a history in immersive theatre, so she understood. She could cut through the effects and access the emotional intentions.'

'But she didn't understand everything?'

'She didn't recognise what motivated me to come back to life, if you can call it that. She didn't understand that all I wanted was to avenge Rashida. I had given up; I was in limbo, waiting for her. Because of what they did to her, she had to live a long, painful, constrained life, and when she died four years ago she came back to me. We loved each other, you know?'

Petra nodded, feeling the woman's pain.

'They broke her, and over the years I watched her constant, vain battle to heal. She had the potential to inspire, to change lives, but they stole it. That night, they drained all the light from her, and she mourned my loss for all those years. But something magical happened when we were together again. On our own, we would have drifted away to oblivion, but clearly the combined energy of our loss and rage and our will to vengeance...' Olivia stopped mid-sentence and shrugged. 'I don't know. I'm no metaphysician. I don't understand the rules of death any more than the living understand the meaning of life. But here we are. Pretty, isn't it?'

Petra glanced at Ellis to see if he was party to Olivia's delusions – looking to him, of all people, for rational mediation – but he was studiously swilling his whisky and avoiding her eyes. 'In other, fewer words, you're admitting that you killed those people?'

Olivia nodded. 'We got it done.'

'Well, *you* got it done, love. I went along with it, I suppose.' This was a woman's voice over her shoulder. She turned to see Rashida Barnes stepping into the room, closing the door behind her as quietly as she'd opened it.

'How can you say that so calmly?' Petra's eyes flicked between the three of them. Suddenly their numbers seemed daunting, dangerous. 'If what you say is true, you seem to think there's nothing wrong with being a serial killer.' Petra felt herself blush; the words did sound ridiculous now they had been formed.

Olivia turned her hands out and shrugged. 'In the greater scheme of things, there *is* nothing wrong with it. Many of our most lauded public figures are mass murderers. For less justification than ours, I might add. Rashida and I are justified, and – for obvious reasons – we have nothing to lose. You gain a certain perspective.'

'Then why wouldn't you just kill Worthing yourself? Why do you need Vincent?'

'We thought we needed him, yes. But from the first time I saw you, I knew you would do even better. I can recognise what you are capable of.'

It was a moment before Petra could breathe. 'What exactly do you think I'm capable of? I can understand Vincent might have reasons to hate Worthing – and I'm glad he's showing that he won't act on that hatred. He's a good man.'

'*Good man?*' Olivia snapped. 'He has the chance to avenge the murder of his daughter and he doesn't want to take it. To me, that's the definition of a coward.'

Petra felt stung. She'd like to think it was because she was defensive of Vincent's honour, but the truth was that Olivia had voiced a suspicion she'd uncharitably harboured herself. 'Anyway, I've got nothing against Worthing.' A spineless attempt to extricate herself from the whole business.

'Really? You took an instant disliking to him. He symbolises so much unwarranted pain. He defines your own exclusion, your serfdom, your pointlessness. You think you deserve more, just because of who you are, where you come from, but you have *nothing*. It seethes in you, that loathing. You don't admit it, but I suspect it will be released soon.'

'Nonsense. I don't *seethe*. I never had any deep feelings about it.'

'If you say so.'

It was as if Olivia was fingering her way into the seam of her soul and ripping it open. Now that it was exposed to the light, Petra realised the truth. This bitterness had been in her all along; she'd been denying it, tamping it down for so long.

'You want to know why they deserve to die. I understand, Petra,' Rashida said. Her voice was nothing like the snappy dictatorian she'd been playing outside; now it was gentle, nurturing. 'You need a reason to do what you know you're going to do.'

'I'm not going to do anything,' Petra said, standing and shooting her gaze between the three of them, feeling like a bug trapped in a jar. 'You're just con artists, preying on Vincent's grief. Making him believe he can speak to his dead daughter. You're torturing him for no reason.'

Rashida frowned, by the looks of it genuinely confused. 'We're not making him believe anything. He is speaking to Beccie. You saw him yourself. You know, many people would give *everything* for a chance to be with their passed loved ones.

Many people do.' She looked across at Ellis, as if appealing for him to explain. 'Surely there would be a little gratitude?'

'I know,' he said. 'This is what we've been saying.'

From her languid fold on the couch, Olivia sighed. 'We're offering both of you the gift of restitution, all wrapped up in a bow, and this is the reaction.'

'You're offering us nothing! Maybe you believe your own delusions, but nobody can talk to the dead.' Petra stepped around the couch towards the door. All three of them were clearly trapped in their own creation, believing to their fibre the story they'd made up. She was done with actors. She was going home, with or without Vincent. 'You can't talk to the dead,' she enunciated as if to a slow child. 'Because they're dead.'

In his corner, Ellis snickered and then a low giggle bubbled in his chest.

'Ohhhh,' Olivia said. 'Now I understand. You won't believe, after everything we've shown you. You still won't believe.'

'We tried to show her,' Ellis sighed. 'We really did.'

Olivia pushed up off her chair and in a single jolt was up and rushing towards Petra; she smacked into her, or should have smacked into her, but it felt more like a sting of scouring sand on a windswept beach, millions of tiny, sharp particles on her skin, into her skin, through her – and then stopping, the particles falling through her body, into Petra's feet and through her soles into the floor. Petra felt grazed and infected in every cell, every corpuscle and nerve ending itching microscopically, and then Olivia was standing inside her, her body pressed weightlessly into her own, an electric buzz sizzling between them. From inside her skull, Olivia put her lips an atom away from her ear where her cold ghost breath rotted.

'Petra,' she whispered directly into her brain stem. 'You *are* talking to the dead.'

Olivia stepped away, pulling the sharp particular charge with her out of Petra's body and off her skin, like a shear of dry wax from every follicle, and then she was disconnected.

Petra ran, propelled by an explosive aversion in every cell of her body. She'd sprinted out of the room and down the main stairwell before she even realised she was in control of her movements. It was only when she pushed through the main doors of the dining room that the nausea hit, along with a sweat-dousing feverish chill. Propping herself against the tiled wall, she recognised the glass panes and steel vats of the brew room that doubled as a kitchen. She was approaching the room from the far side, and ahead of her would be the main lobby and the way to the staff changing rooms and her clothes, the keys to Suki's car. Hearing a scuffle ahead, seeing a familiar shape, Petra hurried across the echoing space.

'Vincent?'

Was that music up ahead? The sound of a harp?

She followed a short passage towards a brightly lit archway; beyond, she was relieved to recognise the narrow, utilitarian passage where she'd looked in on Vincent and Beccie. A little way beyond, the bronze-lit cave was still shining through the window, and when Petra approached, she saw Vincent standing where he'd last been when Beccie had deserted him.

She rushed into the room, shoving the door through the sand caked on the floor, and then remembered with a twinge in her elbow what had happened the last time she'd reached for him. Was this the original cavern or the one that had been projected to her up in the Club Room? Gingerly she felt the air in front as she slowly approached.

'Let's go home,' she said, testing for a reaction.

His back was turned to her, still watching the space where Beccie had merged into the wall, and finally she reached him, feeling for mirror or brick where there should be a human body – but there was nothing. She touched, and she swore she felt something as her fingers pushed through the shape, which turned.

'Don't let her in, love.'

It was not Vincent who spoke.

'Mom! What the… Why are you here?'

As if in answer, her thigh vibrated with an electrifying shock, a thousand trapped insects in her pocket.

Petra pulled the phone out of her pocket and watched the missed message scrolling up on her screen. An unlisted number.

Text message: <*Petra Orff, please call us urgently. Clarendon Hospital.*>

'Oh, darling. I'm out of time. Don't let her in. Go home now, otherwise she'll stay in your head. Please go home, love.'

But Petra was not listening. 'Mom?' Her mind had stopped working – blanked or overloaded. 'Is that you? How can it be you?'

'Get out.' Olivia was in the room and touched Helena on the temple. Her fingers didn't go through her – they fused, and a greenish light flowed from her and through her mother, and Helena slumped forward, deanimated, before dissolving graphically in front of her daughter.

Mom, I don't know where home is.

26 There were about forty people at Helena's memorial service, at the undertakers next to a kitchen out-fitters in a light-industrial estate in Sydenham. They were people who introduced themselves as members of the arts trust and the soup kitchen and the community garden, parts of Helena's life that had only ever been abstract lines in her weekly report, not real living people who would bother to put on suits and skirts and come to this tawdry funeral shop and cry and smile and squeeze the arm of a daughter they had never met. It felt shaming, wrong and deeply comforting all at once to see her mother mourned by these clusters of complete strangers. Suki was the only person there who she knew.

Apart from Gloria. Somehow she'd found out the time and the venue. She'd only been there a minute, standing at the wall by the exit, talking to a woman with short grey hair and a chestful of chunky beads. She caught Petra's eye and came across to where she was standing alone in the middle of the room, burning her fingers on a saucerless teacup whose handle was too small to get her finger into.

'I'm so sorry for your loss,' she said, gripping Petra's forearm. 'Vincent should have come.'

'How is he?'

'He's fine.'

'So he made it home alright?'

Gloria nodded.

'I'm glad to hear that. I went there, you know. I found him. I told him you were worried.'

'I know. Thank you.'

'I was planning to bring him back to you, but then, well...' Petra gestured at the low-ceilinged lounge, looking and smelling like an anonymous reception room in a mid-budget hotel.

'I know. You're a good girl.' And it was this that started Petra crying for the first time today. It was a presumptuous platitude, but right now she couldn't recall Helena ever saying it to her.

'No.' Petra shook her head, feeling the seven-year-old's pout screwing up her lips. 'No, I'm not. At least, I don't want to be.'

A lot had changed in the past ten days, now that she'd had some time to process what she'd gone through. She'd seen ghosts at Sling Sutton – she'd seen and spoken to Olivia and Rashida, both dead actors; she'd seen and spoken to Helena while she was lying dead in the Clarendon Hospital, fifteen miles away. She knew and accepted this now, like she knew and accepted what she'd had for breakfast and what stock she'd unpacked at Needful Things yesterday. She would have expected this knowledge to remodel her entire philosophy, to fundamentally shatter the certainties of her worldview, but it didn't. It slotted in alongside what else she knew of the world. Maybe she was dissociating, maybe was suffering the precursor of a devastating breakdown, but it didn't feel like it. It wouldn't, would it?

'Do you think he'll be okay? He's not planning to disappear again, is he?'

'He's doing fine, darling – he's sleeping better, drinking less, since he went to that concert. So whatever he went for, maybe he found it.'

'Good.'

Gloria took her hand. Her fingers were warm, callused, slick with moisturiser. 'You should spend some time looking after yourself.' With a final squeeze she turned towards the door. 'I'll get him to call you, but I for one won't blame you if you don't want to answer.'

'I didn't know if you would even be... *here* anymore. You were planning to off yourself, weren't you?' He called her less than two hours later, while she was queueing in the bank for a consultant on her mother's account. It was the wrong place, the wrong time, but her anger at him boiled over. It had never stopped simmering.

'I owe you an explanation, a big apology. But do you really want to talk about it, about me, today?'

'Why not?'

'You know, I thought I could find Beccie again. I thought she was calling me to join her, but I was wrong. She didn't need me there, where she is. She only wanted to talk to me – and to ask me something.'

'So it was really her?'

'Yeah.'

'I wasn't sure what I was seeing. I wasn't sure what to believe. I couldn't understand what you were saying. You were acting weird. I guess I was, too.'

'It wasn't an everyday scenario.' He uttered a laugh, then

quickly extinguished it. 'Jesus, Petra, I'm so sorry about your mother.'

She took a long breath in, trying to control her breathing and avoid tears – but if you can't break down here in a fucking banking hall, then where? She let the polite mask fall. 'It was supposed to be routine. We were just chatting away that afternoon. She was fine.' The people around her were shifting awkwardly, the sour woman behind her glaring at her like Petra's sodden sadness was a burden on her – maybe it was. But Petra didn't care; she carried on crying. 'She was going to be discharged. That's the only reason I went to the fucking show…'

'You went there to find me,' Vincent said. 'I don't know how to apologise.'

'It wasn't your fault,' she said. But was it? She'd thought about it a thousand times over the last ten days. Who would she have blamed if Helena had died while Petra was in her flat watching some shit on TV, which is inevitably what would have happened if she had not gone to Sling Sutton. She hadn't been planning to sit by Helena's bedside that night. There had been no reason to. She would have answered her phone, though. Yeah. But Helena died too suddenly anyway. The arrest had been too quick, too sudden – that's what the doctors had said. By the time they called, she was already dead.

'It's not your fault,' she repeated as the banking consultant called her forward.

When she'd signed the forms and got out of the bank, Petra was hit by a cold squall of rain. She huddled in the doorway of the shut-down bookshop and called Vincent back.

'Did Beccie say what she needed to say to you?'

'Yeah.'

'She didn't want you to... join her there. After all.'

'No.'

Wherever *there* was. Now that she was forced to accept some sort of existence after death, some sort of existence alongside us, she still *couldn't* accept it. The idea of Helena floating about in a karmic migrant detention centre for eternity didn't sit well. In the past ten days she'd devised an idea. She preferred to believe that what she'd seen of Helena was the last flash of her physical energy reaching out to Petra's empathetic neurons. Or something like that. In any case, what she preferred to believe made no difference to what was real, what was true. And it didn't explain how Olivia Jouval and Rashida Barnes were playing a vital part in the avant-garde theatre industry after they were dead. She shelved the questions because the answers still didn't match her worldview.

What was important right now was what Vincent preferred to believe – and to try to engage with him on that level. Whatever she chose to believe, it was *his* metaphors that would motivate his actions – and she wanted to know what action Vincent was planning to take now.

'What did she want? Can you tell me?' she asked.

'She asked me to do something.'

'Worthing.' Petra lowered her voice and pressed her mouth closer to the phone, but nobody hunkering past on the pavement was listening. 'She asked you to kill Curtis Worthing.'

He said nothing – a confirmatory silence.

It all made sense. This is how it would have worked with every other show – find a likely perpetrator, seed the thought… then wait. 'Have you done it?'

'Yeah, right,' he scoffed. But when he picked up that she was serious, his tone sounded genuinely appalled. 'Of course not.'

'Why not?'

'Jesus. Because I don't believe it's what Beccie would really want. You were right – they're using her to get their way, confusing her, feeding her lines. Beccie's not like that.'

'But why not, Vincent? He needs to pay. We could find a way. This is what Olivia wants. And she gets what she wants. She can tell us how to do it without getting caught—'

'Petra.'

'They always make it look like an accident, like a coincidence. If we just get in touch with Ellis, he'll—'

'Petra! Jesus Christ. Just stop, will you?'

After a chastened moment Petra said, 'Can you come and see me?'

A long pause. 'Listen, Petra. I'm sorry to say this now, but maybe I should've said it earlier when I realised…'

'Realised what?'

He sighed. 'It's just that I don't think it's a great idea for us to… I mean, for me to see you anymore.'

'Oh.'

'I think you got the wrong idea. You're great, really, but maybe you took it all more seriously than I could. I tried to tell you that. That I… that I couldn't get into anything serious. With anyone.'

'So it's not me, it's you?'

He laughed thinly, relieved at the apparent offer of levity. 'Yeah. Exactly.'

But he'd misread her. 'You know what your problem is, Vincent?'

'Tell me.'

'You're a fucking coward.'

'Sure. Okay.'

Petra said nothing, which was probably a mistake – it gave him time to draw in a deep breath.

'You know what, Petra? All this time, you've never listened to me. You appear out of nowhere and suddenly you want to take on *my* personal battles. You think through the force of your personality, your entitled, newly woken conscience, you're going to make up for centuries of injustice.'

'Hang on—'

'I never needed you to rescue me. I never asked you for help. I never needed revenge.' He paused, building up the final thrust with a tremor of anger she could feel through the phone. 'I never asked for your reparation.'

'Vincent—'

'So now that we're on the topic, that's *your* problem. You can keep your guilt to yourself.'

He hung up.

27 After what Curtis Worthing had done to him? After what he had done to them both? After Beccie had strained beyond herself to give him one final instruction? Did Vincent even understand how lucky he was to know what she wanted from him? She needed him to do one clearly defined thing, and he wouldn't help her. Some people would give anything to know how to help the person they loved.

So it was up to her, then. And Vincent's rejection made things easier. It forced her to reflect; and he was right. All this time, she'd been pretending to empathise with him, with the injustice in his life, but she now realised her rage was hers. She would have to make Worthing pay. For cramping Helena's creative, expansive life to a point of lightless, hand-to-mouth misery, all to afford care that failed her when she needed it. How many people like Helena had Worthing's greed killed? And all the while, he was blithely having his new sports cars polished and his new houses flipped. He shouldn't be allowed to get away with it.

Of course he didn't directly murder Helena, but they never do, do they? They invented a system that destroys lives and gathers profit. Getting rid of Worthing wasn't going to bring the system down, but he was here, brought into her life, and she had to start somewhere.

She consulted the diagram one more time, screwed the twisted copper end of the live cable into the connector and checked the wire's seating in the jack. She traced the circuit up to the headphone speaker where she'd attached the woven tungsten mesh. She'd taken the overpriced marble Sennheisers from the display cabinet at Needful Things, scoured with guilt. It was the first time she'd ever stolen anything, and no matter how her social justifications kicked in to protect her (nobody would be buying them anyway, the headphones would just be gathering dust, Suki didn't need the money and would hardly notice) she felt irretrievably corrupted. But the moral compromise was the price she'd have to pay – she would no longer be a *spectator*.

She double-checked the bypass on the breaker boards and on the console itself. The trick was to make sure the short circuit wouldn't burn the wiring out too quickly, otherwise all he'd get was a painful zap and maybe some attitude adjustment. You needed to make sure the power stayed on. Wisdom from the internet.

Carefully, she packed the headphones back into their gift box, wrapped it in a plastic carrier bag, stashed it into her sling bag and headed for Brook Street. What she'd do with them when she got there was the missing part of her plan. Olivia Jouval and Rashida Barnes and the entire Metamuse troupe seemed to have vanished without a trace, barely any record that they'd ever been there. What was the point of so elaborately priming her to do this deed for them, but then disappearing at the critical moment? She hadn't managed to conjure Ellis Brown for advice. Ida hadn't turned up at the funeral, of course. Petra was on her own. She had no clue whether Worthing would even be coming to the studio today, but action needed to be taken.

Ridding the world of Curtis Worthing would redress evil, she convinced herself on the walk over. Why couldn't Vincent see this? She would do this for Beccie, for Helena – for everyone who'd been processed by Worthing's profiteering system and not come out again. She would help lay all their spirits to rest.

On Brook Street, before she could think any more, she went straight for the red door, trying the knocker first, its welded solidity jarring her fingers. She prodded the call buttons on the keypad and, not hearing any answering buzz or motion inside, hammered on the wood with her knuckles. No response; her showdown wasn't going to happen. If she scurried home, tail between her legs, she would deflate, be gnawed at by the failure, the pointlessness, her lack of any capacity to act. This was what she was here to redress: powerlessness. A decade's worth of being made invisible by a hostile system, the diminishment of her creative, expansive mother to zero by this relentless, abrasive status quo. Worthing was a human point of contact in this murderous system and she had to carry this through.

She'd wait.

Feeling exposed to the channelled wind and squalling rain and the watching eyes out on the pavement, she let herself in through the unlocked garden gate around the corner and took up a position in a small, neglected gazebo at the bottom of the garden. Although the previous night's rain had deposited another layer of slick, cold leaves onto the sludge on the sodden wood, Petra sat flat onto the floor and hugged her knees to her chest, watching the window. It was around noon but under the overcast sky it might have been dusk, and the studio was dark. A rat poked through the garden fence and rooted around the base of some cheerless daffodils as Petra pulled out her phone and looked at Vincent's name.

She thought better of it, huddled in the cold and waited.

For the past several days, she hadn't allowed herself to think beyond the double death of her mother, and the immediate ripples of the manipulative shocks she'd experienced at the Fallout Ball. But now that she had the time and the silence, she started to consider Olivia and Rashida's story, to humanise the monsters. Petra had quit denying that it was all true; it was easier to just give in and believe: the women were dead, their story was a tragedy. She imagined them as young women, the hope of a future laid out before them: Olivia from the complacent classes, and Rashida having grafted her way to her awkward place at Beauchamp. They would have fallen viscerally in love, a difficult truth in those bitter, judgemental years of arch conservatism, but they would have found light and inspiration in each other. Only to have it broken by some entitled men, acting just as entitled men were always trained to act – diminishing and crippling creativity and idiosyncrasy. Worthing and his friends had killed their love and their potential, and they deserved what they got.

She thought of the love between Rashida and Olivia; a love so powerful it resurrected them. Petra would give everything to love like that. She could understand how their love had led to murder; the boundary between a transformative love and furious malice was surprisingly porous.

A dark while later a light came on in the depths of the building – someone coming in through the front door. Petra straightened, made sure she was out of sight, and watched the studio window. A minute later the lights came on there, blaring out a warm yellow over the forgotten garden. A man came into the room and stared around the space. But it was not Curtis Worthing. This man was young, wearing a zip-up hoodie under a red coat, rough black beard, long hair held back with a blue headband.

No.

This was not how the plan should go.

When the man had disappeared from the window, Petra stood and wiped her jeans off, quietly heading for the gate, but when she heard the squeal of old wood she froze halfway across the lawn. The man tapped on the window, as if he was hoping to be let in.

'Hi,' he smiled, relieved, probably, that Petra wasn't a threat to him. 'Can I help you?' A magnanimous question to a soaked and addled apparition in your own back garden.

'Hi, um…' She thought on her feet. 'I'm a friend of Francis Picton's and he was giving me a tour of the studio this morning and I left my bloody house keys inside and I only realised after he'd left and…'

'Francis gave you a tour?'

'Yeah, I'm really sorry. He's been telling me all about the studio and I'm a huge fan of Rovotune especially and, well, he said Mr Worthing wouldn't mind.'

'I'm sure he wouldn't. It's not a problem. Really.'

'Are you Mr Worthing?' she playacted.

'Oh, God no. I'm, well, I'm his son. I'm James. My father's Curtis Worthing – he's just bought this place. Picton works for him and has every right to come and go as he wants. And bring guests, too. But please, come around to the front and I'll let you in. You look frozen.'

Petra collected her bag and found the garden gate. By the time he opened the front door for her, James had found a big towel somewhere and Petra was grateful for it. As she tamped her hair dry, it felt like she was wiping off the thin, manic veneer of vengeful malice too. She tried her best to hold on to it.

'How long were you waiting out there?'

'A while. I phoned Francis and he said he'd come and let me in but he had a couple of things to do first, and I didn't want to wait on the pavement outside in the rain. I hope you don't mind?'

'It's fine,' James said. 'I'm just sorry Picton left you there.'

'Thanks. Do you mind if I just go and get my keys? I remember putting them down in the studio.'

'Sure. I'll get the kettle on. Coffee or tea?'

In the studio, Petra surveyed the headphone jacks alongside the recording booth partition and thought about what she had been intending to do.

'What are your plans for this place?' she asked.

'Well, of course we're looking to start up the studio again. My dad got this great console for a steal. He's converting a couple of flats next door, and upstairs there's loads of space. We could bash out the front wall, make it into windows, change the wood, make it really light. Japandi, you know?'

Petra nodded. She didn't know.

'Dad said he heard someone saying something about art therapy. He put on a strangled accent. "Good way to keep underemployed creatives busy," he said. That could be a wheeze. People will pay good money to soothe their darlings' bruised emotions.'

'Art therapy?' A wheeze. Right.

28   Suki's pain pills were helping. As Petra doodled on a pad at the counter, she sensed the stabs of embarrassment and shame and fear and the fathomless, sucking ache of loss becoming blunter. They kept ambushing her, appearing out of the mist, but right now they sank back again without causing too much harm.

Thank God she'd been careful yesterday. It was luck that James had found her, not Worthing; she hadn't gone to the studio with a plan, but things had resolved themselves. She worked to retain the thought processes that had led her to the studio yesterday, that had led her to think it would be the right thing to electrocute a man for a generalised sin that wasn't directly against her. What had prompted the stupid idea? She concentrated on remembering herself, giving voice and validation to her pain, instead of brushing it off like she had all her life. She was mourning her mother. It was bound to hurt; she was bound to act emotionally. She had every right. Being rejected by someone she thought she really loved was just the dusting on top.

A beam of rage scorched through the haze. '*Art therapy*, can you believe it?' Petra called across to wherever Suki was. 'That was *Vincent's* dream. They obviously heard it from him and jackdawed it, or magpied it, or whatever the hell you call it.' Only now she glanced up to confirm there were no customers in. 'He could work all his life and not have the capital to set up his own practice, but people like the Worthings can just dabble, they can set up a little side hustle for a *wheeze*. A fucking *wheeze*. Like he's a kid in the bloody *Beano*.'

Suki appeared from the back office with a cup of coffee. She leaned over to look at the portrait that was resolving out of the swirls and curls on the page. 'That's nice.'

And it was – no scars or slashes or rips in the skin, no fluid oozing. Just a pretty girl with light in her eyes. Maybe Suki's pills were helping. Petra let a long breath out.

'You know you don't need to be here,' Suki said.

'I really want to be here,' Petra said. Here in the familiar surroundings, Petra's life was beginning to feel manageable again, just about under control. She hadn't told Suki that she'd gone to kill Curtis Worthing, but she'd told her almost everything else. About her mother's death, how she imagined she'd seen her at the show, about Falling Guy and his daughter. She didn't know why she'd battled alone for all this time after her mother died, why she hadn't come straight to Suki, basically her only real friend.

Yes, she did. She thought Vincent would be there for her. She thought if anyone in the world would understand what she was going through, what she'd seen, it would be Vincent.

That's why she couldn't bring herself to tell Suki how Falling Guy had snubbed her, made her feel like a teen stalker obsessing after a one-night stand. It fucking ached.

'Can I bring you anything to eat? There are some Maltesers stashed somewhere, I think.'

'You wouldn't know because you don't touch human food yourself, of course.'

'Exactly. Wine? Another Diazepam?'

'I'm good for now, thanks.' Petra's tentative smile froze when the shop door chimed open.

Instinctively, Petra stood up and stepped across Suki, shielding her from the man in the doorway. 'I don't think you're welcome here.'

Freddie hesitated, glancing around him like a rat in a spotlight. His hand was suspended mid-motion, the door half open and a cold breeze rushing through.

Petra took three steps forward, remembering how he'd locked the door last time. If he tried that again, she'd need to push by him, make sure that door stayed open, get out onto the pavement, yell for help.

'Go on,' she said. 'You'd better just leave.'

Freddie's eyes twitched from her to Suki behind her and down at the floor. 'Wh–what?'

Petra felt Suki's hands on her shoulder, gently, firmly directing her back to her stool. 'Come in, Freddie! Don't worry. Our darling Pet's under the weather. Hasn't been herself the last few days, has she?' She advanced towards the man, ushering him in and closing the door against the weather behind him. 'Come in, love. We've just got a new shipment of *Black Panther Party* and *Dragon Age*. Go have a look. You're welcome.'

Any offence he may have taken from Petra's weirdness was smothered by Suki's unwarranted warmth, and he sloped off to the bookshelves.

'What's that all about?' Suki asked Petra quietly when she got back to the counter.

Petra glared at her. 'You're telling me you're totally over him smashing up the shop?'

Suki was incredulous. 'Who? Freddie?'

'I'm not totally losing it, you know.' Freddie studiously pretended not to be listening, flipping a comic's pages idly through his hands.

Suki sighed and put her hand on Petra's arm, stopping just short of patting her. 'It was a horrible incident,' she said quietly. 'Very frightening. But we spoke about it then, didn't we?'

Petra remembered that they were both badly scared, but Suki was clearly over it, and Freddie was acting like the incident had never happened. 'You're telling me it wasn't...' Petra stopped talking and tried to replay the incident.

'That arsehole won't dare come back here, I'm sure,' Suki went on. 'And if he does, we'll call the police straight away, alright, Pet? He was just a nutter. You can't take it out on poor Freddie, though.'

Petra had been so sure it was Freddie, but now that she thought back on it, she wasn't sure why. He had different clothes, a totally different manner. She'd have to let it go.

Suki slid in behind the counter and propped herself on the stupid stool, and suddenly it made sense. She looked like someone in an advert for designer stools, perfectly poised; the black patterned fabric of her skirts draping in a dynamic swoop to the silver and black thrust of her boots, unifying with the jewellery and tattoos on her bare arms. 'Guess what I got this morning?'

'Tell me.'

'An invitation from your man.'

A brief jolt of hope sparked and sputtered. Suki wasn't talking about Vincent. 'Which man is that?'

'Curtis Worthing.'

'Huh? An invitation? To what?'

'To his birthday party on Saturday, at Brook Street Studios.'

Petra jerked upright. Any last remnants of opiate mist that hadn't been dissolved by Freddie's return were now ripped away. 'Christ, Suki. That's not right. It has to be her.'

'Who, love?'

'Olivia Jouval. Why on earth would Curtis Worthing invite you to an event, here, now? In the place where Vincent and I... It's a setup. It's a trap.'

Freddie couldn't help glancing around at this.

'*Calmez-vous*, darling. I always get invited to these things; a certain middling circle of the well-heeled in the shires. Normally, I just never go. Come with me. I think it will be good for you. Asked around some more; turns out Curtis isn't such a bad old stick. Something of a moral conscience. Quite the socialist compared with many. Come on, Pet – promise me you'll come.'

'What? And go to that bastard's victory party? I may be all over Falling Guy, but I'm not that bitter.'

Petra might be slow on the uptake, but it clicked eventually. Of course she would, and of course she was. The opportunity was serendipitously presenting itself, just as she knew it would, just as Olivia would arrange it.

The cheerful green and blue logo of MyHealth on a letter addressed to Helena changed her mind. A bill for her final hospital procedures. As the initial treatment was logged as an outpatient procedure, and the in-patient accommodation and further surgical interventions were not preauthorised, the patient was subject to penalty payments as stipulated in the hospital-only tier of her medical insurance. Please settle immediately and seek reimbursement direct from the Clarendon Hospital.

It wasn't the money that irked her – though just how the hell she was going to pay this bill was a question she would have to grapple with later – but the fact that the letter had landed on Petra's doormat.

They *knew* she was dead. The fuckers knew Helena was dead and yet they'd addressed the bill to her. They also knew that Helena was no longer in her dingy little flat and knew exactly which other tiny flat to come knocking at for their debt.

They knew Helena was dead, and still they'd addressed the letter to her. They would reach out and strangle her, even in her eternal rest.

They being: Directors: Mary Franklin (US), Roberta Johnson, Marc Peterson (US), Gary Schindler. And Curtis Worthing.

The choice was out of her hands, she felt. Any last qualm affecting her dissipated. Besides, she had precisely nothing more to lose.

The house on Brook Street was glittering when Suki and Petra arrived, golden lights and a gentle thrum emerging through the triple-glazed windows. In the commandeered residents' parking area of a Regency terrace, a man in a sharp tuxedo and a woman in a navy-blue dress and velvet coat stepped out of a burnished, low-slung car. They hurried across the road, the street lights etching the rain in jagged lines through the plane trees' bare fingers, and were swallowed into the red door.

When Suki had pressed the intercom button and uttered something in her low tone and they'd been admitted to the house, Petra couldn't help feeling a little disloyal to Vincent and Gloria and Max's memory. Because this was the way this beautiful space was meant to be celebrated. It was like a scene from an opulent movie set in a time and a place where the world didn't matter – elegant people spritzed with understated wealth, sophisticated lounge jazz resonating richly through the walls like the house itself was an organic instrument, gold and copper and bronze party lights twinkling in soft focus, the clink of crystal and laughter, the smell of fresh-baked vol-au-vent and something roasting. As she hung her coat and hefted the gift she'd brought, beautifully wrapped in gold paper and spangled ribbons, Petra felt like she'd been invited to Nigella Lawson's Christmas party.

She smoothed the electric-blue jersey of her dress down her thighs and checked the ruck at the waistline, trying not to compare her clothes with those of the other women. That was like going to the zoo and envying the tiger's stripes. Beside her, Suki was in skin-tight black trousers, massively bulky biker boots and a black shirt, waistcoat and tail coat, drawing any critical looks away from her. But the temperature was just right inside and the smell of cooking and the mellow music – and a couple of Suki's tranquilisers – were all helping to keep Petra relaxed.

Petra trailed behind Suki, meeting the faces of the guests as they made their way deeper into the house. She half expected to see a flash of orange hair, felt a spurt of adrenaline bubble up as she imagined someone cornering her with a cue. But this was the real world, she reminded herself. She didn't have to play a part, she didn't need to make a good impression.

She was standing among a tight knot of people in a lounge that had been decorated like a ragtime nightclub, her fingers loosely draped in Suki's hand and staring at the framed prints on the wall – black-and-white streetscapes of Paris and New York and Tokyo – when Suki drew her towards the bar counter at the edge of the room and she heard the familiar voice.

'What can I get you?'

'Vinnie, darling! There you are.'

'Heya,' Vincent said. He was wearing a suit with a white-banded fedora that he might have borrowed from Ellis Brown's collection. Suki was stretching across the drinks table to grip his face and kiss him on both cheeks. Defensively, Petra held the gold-wrapped box in front of her.

'Snazzy getup,' Suki said.

'Yep,' he said, twisting his lips. 'You know how it is. I've been asked to wear worse.' And it was only now, as he shifted his view, that he recognised Petra. 'Oh, hi.'

'Hey,' she said. 'Do you two know each other?'

'Yeah,' said Vincent. 'We've worked together. On and off. For a long time.' Suki was checking the glance between them.

'*Oh. My. God.* This is your falling man? Our Vincent?'

Petra blushed. Vincent's eyes dilated. She could swear on it.

'The way you described him, I could have sworn you'd fallen in love with Adonis.' Petra crushed Suki's fingers. 'Not this battered old model.' She paused, staring at each of them in turn. 'But, fuck, it makes sense now, doesn't it? This calls for champagne, I think. Coincidences always indicate the opening of a new pathway.'

'I won't have anything, thanks,' Petra said.

'God, darling, how insensitive of me. That's thoroughly inappropriate, given your state of mourning.'

'Christ, Suki,' Vincent said. 'Always so bloody tactful.' He darted a look at Petra, the dress highlighting what he'd given up, and looked away.

Suki didn't pause. 'But it might help, you know. Coming out, letting yourself forget your troubles for a while. I see Curtis is offering Georges Perpignan – lovely choice. You can't say no to that, surely. Leave that behind the bar,' she said, indicating the golden gift. 'Vinnie will look after it, won't he?'

For some reason, it sounded like a good idea. If some unpronounceable alcohol would re-establish that padded feeling of peace she'd just enjoyed, what the hell. She shrugged and Vincent poured them two glasses. Suki grabbed the bottle and led Petra through the kitchen and out to the back garden where a marquee had been set up, warmed with space heaters. It was fresh and calm out here, barely recognisable as the neglected patch where Petra had sat on her murderous vigil just three days ago. Apart from a couple of smokers on the back step, there was nobody else out in the garden. Suki and Petra sat in a couple of the cushioned garden chairs under the marquee and Suki topped up her glass and proffered the bottle towards Petra.

Petra shook her head. 'How do you know Vincent?' Petra didn't believe in coincidence anymore. This last month, she'd been yanked around like a marionette. A gullible, naive fool playing a part in somebody else's game. She would have just walked away from it all – the game had nothing to do with her – only it had sucked her mother in, and now she had nowhere else to go.

'I've known him for several years. He's a collaborator in Line Logistics. He's a documentarian. All the images on the website, that's him. And lately he's been doing overnight research – ever since poor Beccie, he hasn't been able to sleep at night. But it blows my mind that he's your man. I mean, there's no reason you shouldn't like him – he's lovely. But what are the chances?'

'That's exactly what I'm asking myself. Are you expecting me to believe it's just a coincidence that you know him? Why didn't you say anything?'

Suki put her hand on Petra's arm. 'I had no idea, darling. How was I supposed to guess? You never mentioned his name. You did tell me he was a photographer and an oddjobber, true, but there are plenty of those in this town.'

Petra scrutinised Suki's face. In all the years they'd known each other, Suki hadn't lied to her. She didn't lie. If anything, she erred in stating her truth too bluntly. Petra sighed. 'Okay. Still, it's very weird. Anyway, if you're besties you'll know that he dumped me.'

Suki frowned. 'Silly man. We're not that close. Not the full-frontal-personal-details sort of acquaintance.'

'But you know about Beccie.'

'Yes.' Suki stared out into the garden, at the run-down

gazebo in the shadows, with an expression so unguarded it unsettled Petra. Autonomously, she took a sip of her champagne. 'Well, as much as he's told me.' She put her hand on Petra's forearm and squeezed. 'Things aren't always as haphazard as they seem.'

As Petra opened her mouth, still processing an unformulated response, but they were interrupted by two men entering the marquee. Suki stood up and Petra turned.

'Susan, it's good of you to come.'

'I wouldn't miss it,' Suki said, kissing Curtis Worthing on both cheeks. Next to him, Francis Picton put out his hand and Suki shook it. Petra stood, shielding herself beside Suki's shoulder so she only needed to nod at Picton. She knew he wouldn't recognise her.

'Miss Orff.' Worthing turned to her. His eyes were soft in the gaslight and the lines around his eyes made a good impression. 'I'm desperately sorry to hear of your mother's passing. If there's anything I can feasibly do, anything at all, do reach out.'

Instead of saying the first several things that came into her head, Petra nodded and blushed, the docile citizen consumer in the face of imperturbable power.

When Worthing and Picton had gone back towards the house and were greeting the smoking guests on the stairs, Suki said, 'That's nice, isn't it?'

'It sounded very nice, yes. Very authentic. Just like the well-schooled men on the Parliament Channel. You're taught Convincing Authenticity in your upper-class debate clubs, aren't you?'

'Yes, darling. Yes, we are. Let's go inside.'

'I still don't understand why Vincent works for him,' Petra said as they walked back to the house. 'He could do odd jobs for anyone else.' She paused. 'For you, for example.'

'He doesn't work *for* me, Pet. He works with me.'

Inside, most of the guests were gathered in the studio, where Picton was on a small stage near the control-booth window, tinging a spoon on a champagne glass. The thirty or forty guests crowded into the rehearsal room settled down to a murmur but still there was a lot of noise from the other rooms in the house.

Picton tapped the microphone and yelled into it with an air of joviality that didn't do enough to hide his aggression. 'Oi. Oi! Keep it down.' He was answered by laughter from another room. 'Shut it!' He spotted one of the catering crew at the studio door. 'Get that bloody music off, would you.'

Tapping the mic again, enjoying the rich sounds he was making, he put on a drunk-karaoke baritone, pressing his lips to the mesh. 'It's time to hear from the man himself. Our good friend, without whom none of us would be here...'

'Clearly,' Suki murmured.

Now Petra turned to shoulder her way to the door. Suki sent a *where-are-you-going?* frown after her and Petra replied by holding up a *just-a-moment* finger.

'The one, the only, birthday boy, twenty-one again, let's give it up for Curtis Worthing!' Gripping his emptied glass and a knife, he tried to clap into the mic as Curtis Worthing stepped up onto the dais. Petra glanced around the room and noticed James Worthing standing by himself in the furthest corner of the studio, near the window she'd climbed through the other day. He was wearing jeans and a stylish casual jacket over a T-shirt, a small circle of space carved out around him. When he noticed Petra looking at him, he raised his beer bottle towards her with a smile.

'Thank you, Francis,' Curtis said. 'It's good of you to arrange this, and good of you all to come. I don't want to spoil your evening with speeches. Tonight is just a small acknowledgement of a significant milestone. As you know, now that I'm of pensionable age, I'm winding down my involvement in the MyHealth group. I'll be leaving the company in good, strong hands and in rude health.' Applause from the crowd. 'While we never forget all the sacrifices that have brought us to this position, I pride myself that I have helped build a company based on care. From just a few hundred employees when I came on board, to a public-traded corporation of over a hundred and twenty thousand dedicated employees – all with the nation's health in our hearts.' He paused to tap his palm against the left portion of his chest, to another round of applause and some hearty whoops. 'Now it's time to reap the rewards of that rather single-minded period of my life.' Here he raised his glass towards James at the back wall, who responded with a gracious nod. 'It's time to spend this next season of my life on some things that really matter to me. I plan to travel the world and see beyond boardrooms, and at the same time I'm coming home, and this beautiful house will be a part of my home base. Thank you for helping me celebrate it in such a fitting way.' He raised his glass. 'Now, for the love of God, Francis, please get that music back on.'

As the applause rose, Petra made her way to the stage with a brightly wrapped object in her hand. Vincent had trailed her to the rehearsal room and was watching from the doorway. Petra found Suki's eyes in the crowd and offered her a nod and a small smile. Francis Picton swerved in front of Petra with a sour glare, but after Petra said something close to Picton's ear, he took the package – it was the gold gift she'd been carrying – and stepped up to the microphone next to Worthing.

'One more thing. Hang on, one more thing, everybody. As you know, this is not just a birthday party and a housewarming party and a homecoming party. It's also the official reopening of the Brook Street Studios, which were quite famous in their day. Soul music and so on. I know one of your retirement projects is to make it a going concern again. This, apparently, is a gift to help Curtis inaugurate the studio. State-of-the-art audio equipment from a fellow music-lover.'

At this, loudly enough to be heard through the whole room, with a striking, calm certitude, Petra said, 'Happy birthday, Mr Worthing, from all our families.' She turned and found Vincent's eyes, making sure to hold his gaze for one last time.

'It's heavy,' Curtis smiled and tore open the wrapping, setting the box down on the stool next to him and opening the lid to reveal a pair of luxurious-looking headphones in a marbled case. 'Beautiful,' Curtis said.

'Wait. Stop,' Vincent said, trying to push into the room, but nothing did.

'Sennheiser Orpheus,' Petra said as Worthing slid the phones over his head. 'Eight valves. Carrara marble chassis. For the man who wants to be famous.'

Worthing unwound the cord and handed it to Picton to slot into the headphone jack.

It all happened too fast for anyone to save him. But Petra had time to look around to James, who kept leaning against the wall for several slow seconds, watching with a disembodied interest, before moving through the screaming, jostling crowd. It was too late, anyway – Curtis Worthing was dead before he hit the floor, before the acrid stench of melted plastic and burned hair and singed skin had wafted through the air into Petra's face.

One struggle resolved itself against the uncoordinated flurry of people scattering out of the studio and clustering around Worthing's body: Petra in her electric-blue dress being manhandled by Frances Picton. She was trying to slip through the connecting door into the control booth and Picton was yanking her back, one arm around her neck and his other hand grabbing at her hip. Vincent was there too, scrabbling at the back of Picton's jacket.

Petra aimed an elbow into Picton's gut and raked a heel down his leg, gaining enough traction to make him let go. She shimmied out as Vincent delayed Picton for just a couple of seconds, before Picton planted a vicious punch in the centre of Vincent's face and sprinted to catch up with Petra. 'Come back here!' he was yelling, louder even than the noise of the panic.

The passageway to the front door was blocked with party-goers finding their phones and their keys and their coats – the animal fear already settling into an organised, genteel, self-protective evacuation – so Petra hared up the stairs, only half aware of Picton and Suki and Vincent thudding along after her. Outside, slamming doors, the hiss and the growl of expensive cars vacating the scene.

She made her way up the stairs and stopped on the landing, casting left and right for a clear route, and finding an empty front room. Quietly, she closed the door. There was no furniture to barricade the door, so she simply backed away and waited in the empty room tinged blue with stark light from outside. Petra in her blue dress in the blue light. The scuffling rattle below had stilled, the chasing pound of feet gone off the opposite way then dying. The few seconds granted Petra stretched unnaturally, but not long enough to think anything appropriate. Now, the careful creaking tread and low, urgent voices approached.

The sash window ground open with a resonant shear, and in answer she heard the footsteps shift and turn, Suki's heavy, hard-heeled boots among them, a comforting *clunk* she'd heard so often in the shop without even realising its familiarity. Petra was glad Suki was here, at least.

And it was Suki, bless her, who pushed the door open, peering inside, taking one tentative step towards Petra by the window, before she was shoved aside by a pounding and incoherent yell, a heavy, grappling shape bursting the air behind her. Gasping, Suki pressed herself against the wall as it bundled past, like an underground trackwalker avoiding a hurtling train. The wrecking ball of noise and energy was Picton and Vincent wrestling and writhing their way from the stairs and chasing into the front room.

'Petra!' Vincent called. 'Look out!'

Picton had got out of his grip, and he was weasel fast, already slamming through the door and grappling at Petra's blue form as she worked the sash window up.

They sped towards her, the three of them – Picton, Vincent and Suki as they saw her perched on the sill, looking for a safe way to get down.

'Stop!'

'Don't!'

'Hey!'

But all their shouting and their muscling couldn't change the fact of gravity as Petra flinched and lost her grip on the slick sill and plunged through the air out of the window like a shimmer of ghost lightning through the sodden sky.

Petra fell precisely where Vincent had fallen just forty days before, on the hard tar, but she fell less kindly.

DEATH IN THE STUDIO

SHOCKER! Medical magnate electrocuted to death by his OWN present at LAVISH birthday party

Sun & Star, 22 March

A POLICE PROBE has been launched after a sixty-year-old man was electrocuted to death and another guest died in an apparent fall at a plush birthday bash in Leamington Spa.

The incident took place around 10:45 p.m. at the upmarket celebration in the leafy Warwickshire locale, where townhouses sell for more than £1 million.

The male victim, the host of the party, whose identity is being withheld until next-of-kin have been notified, is a senior executive at a major medical insurance company. His guests at the party included members of the corporate elite from as far afield as Moscow and Manila.

According to eyewitness accounts, the victim was killed by a set of faulty headphones he received as a gift. Police have not confirmed whether they are treating the death as accidental or suspicious. No arrests have yet been made. The headphones in question retail at over £50,000.

One traumatised guest described the horrifying scene: 'He looked like his brain was on fire for a second, then he just collapsed.'

Eyewitness reports suggest that the second casualty, a woman of around thirty years of age, attempted to flee the scene of the electrocution and deliberately jumped from the upstairs window, but died on the scene of her injuries.

A shocked neighbour explained how the male victim had pre-warned them of the party. 'His note was very civil. Everything was relaxed until when it must have happened.

'There was a lot of screaming and shouting. The police arrived a few minutes later. The road was closed off all night and even now there are twelve police cars parked outside.'

Police are appealing for anyone with information to get in touch, and appeal to the public not to speculate.

Chief Superintendent Tony James, of West Midlands Police, said: 'The investigation is in its very early stages and our thoughts are with the families of both of the deceased.'

29 *Seven months later*

'Welcome to Ghost Town Studios.' James Worthing opened the red, imp-adorned door wide, and stepped back to let Suki in. He'd cut his hair and shaved his beard, and it suited him. He looked good, confident, adult. His hand-stitched indigo linen jacket, fine silver denim trousers and canvas sneakers were trimly elegant and spoke of a sense of style he'd clearly retained from his sojourn in Japan. You don't learn that shit in the Midlands.

'Thank you,' she said with a warm smile. 'It's been a while.' *Precisely since the night your father died*, she didn't say. 'How are you keeping?'

'Well, thanks,' James said, before checking himself. 'Of course, it's taken some time to get over the shock and all that.' But it was clear to Suki that he was recovering just fine; thriving, in fact, now that the overbearing paternal shade had cleared.

As if recognising what Suki saw in him, James expanded. 'My aunt's still out for blood – she's suing Picton and the contractor for criminal negligence.'

'What? She doesn't accept the findings of the investigation? That it was an unfortunate accident?'

James tilted his head, evidently replaying what had

happened that night. Petra's urgency to get the headphones to Worthing. 'She doesn't – we don't – believe that was all there was to it.' Suki's breath hitched before James continued, 'The bastards were taking shortcuts. Picton apparently paid this guy to sign the electrical compliance off, but the wiring was riddled with faults. If it wasn't that socket, it would have been another. We had it all stripped out and replaced.' He paused. 'But of course, none of that will bring him back.'

So, if Petra hadn't run, she might have got away with it. Stupid girl. Suki sighed and the lump inside her throbbed.

'No,' she said, swirling around and expelling the dark past. 'It looks wonderful in here, James. It feels really open.' The main passageway felt wider and natural light was cascading down the stairs.

'Yeah, it took some work to make it accessible.'

'And it's so light.'

'Yeah, we've installed some skylights, made the windows bigger, changed out some of the gloomy, overstained old wood for lighter cedar and pine. It's been crazy bright over the summer but as you can tell, it really does its work when the nights start to draw in. The kids love it.'

'I can imagine. They probably don't want to go home. Can I have a snoop around upstairs, or is he busy with a session?'

James checked his watch. 'I think they're on a break, so feel free. Come through and see us when you're done. The coffee's already on. It's always on, I should say.'

He headed back and Suki made her way up the stairs towards the top floor. This was the staircase she'd chased up all those months ago, trying to stop Petra. That night had been such a clutter of indecent people and smell and noise and now it was unrecognisable. Walls and partitions of the poky rooms had been swiped away, the front wall had been blasted out and replaced with modern, minimalist luminescence, a glass wall framed with chunky stripped-timber beams. It was hard to tell where precisely the narrow sash window had been where Petra had attempted her escape.

A prize swathe of October afternoon sunlight spread itself over the stripped, sanded and sealed floor and the lightwood accents picked out the yellowed plane leaves, making them new. The room felt like a breathy Shinto temple, a million miles away from the stifling density of her home. Suki approached the glass and looked down to the pavement below, lost in thought for a moment before turning.

They'd hewn another large room out of the subdivided jumble of this level – the eastward room, the morning room – and this is where she'd find Vincent. As someone opened the door, she could hear the voices of the kids who'd come here to play. In the anteroom, a mother sat on the nutmeg-upholstered Japandi sofa, scrolling on her phone, a cup of green tea on the little round table beside her. The stylish sign on the wall behind the sofa – *Vincent Rice Creative Therapies* – was illustrated with one of his photos: mist-shrouded neon darkness on one side, resolving to an image of happy children running in sunlit uplands on the other. Suki nodded to her and slid the double-glazed glass door open.

Vincent was sitting at a long craft bench with four children of between eight and probably fifteen, cutting shapes out of large photographic prints. He smiled up when he heard her coming in.

'I hope I'm not interrupting,' Suki said, awkward around the small people. 'James said you were on a break, but...'

'We don't mind if you join us, do we?' he asked the kids.

The older two kids shook their heads wordlessly as they continued with their crafting, while the younger two stared at her. They assessed her for a full ten seconds before the youngest kid adjudicated: 'Nah, you can stay.'

'See? There you go. Come, sit. Grab a knife.'

Suki didn't sit. 'Really, it's fine. I'm actually... I just came for a quick look. I hadn't seen the studio since... I'll see you soon, all right.' She backed out of the room and headed through the waiting room to the stairs.

Vincent had followed her and hurried to catch her up. 'Hold on. Wait a sec,' he called to her.

She stopped by the window, eyeing the route down the stairs.

'Are you okay?' he asked.

'Yes, of course... No. No, I'm not really, actually.' She turned to look out of the vast window over the planes.

Vincent looked at her.

'It's exquisite here, Vinnie,' Suki said. 'I don't know why it's taken me so long.'

'It hasn't been that long. We only opened in August.'

'I could live here. Honestly.'

'Well, you know they're doing the apartments next. The offer stands... until they're sold, that is.'

She sighed the platitude away, her anger getting the better of her for a moment. 'She just disappeared, didn't she? We chewed her up and spat her out. She tried so hard... to carve a space, to belong. But she disappeared, and it's like she never existed.'

'That's not true,' Vincent said. 'She's here. I think of her a lot. Although…'

Although I owed her nothing. He didn't say it, but the meaning still resonated and batted against the glass pane.

'I'm glad it worked out for you and your grandmother,' Suki said. 'You deserve that.'

'*Deserve* means nothing. People don't get what they deserve,' he said. 'You know that.'

'You'd better get back to your troubled, needy children.'

Feeling the acid in her comment, Vincent opened his mouth, decided against it, and walked away.

Suki made her way downstairs, where James and Vincent's grandmother were busy in the control booth.

''Scuse me.' A woman with a mug of coffee angled past her into the studio, and sat down in front of a microphone.

The secondary stage near the control-booth window where Curtis had stood and died in that ghastly accident was now occupied by a collection of audio equipment, all angles and jags and LEDs. Suki gazed at it, remembering the smoke and the panic, before flushing it away with a pre-prepared ideation: stupidly, a swan on the mist-shrouded Avon. Wilfully editing out the trash choking the riverside reeds, the shit that bobbed in Shakespeare's river.

She turned and headed towards the red door.

'Ready?' Gloria's voice sounded behind her back. 'Track seven, secondary vocals. From the bridge. Let's start with "Falling".'

ACKNOWLEDGEMENTS
AND INSPIRATIONS

Bronwyn, when we got together I was battering away at an old computer at a tiny desk with no expectations while you waited outside my door with generous hope, and I close this circle the same way. You read me, you saw me, you got me; you've worked through my plots with me with more love and attention than they deserve. Thank you for being my ideal reader.

Sam Greenberg and Adam Greenberg, thank you for giving me the support and hope I needed to write on, and the reason to keep seeking out meaningful ways to live.

Of course, Rosa and Houdini still sniff and scratch and woowoo their way between these lines.

For what it's worth, this book is dedicated to you all.

Publishing is an act of collaborative magic. To everyone who's worked to put my books in readers' hands: Oli Munson and all at A.M. Heath; Conrad Williams at Blake Friedmann; Cat

Camacho, Joanna Harwood, Dan Coxon, Julia Lloyd and the whole Titan team; and to every printer, warehouser, librarian and bookseller who's passed this book or its metadata through your fingers – thank you.

And especially to every reader who's spent time bringing my words alive with their minds, thank you.

The immersive theatre described and alluded to in the book was founded on descriptions and reviews of the immersions of Rotozaza, Autoteatro, Punchdrunk, Lundahl & Seitl, Adrian Howells, WildWorks and Ontroerend Goed. Many of these productions are helpfully introduced and discussed by Josephine Machon in *Immersive Theatres*. A masterclass in set design at Punchdrunk Studios in London offered me a valuable behind-the-scenes glimpse into their process.

The lines of conversation about Ukraine and frozen grass are remixed with kind permission from the script of the fascinating short film *Skwerl* by Brian and Karl.

Tricks of the Mind by Derren Brown and *Sleights of Mind* by Stephen Macknick and Susana Martinez-Conde were accessible, informative and smart primers on mind-control tricks, con jobs and cold reading.

The descriptions of Vincent's photographs are inspired by the moody, misty photography of Elsa Bleda; Petra's artwork is inspired by the lush graphics of Taozipie and Tati Moons, and by Haris Nukem's portraits. These artists had nothing to do with the drafting of this book, and they'd probably be appalled by my misuse of their magical images.

Brook Street Studios is a gratuitous, fanciful and factually aberrant reimagination of Leamington's Woodbine Street Studios. I lifted one of its most famous recordings, 'Ghost Town' by The Specials, for my story. I was planning to fictionalise the song's title and the band's name, but it deserved to stay intact, however mangled. The Coventry Music Museum also offered an inspiring journey into the region's musical significance.

Leamington and Warwick, the stage for this story, are planted in the (hotly debated) geographic centre of England and can well serve as its symbolic and aspirational heart too. I fictionalised some of its local shops, pubs and restaurants, and readers from the area may recognise them. Instead of advertising them each by name, I'd encourage you to support your local independent businesses, wherever you are.

ABOUT THE AUTHOR

Louis Greenberg is a Johannesburg-bred author, editor and writing tutor. He was a bookseller for several years, and has a Master's degree in vampire fiction and a doctorate in post-religious apocalyptic fiction. His first novel, *The Beggars' Signwriters*, was shortlisted for the Commonwealth Writers' Prize, and he's also the author of *Dark Windows* and *Green Valley*. As S.L. Grey, he co-writes horror fiction with Sarah Lotz, including *The Mall* and *The Apartment*. He lives in the middle of England.

For more fantastic fiction, author events,
exclusive excerpts, competitions, limited editions and more

VISIT OUR WEBSITE
titanbooks.com

LIKE US ON FACEBOOK
facebook.com/titanbooks

FOLLOW US ON TWITTER AND INSTAGRAM
@TitanBooks

EMAIL US
readerfeedback@titanemail.com